My Royal Showmance

Also From Lexi Blake

ROMANTIC SUSPENSE

Masters and Mercenaries
The Dom Who Loved Me
The Men With The Golden Cuffs
A Dom is Forever
On Her Master's Secret Service
Sanctum: A Masters and Mercenaries Novella
Love and Let Die
Unconditional: A Masters and Mercenaries Novella
Dungeon Royale
Dungeon Games: A Masters and Mercenaries Novella
A View to a Thrill
Cherished: A Masters and Mercenaries Novella
You Only Love Twice
Luscious: Masters and Mercenaries~Topped
Adored: A Masters and Mercenaries Novella
Master No
Just One Taste: Masters and Mercenaries~Topped 2
From Sanctum with Love
Devoted: A Masters and Mercenaries Novella
Dominance Never Dies
Submission is Not Enough
Master Bits and Mercenary Bites~The Secret Recipes of Topped
Perfectly Paired: Masters and Mercenaries~Topped 3
For His Eyes Only
Arranged: A Masters and Mercenaries Novella
Love Another Day
At Your Service: Masters and Mercenaries~Topped 4
Master Bits and Mercenary Bites~Girls Night
Nobody Does It Better
Close Cover
Protected: A Masters and Mercenaries Novella
Enchanted: A Masters and Mercenaries Novella
Charmed: A Masters and Mercenaries Novella
Treasured: A Masters and Mercenaries Novella

Delighted: A Masters and Mercenaries Novella
Tempted: A Masters and Mercenaries Novella

Masters and Mercenaries: The Forgotten
Lost Hearts (Memento Mori)
Lost and Found
Lost in You
Long Lost
No Love Lost

Masters and Mercenaries: Reloaded
Submission Impossible
The Dom Identity
The Man from Sanctum
No Time to Lie
The Dom Who Came in from the Cold

Masters and Mercenaries: New Recruits
Love the Way You Spy
Live, Love, Spy
The Bodyguard and the Bombshell: A Masters and Mercenaries:New Recruits Novella, Coming August 6, 2024
Sweet Little Spies, Coming September 17, 2024

Park Avenue Promise
Start Us Up
My Royal Showmance,

Butterfly Bayou
Butterfly Bayou
Bayou Baby
Bayou Dreaming
Bayou Beauty
Bayou Sweetheart
Bayou Beloved

Lawless
Ruthless
Satisfaction
Revenge

Courting Justice
Order of Protection
Evidence of Desire

Masters Of Ménage (by Shayla Black and Lexi Blake)
Their Virgin Captive
Their Virgin's Secret
Their Virgin Concubine
Their Virgin Princess
Their Virgin Hostage
Their Virgin Secretary
Their Virgin Mistress

The Perfect Gentlemen (by Shayla Black and Lexi Blake)
Scandal Never Sleeps
Seduction in Session
Big Easy Temptation
Smoke and Sin
At the Pleasure of the President

URBAN FANTASY

Thieves
Steal the Light
Steal the Day
Steal the Moon
Steal the Sun
Steal the Night
Ripper
Addict
Sleeper
Outcast
Stealing Summer
The Rebel Queen
The Rebel Guardian
The Rebel Witch

LEXI BLAKE WRITING AS SOPHIE OAK
Texas Sirens

Small Town Siren
Siren in the City
Siren Enslaved
Siren Beloved
Siren in Waiting
Siren in Bloom
Siren Unleashed
Siren Reborn
The Accidental Siren

Nights in Bliss, Colorado
Three to Ride
Two to Love
One to Keep
Lost in Bliss
Found in Bliss
Pure Bliss
Chasing Bliss
Once Upon a Time in Bliss
Back in Bliss
Sirens in Bliss
Happily Ever After in Bliss
Far from Bliss
Unexpected Bliss

A Faery Story
Bound
Beast
Beauty

Standalone
Away From Me
Snowed In

My Royal Showmance

LEXI BLAKE

My Royal Showmance
A Park Avenue Promise Novel
By Lexi Blake

Copyright 2024 Lexi Blake
ISBN: 978-1-957568-73-7

Published by Blue Box Press, an imprint of Evil Eye Concepts, Incorporated

This is a work of fiction. Names, places, characters and incidents are the product of the author's imagination and are fictitious. Any resemblance to actual persons, living or dead, events or establishments is solely coincidental.

Author's Acknowledgements

I usually have something I'm working through in my personal life when I write a book. I struggle to find the words to explain something deep in my soul. I've worked through grief and imposter syndrome and my fears that I'm going to break the people I love. So when I breezed through *My Royal Showmance* I was worried I'd missed something. Does this story have a deeper meaning than a funny young woman finds herself in a wacky reality show trying to marry a king? And then I realized I had made the mistake of equating trauma with emotion. I realized there's more to me than what I've survived. There is something so important, and this book addresses that subject.

Friends. Loved ones. The people around us.

They are the ones who make survival possible. Who make our lives rich beyond compare. The older I get the less I think about the people who harmed me. More and more my memories, thoughts, actions, orbit around my friends. I love my family and of course they come first, but oh how my friends have been the strong ground beneath my feet. And that is why this book felt effortless. Because my love for my friends is as easy as breathing. So this book is dedicated to my circle of friends. None of this is possible without you. Thank you for making my life better than any television show.

Chapter One

"Do you understand what I'm asking you to do?"

I stare at my boss and wish I could say no and that I'm just not up to this new assignment she's giving me. Not that it's all that new. She gave me a week to think about it, and I can't figure a way out that doesn't involve me leaving a job I love. I've been with Pinnacle Productions for five years now, and I'm so close to getting to where I want to be.

But where I want to be isn't where she wants me to go for the near future.

"You want me to figure out if Joseph Helms is sexually harassing his crew because you can't afford to hand over a multibillion-dollar franchise to him if he's going to cause a scandal."

Joseph Helms had been Hollywood's golden boy until he'd gotten too invested in vodka. Now, he's making something of a comeback. Pinnacle recently invested millions of dollars to acquire a super popular video game franchise, and the rumor is the board wants Helms to direct.

Yep. That's why she wants me to put my career on hold. Not hold, exactly. It's worse. I'm taking a step down.

All in all, not how I'd expected my year to go.

I'd started the year with the highest hopes. I'd gone to my bosses with a couple of projects I thought I would be good for. I've spent the last ten years in the trenches. First as an intern to a big network known for its educational and reality TV shows, and then as a production assistant on several projects. I've become well known as everyone's Girl Friday. Need a latte at three in the morning because you have an early call and forgot to fit in some sleep? Call Anika Fox. Does the writer need to be soothed into coming up with a fourteenth draft? Anika is every writer's best friend. Need someone to manhandle a morning news host out of a night club? I'm short but I put some time in the gym, and I can be persuasive.

The woman in front of me often calls me her secret weapon, and it looks like I'm about to be deployed.

Jessica Wallace has been the force behind Pinnacle Entertainment for the last thirty years. Her father had started the studio in the forties, and everyone had expected her brother to take over when he died. I'm still not sure if she had some shit on him or if he really did want to run away to Boca and retire at a young age, but when the board voted, Jessica had come out on top. She'd taken power when women were still mostly on the sidelines. Those are actual Oscars on the wall behind her. In an office that screams power and status, those golden men are hung almost perfectly like horns she could use to headbutt her way through anything. She sits back, looking comfortable and as casual as she ever gets in slacks and a silk blouse, her perfectly silver hair in a chic bob. "Yes, that is the general gist of this assignment."

"And I have to pretend to be a production assistant on the reality show he's directing in order to..." I need things to be made perfectly plain. "Am I bait?"

She stares at me for a moment as though trying to figure out how to handle me. "I wouldn't call you bait, Ani. I hope you know I wouldn't put you in a position I didn't think you could handle. I have no idea if you're his type, but you are everyone else's, and by that I mean people will talk to you. People confide in you. They trust you, and I want you to let anyone who needs to be heard know that you are listening."

Well, there's a reason she's reached the heights she has. She knows how to get a person on board. If there are women out there being harassed, they're probably a lot like me. And she's right. People do tend to talk to me. I think it's because I'm one of *those* women—pretty but not too pretty, smart but not intimidating. I sometimes worry I'm a little mid, but I'm also comfortable being who I am. I'm on the basic side, and that's okay with me.

Which is likely why people I've only recently met sometimes tell me their life stories.

"I'm not even certain anything is happening, though it wouldn't surprise me," she continues. "Joseph is an old friend of my husband's. His wife is… Well, I would certainly cheat on her."

"Jess," I begin, because one of my jobs is to remind her this isn't the eighties and we're not all high on cocaine and meanness.

A slender shoulder shrugs. "I wasn't talking about her looks. Sylvie is fine if one enjoys the crunchy-vegan look. I'm talking about her personality. That's still fine to remark upon if one is not discussing something one can't help. She could be less boring. And seriously, you need to loosen up. I don't understand your generation. No one in mine was allergic to gluten. Sylvie goes on and on about gluten. Isn't that one of those things that people make up?"

I shake my head because we've gone over this. "Nope. It's real. Always has been, and if she's allergic to gluten, then you shouldn't make fun of her. We were talking about Joseph Helms, not whether or not his wife deserves to be cheated on. Which is also not what we're talking about. Cheating implies the other party is interested. Sexual harassment is the better word."

Jess sighs as though I've deeply disappointed her. "It's a word that's going to cost me a lot of money if I make the wrong bet. Look, Ani, you've heard the rumors."

"No, I haven't," I reply. "All I've heard is what a great guy he is to work with when he's sober, and not so fun when he's not. I've heard he's relatively happily married. I know he employs a lot of women on his production teams. I know he's had a problem with alcohol in the past."

Jess waves that off. "Everyone in this town does. Joe has done his time in rehab. He's brilliant, you know. He's slumming on this show."

"Because he had a meltdown on his last film, and no one wants to work with him," I point out. I do know his work, and he's one of the reasons for those Oscar horns. I think it's the one on the right. Needless to say, Jess is invested in Joseph's career. Much of Pinnacle's respect in the industry comes from those films directed by Joseph Helms.

The money, however, comes from a whole lot of television, including the over-the-top dating shows that bring in ratings and bank.

I've been working in the film side of the business for the last two years, specializing in movies made right here in NYC. I've done some TV and worked on the lower ends of film production. I have my first script ready and my dream staff as a list on my phone. I'm supposed to be ready to produce my first film, the start of my real career.

Then I hit this roadblock.

"Joseph isn't the only one taking a step down," I point out. "This is low-level production assistant work. Not that there's anything wrong with that, but I've put my time in here."

"I know and I understand your frustration, dear, but you are the only person I trust with this assignment."

"Hailey's show wrapped yesterday. I know she's looking for something new," I offer. Not only because I want out of this assignment, but because if anyone deserves to be shoved onto the hellscape of taping a bunch of women dating one European royal in the hopes of finding...I don't want to say *love*. I think I might be contractually obligated to use the word *love*. But I think it's mostly screen time and maybe a crown. Anyway, if anyone deserves that, it's Hailey.

Jess's lips form a straight line. "Hailey would bully the poor women into silence if she thought it would take her another rung up the ladder, and she's got movie dreams. I can't trust her to not side with Joe. The same with the men in your position. I understand that you do not deserve this, Anika. You're smart and capable, and unfortunately you have a deep sense of morality that is not often found at this level of the entertainment industry. I did not fight tooth and nail for this seat so some old man can harass the young women beneath me. I would simply turn him away, but as I said, he's a friend of the family, and his name has meant something to this company."

She's right. Damn it. She's always right. She's been my mentor, and she didn't have to be. She's the head of one of the world's premier entertainment companies. And she doesn't have to take time to meet the new crop of interns every year, to make sure there are always as many women as men, to take a few she sees promise in under her wing so they don't get lost in the everyday shuffle.

The truth of the matter is I owe her.

"What are you hoping for, Jess?" Not that what she wants will change the nature of my investigation. I'll be honest about what I discover.

She seems to think about the question for a moment. "I suppose I hope it's all rumors. I've never seen this kind of behavior out of him, but I had power when I met him. Men's behavior can change when the power dynamic is in their favor. I know I can be a bit much, and I don't apologize for that. I had to be to make it where I am. But I'm not one of those women who thinks my daughters and granddaughters should suck it up because I had to. What am I hoping for? A different world for this generation. One where they don't have to worry their boss will harass them. It's a whisper right now, and that could be jealousy. No one has stepped up with an accusation, but I want to be prepared. I know you think this show is dumb."

"I didn't say that." I didn't think I had to. It is called *The King Takes a Bride*, which is perfectly fine if we're talking about a Broadway revival of some fifties musical. But no. This is a reality dating show complete with a whole bunch of hot tubs I will be responsible for ensuring get cleaned.

I kind of want to cry.

"Of course it's dumb, and I don't know what the executive producer has over the king's head that he felt he needed to do this," Jess says. "His Majesty Reginald Lucannon St. Marten of Ralavia is gorgeous and has a crown on his head. He's not known to be wild. Of course, it's not like he's Prince Harry. I think there are three hundred people in his country, so it's not surprising the press isn't all over him."

"It's around a hundred thousand," I correct, though she's right about the tiny principality not being big in the news cycles. I remember there being some kind of flooding in that part of Europe a couple of years ago, but otherwise I suspect it's all castles and cobblestone streets and tons of tourists.

"Anyway, I wonder. The man is stunning, and if he'd been lucky enough to be born in a country that mattered, he would have been on the cover of every magazine, celebrated for his royal blood and a nicely made six-pack," she says with a sigh.

I raise my brows.

She shakes a well-manicured finger my way. "That is not harassment or sexualizing him. He did it to himself when he posed for all the publicity photos."

"I haven't seen them." The truth is I could do this particular job in my sleep. My nightmares. I haven't studied up on the king because I don't need to know more than what kind of drinks to order for him and if I will have to keep his drug dealer away from the set. I know that sounds crazy, but I've had to in the past. Like I said, most people underestimate me, but I know my way around some unsavory situations.

"Well, you should. They're fabulous. The king himself is…not what I expected. He's an interesting man. Not that it matters. You won't be around when the show comes out," Jess promises me. "Ani, you're my best producer. Do this for me and I'll green-light your movie. The silly one about… What was it about?"

"It's the story of one of New York's first woman firefighters. Her life and struggles." It is my dream project, and it certainly isn't silly. It's about empowerment and the fight against discrimination in the workplace.

Jess's surgically perfected nose wrinkles slightly. "Could she be fighting aliens?"

I growl. It's an alpha sound I've worked on over the years since no one takes a small blonde woman seriously in my business until they catch sight of our three rows of teeth.

Not that I'm like that in my normal life. I'm a regular young woman. I try to be nice and kind to everyone around me, and if they cross me, I will bury them and no cop will look in my anime eyes and think me capable of murder.

Sometimes the patriarchy works in my favor. Not that I want to give up bodily autonomy and equal pay just so I can murder someone a little more easily. But for now I'll take what I can get.

"Fine." Jess has her hard negotiator expression on. "What's the budget?"

I can do it for ten million, but she's sentencing me to six weeks of dealing with women who think they are going to end up being queen. It will be spray tans and claws, and I will hear the words "the right reasons" so many times. "Fifteen."

Her eyes narrow like she knows exactly what I'm doing.

I sit and wait. Like she taught me.

Don't show a minute of your emotions, Ani.

"Fifteen," she agrees. "And you'll be fast-tracked. If you get this done, I might even be persuaded to tell publicity they have a slightly larger budget."

She really wants this.

I wish I could talk to my friends, but I know what's at the end of this conversation. I won't be able to explain why I'm taking a crappy assignment. Ivy has her own issues and won't question it. She'll be all "rah-rah, girl power," but Harper likes a mystery, and, even more, she loves to point out when things are going wrong.

Still, I'd like their advice, but I'm not going to get it.

I'm on my own. "I'll do it."

Jess smiles like she would have gone to twenty.

She wouldn't have, but I give her a frown because it's always good to let the boss think they're still in control.

"One more thing, dear," she says, sliding a stack of papers my way.

Yep. There's the very long and binding nondisclosure agreement. My mouth is going to have to stay closed. But my eyes will be wide open.

Chapter Two

"So you start Monday?" Ivy looks at me across the table, a glass of Pinot Noir in her hands. Ivy Jensen is one of my two best friends. She works in the tech sector and is in the middle of a huge comeback project with her boyfriend, Heath. He's the coder, though she's damn good at it, too. Ivy is also excellent at running a business and raising funds.

We're sitting in a bar in an upscale hotel in the middle of the Upper East Side. Not my usual neighborhood, but we attended a party thrown by Ivy's mentor earlier this evening, the fabulous CeCe Foust, and a debrief had been required. Hence this swanky bar and overpriced drinks.

I live in what passes for an "apartment" in Greenwich Village. It's more of a room with an even tinier room attached, so they can say there's a full bathroom. I wouldn't use the word *full* in association with my place, but it's home and I mostly work.

"Yes, she starts the mystery job on Monday." Harper Ross is my other bestie. We've known each other since first grade when we both attended PS 111 and were placed in Miss Nixon's class. She was a newbie, and to say chaos ruled would understate the situation. Harper had taken my hand that first day on the playground, and we had Hunger Gamesed our way to the end of the school year and have been together ever since. We've gone through my parents' divorce, her dad's death, countless boyfriends, and career setbacks together.

So there's a reason she's upset I won't tell her why I'm suddenly back in the reality dating trenches. She's protective. Harper is that friend who steps in front of you when danger feels close. She's also a control freak. I think they go hand in hand.

"You know why," Ivy says, her eyes widening like they've been over this a couple hundred times. And they probably have.

I've read that it takes a person about eight times to grasp a new concept. When that concept is releasing control over things that could happen to people Harper loves, the number goes up significantly.

"Is this about that NDA?" Ivy's boyfriend Heath is with us, though he'd offered to stay home and play video games with his best friend so we could have a girls night.

Mostly because CeCe scares him and calls him "Ivy's Side Piece," even though they're living together and firmly committed and stuff. CeCe's not great with names, and she doesn't always understand slang. Like in any way. But she does love to use it. She calls me "Tiny Blonde One." Harper is "Ivy's Friend Who Could Use Some Blush," so I think Heath got off easy.

"I thought we all agreed we weren't giving Ani a hard time." The reason why Heath had no easy way out of the fancy party we'd all gone to sat beside him. Darnell Green rounds out our group. He's a coder by day and speculative fiction writer by all the times he's not coding or making sarcastic remarks. He's excellent at those.

He also loves a good train wreck, and he'd shoved his best friend right under a bus when Ivy offered to let him come if he could get Heath to go.

And what a beautiful train wreck it had been. We'd had some delicious food and expensive booze as we'd watched a couple of Broadway stars figure out they were both screwing the same director. CeCe had announced she wouldn't be backing a local politician because he was an ass. He was in the room when she said it over the loudspeaker she was experimenting with. He had not been happy, and that was when the man CeCe calls Lawyer had been introduced.

All in all, it was a chef's kiss of an evening.

And all I can think about is the fact that I have to deal with thirteen overly dramatic wannabe reality TV stars come Monday morning. I'm coming in at such a low level that I don't even have to be on set until filming starts. It's embarrassing, and I have to tell myself that I'm sacrificing for the sisterhood. It's worth it if I can save someone from a sexual predator.

Hmm. If I were CeCe Foust, I would call Joseph Helms Sexual Predator and nothing else.

Which wouldn't be fair because he could be innocent.

Maybe.

"We've lost her," Ivy says with a sigh. "Probably because the last thing she needs is another lecture from Harper on how she shouldn't sacrifice her career for whoever Harper's decided is the villain of the piece this time."

"I know who the villain is," Harper declares, pointing to Ivy over her Hendrick's martini up with a twist. "Jessica Wallace."

I roll my eyes. "She's not a freaking villain. Why is my mentor a villain but CeCe is okay?"

Harper's dark bob shakes. "I never said CeCe wasn't a villain. She's like the supervillain of our world, but she's kind of *our* villain. Watching her with the moms is cool. Even when Ivy's mom is lecturing her on karma and how she treats people, and then Heath's grandma talks about what God's going to say to her when she gets to heaven."

"CeCe does not plan on dying, so she's going to avoid all that," Ivy says like that's a normal thing. "And Jessica's pretty cool."

"I just think it's weird to think of *the* Joseph Helms directing a reality show." Heath shakes his head and exchanges a look with his best friend.

Darnell nods as though they've discussed the situation before. "*A Far Planet* is one of the greatest science fiction films ever made. I'll admit I wasn't into all those films he made about how angry white dudes are, but that one was excellent."

The angry white dude films are the award-winning ones, and yes, that says something about my industry.

Heath sits back, his hand on the beer in front of him. He's what I like to call generic cute boy. He would have ruled the CW airways back in the day. But I've come to learn that's merely his looks. Heath's surprisingly perceptive about more than just his code work. He's good at analyzing a situation and the people in it.

I realize a second before he speaks that he's probably the most dangerous person at the table.

"You know I've heard a rumor that Pinnacle is developing a film based on *Red Haze*," he muses.

It isn't a rumor. It hasn't been announced yet, but I happen to know that they already have scripts for three movies based on the world's best-selling video game, and they're putting about a billion dollars into building the franchise. "Huh, that sounds like something Pinnacle would do. I won't be asked to work on that one and I'm cool with it. I like working with small-budget films. More freedom to tell a good story."

Ivy's head comes up, a spark in her eyes.

She's curious, and I pray she lets it go. Ivy's the one who backs me on the whole NDA thing. She's signed many nondisclosure agreements herself. Harper works in construction. They aren't big on keeping secrets. People in Harper's industry tend to want everything out in the open, but Ivy understands.

She also loves to be a smarty pants who figures out a puzzle.

"Didn't Helms's Oscar film come from Pinnacle?" Ivy asks, and Heath nods her way. "And he's directed big blockbusters."

"But then he had to go to rehab," Harper points out. "I think that's why he's working on the reality show. I think it was all he could get because no one will insure him."

Insurance is a big thing in my industry. Oh, we don't like to talk about it because we want to seem all artistic and bohemian—let the art lead the way—but we mostly let the money lead the way, and protecting those big bucks is a whole vibe. Harper's right. I happen to know that Jessica had to work some magic to get Helms insured for this show.

She can't get it for the big movie unless he proves himself.

"But if he did want to make a comeback, it would go a long way to prove he's clean and sober," Ivy continues. "They wouldn't use a big budget project. They would need something smaller."

Harper's mouth drops open, and she looks my way. "You're babysitting."

I let my head fall to the table. "NDA."

"You are totally babysitting," Harper says with a bit of triumph in her tone.

Not that she figured it out. That had been a combo of Heath and Ivy. And I'm not babysitting, exactly. That job will be left to his sober companion and all his assistants.

"Guys, leave her alone." Darnell is the only one who defends me. "Our little mirror ball needs some space. If she signed an NDA, there was a good reason for it."

Seriously? Wear an overly sequined mini dress one time and they never let you hear the end of it. I sit back up. Tonight my mini dress is sequin free, though it does have some bling on the hem. "Thank you, Darnell. Obviously I will be honoring the NDA I signed."

Even Ivy groans at that. "You know we won't tell. NDAs are a dime a dozen. No one doesn't talk."

I'm kind of a rules follower. Most of the time. I believe society has some good rules and some bad ones. Not committing undeserved murders falls into the good rules. Dress codes are for Victorian pearl clutchers, so I don't pay a lot of attention to those. However, when one signs a document stating plainly they will not talk about a particular situation or they will get the holy hell sued out of them, I tend to believe the document. As I do not have a man or woman I call Lawyer on staff, my lips are sealed.

Besides, I don't think it's fair to talk. Rumors like this can ruin careers, and I need to think of this man as innocent until proven guilty.

"I can't, guys, and I need you to accept that," I say. It's not late, but we're one of two tables of drinkers, and there's only one person sitting at the bar. A light rain has started, pebbling against the windows and turning the street outside into a soft splash of neon from the lights around us.

The prettiest man I've ever seen is sitting there, staring down at his phone. The bartender slides a cup in front of him. Coffee. He looks up, and a smile comes across his face.

My jaw kind of drops because it's one of those moments when time seems to stand still and music plays in the background. It's the moment when the heroine looks across the crowded room and sees Prince Charming for the first time, and the world seems like a better place than it had been before.

Or I'm really horny and he's gorgeous.

"Wow." Ivy is staring his way, too. "That is a stunning man. I don't think I've ever seen a dude take Anika's breath away."

"My breath is in my lungs, thank you." I'm not gaping at the dude or anything. He's obviously out of my league, but I appreciate a lovely work of art. I can't tell how tall he is, but he has dark hair and a jawline that would make Superman envy him. He's maybe thirty-five, though clean living could age him up a bit. He's wearing slacks and a button-down, as though trying to blend in with the afterwork crowd.

That man couldn't blend to save his life.

Harper sits up, a grin lighting her face. "Are we wingmen?"

Dear lord. That's the last thing I need. The poor man is probably in town for a conference or something and he's trying to wind down. He doesn't seem to have a companion, but maybe his wife or girlfriend or husband is somewhere else and he's waiting on them. "No. I just…I mean, look at him."

"I am," Ivy assures me. "Hence me being willing to back you up."

"Or you could remember your boyfriend is sitting right here," Heath says with a frown on his face.

Ivy turns her boyfriend's way and puts a hand over his. "Sorry, babe. You know you are the only pretty man I need in my life, but you have to admit he's kind of hot."

Heath's lips curl up. "He is striking, if you like the male-model type."

I shake my head because he's wrong. This man is gorgeous, but there's character in there, too. Like he's seen some things, but he handled them all. The way he's smiling at the bartender makes me think he's kind. She says something and his expression changes. He leans in, really listening to her, and then there's compassion in the way he takes her hand. I can't hear what he's saying, but I imagine it's words of support because the bartender is suddenly smiling and thanking him. "He's not a model."

"Bet he is," Harper says, challenge in her voice. "I bet he's in town for a shoot. Or he's meeting his older, wealthy lover right here in this hotel."

"Or he's in town on business and getting ready to head home to his wife and kids," I shoot back.

Ivy shakes her head. "I don't see a ring on that finger."

"Hey, how about we head over to that diner two blocks over?" Darnell downs the rest of his beer. "Those appetizer things CeCe served were good, but I need man-sized food."

I don't want to leave because the view here is so nice. Still, I'm hungry, and if I sit here I'll likely stare at the man long enough to make him uncomfortable.

It's not like I planned our wedding and two point five highly gifted children in those few seconds.

I need a boyfriend. It's been a while for me, and the last guy couldn't handle my slight eccentricities. "Sure."

Darnell slides out of the booth. "I'll go hit the bathroom, and then we can go. I can already taste that burger."

Actually, now that he mentioned it, I can, too. I'm kind of hungry and will likely be eating nothing but craft services for the next six weeks. On a show like this the crew films eighteen hours a day, seven days a week. A late-night burger with friends sounds good.

If they don't keep pushing me to talk.

"I think you should go introduce yourself to him." Ivy slides her arms into her jacket.

"Ivy's right. He's sitting alone in a bar," Harper points out.

"What is that supposed to mean?" Heath finishes up his beer.

Ivy shrugs. "He's sitting in a bar on a Saturday night looking like that, and he doesn't have earbuds in. He looks like he's…looking."

"I think the earbuds thing is a girl hack," Harper replies. "He's definitely lonely. Ani, you should offer to buy him a drink."

"I'm not going to bother the man." Just because he's a guy doesn't mean he's looking for a sexual partner for the night.

I'm not the kind of girl who picks up a guy for sex.

Though now I wonder why not? I'm single. I'm apparently in desperate need of stress relief, and I don't do things like go to the gym. I'm more of a read a romance novel girl. The dirtier the better, and I do not apologize.

However, the latest book I read about a badass chick who gets railed hard—and lovingly—by her three werewolf fated mates has done nothing to alleviate my need for physical affection.

My taste in literature is one of the things the last guy had been opposed to. He'd told me that women who read romance novels are obviously lacking something in their lives. And then I told him I didn't read mysteries because I didn't lack murder in my life and that he was made of misogyny, and we broke up.

The stunning man across the bar wouldn't ever have to deal with my reading choices, nor would he ever have to know that there are some candies I eat like a polite squirrel. He'll never have to know that I don't like prime numbers. They're scary, and I don't want the volume to be left on one of them. Six or eight are perfectly fine volume numbers. If I had any courage at all, I would walk up to him and ask him if he wants to hang with me for a couple of hours, take out my frustrations on his hot bod, and then we would both have a good memory.

But I'm not going to do that because deep down I do believe those romance novels. I want a connection with someone before I hop into bed. Not a forever connection. I like to think I have a healthy relationship with sex, but I do like some real conversation first. I like to think the person I'm going to bed with is nice.

"Hey, if it helps at all, my grandmother says she's got a couple of matches for you," Heath offers.

I feel myself blush. Lydia Marino is Heath's grandmother and one of the last great matchmakers in New York City. She's been connecting people for over fifty years, and she's got a whole system in place. When Ivy and Heath had gotten together to build an AI matchmaking program, they'd used a lot of Lydia's work to train the system. And Lydia had asked Harper and I to fill out her forms. For fun, she'd said.

It hadn't been a lot of fun. It had been weird and made me realize I have a lot of baggage. And some quirks.

It's been weeks and nothing, so I thought Lydia had been telling me the truth and she just wanted to get to know us better. The fact that she's been trying to match me up scares the crap out of me. "Oh, I have to work. No time to date. It's all work all the time for the next couple of months."

Harper snorts and pokes my arm like we're twelve again. "Lydia found you a boyfriend."

I shake my head. I do not need this. I have sworn off all dating apps and going out with men my mom meets at church. Nope. I'm good on my own. Book boyfriends are all I need. Fictional men never ask me what my favorite bible verse is or if I want to split the check because I'm not as hot as I was in my profile.

Fictional men truly are superior, and that's why I'm playing this smart. I'm not going to introduce myself to Hottie McHotterson, who probably will turn out to be a serial killer, with my luck.

I've never dated a serial killer, but it feels on brand for me. I did date a guy who tried to rob a bodega with a water pistol. I heard he did well in rehab.

"Thank her for me, but this job is going to take all my time for the foreseeable future," I explain as politely as possible because while I might not want Lydia's matchmaking services, I do like her lasagna, and at least once a month she invites us all to lunch.

"I'm sure you'll have some time off." Harper knows how hard work is going to be for me, but she's got a look of mischief in her eyes I rarely see these days.

She's enjoying teasing me, and I find I can't quite shut it down, but I can make a point. "You know you filled out those forms, too."

"Yeah, but I was totally honest, so she's never finding a dude for me," Harper shoots back.

"I wouldn't bet against Lydia," Ivy offers, checking her purse before looking up. Her eyes go wide. "I thought Darnell was going to the bathroom."

That's the moment I realize Darnell has, in fact, not gone to the bathroom. No. He's standing at the bar, a wide smile on his face as he points back to our table. He's talking to the object of my gloriously brief mind affair, who smiles and shrugs as if saying, sure why not.

We have a tagalong.

I am going to kill Darnell.

Chapter Three

The man is even more devastating up close than he was across the bar.

An hour later we're sitting in a big booth at The Red Eye Diner, and my belly is full of the excellent cheeseburger I ate and butterflies. Because he's kind of everything.

And that's why I should be wary, but it's okay. The man's here for work and won't be staying long.

Luca. He'd introduced himself as Luca Martin, and he'd zeroed in on me in a way that told me Darnell had absolutely explained my prior drooling situation. Which I really hope I've stopped doing.

My friends are terrible, wonderful people who'd asked Luca a whole bunch of questions, eaten quickly, paid the bill—taken at least one surreptitious picture of him in case I got murdered—and then left Luca and I sitting here as the evening lengthened to night. I can't quite make myself leave. I worry I'm about to make a complete fool of myself over this guy, and I can't stop it.

"Your friend," he begins with the most perfect British accent, "she seemed familiar. I think she called herself Ivy. She mentioned she worked in tech. Was that Ivy Jensen?"

So he follows the business world, more specifically the tech industry. I nod. "Yes, she used to run a company called Jensen Medical."

His fingers snap in recognition. "Yes. She was at the top of her game. I was sad to hear she lost her company. Her software works brilliantly. Our hospital system uses it. The local system that is. She's quite intimidating. I've been told my picture was taken at some point in time this evening, and if you go missing, she will put me on something called *Dateline*."

That sounds like Ivy, but I don't want to scare him away. "Don't worry about her. She's only watching out for me. Do they not have *Dateline* in England?"

He shrugs slightly. "I might have heard of it, but I've never watched it. It sounds very informative. I prefer something more entertaining. I do quite a lot of reading."

"I bet you're into nonfiction and like Nobel Prize-winning literature." He would certainly not approve of my latest read, *Their Virgin Mate*, and that's a shame because I learned a lot from it.

He shudders, an oddly masculine gesture on him. "Not since I finished university. Give me a murder mystery or a good graphic novel. My adv…coworkers always lament my taste in fiction. The only reason I don't watch a lot of telly is time. My job can be a bit intense. When I have some down time, I enjoy… What do you call it here in the States? Binging?"

So he's not an overly intellectual snob. He's ticking off all the boxes on my list while presenting me with zero red flags. He'd been charming with my friends and attentive with me. He hadn't even said anything when I'd gotten ketchup on my dress. He'd simply taken his napkin, soaked it in his water, and told me to pat. The man knows how to take care of semi-fine fabrics. "Yes, I like a good binge. I once locked myself in my apartment for a weekend and shut off all social media so no one spoiled *Stranger Things* for me."

"That's the worst. Although it's a fine line, isn't it? When does a spoiler become a normal, everyday reference every human should understand?" There's a mug of coffee in front of him and an empty plate that used to house a big piece of chocolate pie he'd declared delicious. "I have a friend who still hasn't watched *Game of Thrones* and gets upset when we talk about it around him. Sorry, mate. That ship has sailed."

Oh, I like him so much. He's laid back and seems real to me. The haze of his hotness is still there, but there's also an ease between us that does something for my soul. In the last hour we've talked solidly thanks to the gift Heath left for us.

It's a game he sometimes carries around when we're all going out to dinner. It consists of a bunch of cards with get-to-know you questions. Like *what's your favorite type of weather*. His—rainy with a hint of a chill.

Mine—a fall afternoon when the air is crisp but the sun warms me while I'm walking through the park.

It's odd because those questions Heath left us don't cover the basic *where do you live, where did you go to school, who are your friends* type of things that normally get asked when you first meet someone. I suck at those first awkward conversations because I usually say something weird.

A regular guy would have tossed the questions aside the minute Heath and the gang had left us on our own, but Luca seems fascinated with the cards. He holds out the stack. "It's your turn."

It's getting late, but he shows no signs of wanting to leave. The waitress has long since given up on us, leaving a pot of coffee on the table as she starts to clean up. I reach out and take a card from the middle, hoping it's a good one. Luca doesn't allow mulligans. I glance down. "All right. *Where is your favorite vacation spot and why?* It has to be a place you've been to, not an aspirational location."

He sits back, and a soft expression comes across his face. "Santa Maria. It's an island in the Azores off the coast of Portugal. My uncle lived there for most of his life and when I had school holidays, I would sometimes go and work at his vineyard. I suppose it was the time I felt the most free. My parents were particularly invested in me doing well at school. Boarding school in England is… Well, there's a reason *Game of Thrones* resonated with me."

"Boarding school?" I can't imagine not being able to go home at night, not having that firm boundary between school and rest. Not that it would have been possible for me. My parents had been solidly middle class, and rent control is the only reason my mom still lives in her two bedroom in Hell's Kitchen. Luca's family apparently had money.

He nods, pouring another cup of coffee. "Yes. I went away to boarding school when I was eight. I only saw my parents on breaks after that, and when they were busy, I would be sent to my uncle's. I have to admit, I preferred that. My uncle was more laid back, though he worked hard. He taught me a lot about wine and how to grow it, how it represents the land and the history of the people who make it. For my uncle, wine was a living history."

"Was?" I ask, knowing the answer.

He nods. "Yes. He passed a few years ago, my father before him. Cancer. My mother died last year. She had a stroke that she never recovered from."

"I'm sorry to hear that."

A soft expression crosses his features. "I wish we'd had a better relationship, but that's in the past. So now you know why I love Portugal, despite my love of rain and gloomy climates. How about you?"

He's been so open with me. I want to say Disney World because of fun. I went once with Harper's family, and we had the best time. We'd been eight years old and made it a point to try to make each other throw up on the tea cups.

But that isn't the place that still calls to me. "My dad's family had a big cabin in the Poconos. That's a place in Pennsylvania. It's beautiful. Mountains and lakes, and it's so green in the summer. He grew up in Scranton, but he spent his summers there with his parents. So when I was young and my grandma was still around, we would go for a couple of weeks every year."

"And you had fun running around the forest?"

I sigh because it's more than childhood fun. "It was the only place where my father seemed happy. He was a complex man. Is still a complex man, I assume."

"He's not in your life?" Luca asks.

We're getting deep for only having met a few hours before, but I also think this will be our only night together, so it feels strangely right to confide in him. Like he's a safe place to put some of my emotions for the simple fact that I won't see him again. "He left my mom when I was twelve, but the marriage was shaky before then. It was kind of toxic. Not kind of. Just plain toxic. I don't think my father liked how his life turned out. He always made it clear to my mother that she wasn't his first choice. The problem was he was hers, and no amount of bile he spit her way changed that for her. But those weeks when he was back around his old friends he seemed like a different man."

"Why didn't he move back to where he was happiest?"

"Oh, the family home was gone by then. They'd all had to leave the area to find better opportunities. He did finally move back a couple of years ago. He's working at a resort and seems to have gotten some of his issues under control." I have probably said way too much. I give him what I hope is a bright smile. "Anyway, I loved rafting and hiking, and there was this place that had the best cinnamon rolls. Big as my head at the time, and my mom would get one and I would eat on it all day. It was fun. Now if you ask me where I want to go today, I would absolutely say someplace like Hawaii or Fiji. Somewhere beachy, with a fabulous spa."

He reaches out, his hand covering mine. "I know what it's like to have complicated relationships with parents. It's hard. Thank you for sharing that with me."

I feel vulnerable in that moment. He's looking at me with soft eyes, like he's never had a woman open her soul to him, and he probably hasn't after knowing her for such a short amount of time. "It's your turn."

I take the cards and fan them out, turning them his way. He hesitates, and I wonder if we're done for the night. By night I mean forever. I won't see this man again. He's explained that he has a big project he's working on while he's here in the city, and this is his last free night. When the job winds up, he'll head back to England. Though he simply called it Europe.

He reaches out and takes a card, turning it over and frowning. "What's your biggest fear?"

"Spiders." I hate them. They're gross and build webs to trap you in and have eight eyes, and that seems like an unfair advantage in this wildlife documentary we call life.

He frowns my way. "That is not your biggest fear."

"How would you know? You met me a couple of hours ago. I could have gotten bitten by a tarantula when I was five and still bear the scars of that trauma." I hadn't. I'm smarter than that. Tarantulas are large and easily avoidable if one is always on the lookout for arachnids. And I am. No. It's the small ones I truly fear. Not to say I won't girly scream and get my ass out of there if a tarantula shows up, because I will.

Luca is staring at me like he can see through to my soul. "We talked about your parents and my parents, and if you're not afraid of becoming your mother, I'll eat that special thing they have on the menu."

It's fried pickles slathered in sriracha, and Luca had seemed both fascinated and horrified at the thought. I rather thought they'd shut down the kitchen at this point, but I get what he's saying, though I stand by my arachnophobia. "Fine. I do worry I'll end up in that kind of relationship. She was devastated when he left. I don't know what she would have done if she hadn't had her business partner. Tonya's been her best friend since high school. She held us all together while Mom worked on some stuff. It was hard because right after the divorce, Dad insisted on a strict custody schedule. I think he did it to punish her."

"Why do you think that?" Luca asks.

"Because he wasn't interested in spending time with me." It had been a difficult era for me. He moved out of the city so when I was at his place, I didn't have Ivy or Harper. I was alone. "I don't think he hated me. He was kind of neutral when it came to me. I think he was far more interested in punishing her for not being the woman he wanted. And this is why I put all the weird stuff out at the beginning. I think that's what my dad did wrong. Or maybe it was my mom. She said he changed after they got married, and again after they had me. I don't think people really change. I think they get comfortable enough to show you who they are. I make it a point to simply be myself the entire time."

He seems to think for a moment. "Sound reasoning, although for some people there is a hidden self. One they must show to the public, and a more private self."

I don't buy it. "Why would anyone want that kind of life? I mean, I get it. You're talking about politicians or like an actor or something. I deal with a lot of those, and I know they don't present the same face to the world they do in private, but that's work. You're never going to be the same person at work that you are at home. Not entirely."

He seems to think about what to say, leaning over, his deep brown eyes searching mine. "But what if your work is always with you? I don't think King Charles would say he gets much of a private life."

"Yeah. It would suck to be royal."

"Yes, it would," he agrees. "Although there are some compensations."

I can't think of one, and I am about to have to deal with a horny king, so I'm ready to get off the topic of royalty. "Well, I'm not worried about ending up in some royal family, but I do worry I'll find myself in love with someone I don't truly know."

He stares at me for a moment. "So you try to be yourself always."

"Always. Though you should understand I truly am afraid of spiders. They're not natural. You shouldn't be able to have eight legs and a million eyes and be hairy under a microscope."

"Well, if we see any I will slay them for you," he offers gallantly.

"I didn't say I wanted them dead. Just not in my house. Or whatever space I'm in. I read somewhere that at any moment in time your house has an average of eight spiders in it." I shiver at the thought. "Maybe not mine, though. It's very small, so maybe mine is only like one or two."

A grin flashes across his face, and I swear my heart reacts to how glorious he is. The thump in my chest isn't something I can ignore. This man does it for me. The elusive, undefinable "it" we're all looking for.

"I've heard the lodgings in the city can be somewhat small," he remarks.

"Try excruciatingly tiny. I have to move my sofa in order to bring down my bed to sleep. But it's in a great place for me workwise. I can get everywhere I need to be quickly, and I'm close to my friends, though I worry someday Ivy and Heath are going to make some super-smart babies and leave for Connecticut. Don't tell her that. She would find it horrifying, but I suspect one day she might even buy a minivan. Did you know Connecticut is called the Nutmeg State?"

If he's shocked by my weird turn in conversation, he doesn't show it, merely looks at me like I'm fascinating. "I did not."

Like I said, I put my oddness out there for all to see. Strange facts are a part of the package. You learn a lot in the industry I work in. A lot of useless facts, though I think I might do well on *Jeopardy*. "Yes, it is, and I find it interesting that nutmeg, while everyone thinks it's just a part of a pumpkin pie spice combo, is actually a toxin if it's not processed properly. If you consume it in large amounts, it can give you hallucinations, and I think that's why people from Connecticut always seem so happy. They have too much nutmeg in their systems."

He sits back and laughs, the sound booming through the small diner. I like the sound. "You are the oddest woman I've ever met."

Not the first time I've heard that, but he doesn't say it like it's a bad thing. I think he might be a man who can handle some odd. "You obviously don't get out much."

"You do know it's almost one in the morning." The waitress looks tired of our antics. "And everyone else is gone. We close in twenty minutes. Or in five, if you decide to leave."

I don't want to leave.

Luca pulls the cards into his hands. "We haven't finished the game. I think you're going to have to show me this tiny space of yours."

When he offers me his hand, I take it.

Two hours later we've gotten ice cream and walked around Rockefeller Center, answering more of those silly questions while sitting on a bench. Usually the late-night crowds would bug me because at this hour they tend to be drunk or obnoxious, but the truth is I don't see anyone but him.

We've talked about what world peace would look like for us—a weird question that he answered beautifully and I mentioned the words free candy—discussed our childhood pets, and whether or not we have siblings. No for both of us.

We have a lot in common. It's all I can think about as we approach my building. The night seems magical, and I don't want it to end.

"This is me." I reach inside my teeny tiny bag that basically only holds my phone, ID, and the key to my apartment.

He glances up at the building, and I wonder what he sees. It's an old building, bearing the marks of decades and generations. There are certainly prettier buildings. Like the one I'm going to spend a bunch of time around soon because it will play host to a group of wannabe queens, while their king stays at a luxury hotel.

I don't want to think about that right now. I want Luca to kiss me and come upstairs, and we can forget everything for a couple of hours. I know we're not starting some grand romance. He can't stay in New York, and I won't be moving to England anytime soon, but I've so enjoyed the feel of his hand in mine.

I want to not be lonely for a little while.

"This has been the best night I've had in a long time," he says quietly, his fingers disentangling from mine. "Thank you. I so often find myself in stuffy places with stuffy people. It's my line of work."

He described it as a combination between publicity and diplomacy. I picked up that he works for his government, and likely in a high-level position.

I'd explained my dream job to him. Not the one I'm about to do. We talked about my upcoming film project, and he agreed that it probably didn't need aliens. Probably. He really does like science fiction. "No stuffy people around here. Only weirdos."

He looks down at me, his fingers coming up to brush the line of my jaw. "I like weirdos. I enjoyed being in your world for the night, Anika. I wish I could stay longer."

I don't like the sound of that. "You could come up for a nightcap."

That will lead to sweaty, glorious, nasty sex, and an exchange of phone numbers.

Damn it. I'm thinking beyond the night, and that's so foolish of me. He told me he can't hang out. He's been clear, and I should know better.

He sighs, a look of regret in his eyes as he stares down at me. "If only it was so simple. The funny thing is I thought I would be walking up those stairs with you. Or I would convince you to come back to my room. I looked across that bar and thought I might be able to fit one good night in."

Despite the fact that I've just admonished myself for overreaching, I leap at the opportunity. I still want him even though I'm pretty sure he'll break my heart. "So come upstairs with me. It's small but cozy, and I think I've got some wine."

It might be in a box. I hope it's not in a box.

"But then I got to know you," he says, stepping away. "And I know what a sacrifice I'm about to make. I have things I have to do, things I don't want to do. However, I will do my duty, and one of those things is going back to my hotel room alone. It was such an honor to spend time with you, Anika Fox."

He's going to leave and he's not even going to kiss me.

I thought for sure he would kiss me.

He seems like the charmingest of princes, and now I realize I've been playing out a fantasy in my head. A rom-com where we both go in without the intention of falling in love, but in the morning he would know he can't leave.

I'm still that little girl who wants so badly to have an epic love story because the world seems so cold.

He's doing me a kindness because he isn't playing into my fantasies.

"It was good to spend time with you, too, Luca." I give him what I hope is a bright smile.

He takes my hand in his and brings it to his lips, his kiss sending warmth through me. "Know that I am going to regret walking away from you for a very long time. Have a good life, Anika, and I'll look for that movie of yours."

He backs away, and I watch as he hails a cab. He waves to me and then he's gone.

I stare for a moment and then walk slowly up the steps, hating the fact that I have tears in my eyes.

I don't know that man. Not really. I mean I know where he likes to vacation and that he felt lonely most of his life. I know he views his job as something he can't step away from. I know his parents didn't give him the best model of a relationship.

So it's strange that when I think about it, I have to admit that I know more about him than my last boyfriend, and I dated him for half a year. We'd done all the *where did you go to school and who are your friends stuff,* but we'd never gone deep. Not the way Luca and I had.

I sniffle and realize how late it is. It's time for bed. If I can sleep.

I buzz into the building, and there's a woman sitting on the bottom step. She's still dressed for the party we went to earlier, and I wonder how long she's been sitting here.

"Harper?"

Her head comes up, and her face falls as she realizes I'm alone. "Oh. Did you already go back to his place and now you're walking in here all happy and satisfied? Except you look ready to cry."

I am so relieved to see my friend. She stands, and I cross the space between us, throwing my arms around her. "I liked him so much, but he didn't even kiss me. We walked around the city and asked each other all those questions and then he left me here."

Harper's arms close around me. "Oh, sweetie. I'm so sorry, but if you're this invested already, it's for the best. I was waiting because I knew how much you liked him, and I was either going to let him know I was hanging around in case he thought about hurting you or for this. I can kill him if you want. I know how to use a nail gun."

She does, but there's no reason to want vengeance. He's a nice man who didn't take advantage of me. He gave me a great night and a wonderful memory. I wipe away the tears I shouldn't be shedding because I barely know him.

Except it doesn't feel that way.

"Come on," Harper says. "I swiped a bottle of wine from CeCe's. It's been in my tote bag most of the night."

"You did what?" I ask.

Harper grins. "Well, I was going to swipe another bottle, but CeCe caught me and told me I was an idiot and gave me this one instead. It's old. Should we drink wine from 1947?"

"Yes." My best friend mostly drinks beer. I happen to absolutely trust CeCe to give up the good stuff. She can be intimidating, but she genuinely enjoys sharing the things she loves with people she doesn't want to murder. That bottle of wine is practically a declaration of love. "We are definitely drinking that wine."

It will be the perfect end to a glorious evening.

I sit on my fire escape, watching the night ease toward morning, talking to my friend, drinking wretchedly expensive wine. And wondering what Luca is doing.

Chapter Four

I walk into work Monday afternoon having spent the majority of the day sleeping in to get used to the schedule I'll have to follow the next few weeks. There are a lot of night shoots on a show like this, and the first shoot here on set is one of them. They've already done all the getting-to-know-you shots. Those had been done in more formal studios before the cast was required to be in the city.

There's a reason most reality dating shows don't take place in New York City. They find mansions in California where they have tons of room to film, but for some reason they think this one can work.

"Can I see your ID?" The security guard's question reminds me I'm here for a reason.

I stand in the studio space. From what I understand the contestants will be staying in a gorgeous Gilded Age mansion, one of the few left that hasn't been broken up and redone as apartments. There are still a few left standing, and this one has a place in my heart. I hadn't recognized the address, though I suspect Harper would have if I'd told her.

Once my two best friends and I had stood in that mansion when we visited it on a class trip. We'd snuck away and promised to always stick together.

Maybe it won't be so bad since I'm here and I know they are, too. Somewhere in the city we live in, Ivy is getting a taco and Harper is installing drywall. Not really since they're both probably getting ready to end their workdays, but you get the point. This place tied us together once, and even though they can't be here with me, I feel better.

It's not like I'm going into a battle.

I'm going into work, and everything will be fine. It's six weeks of my life. That's all. And then I'll be back on track and I'll have either saved a man's career from bitter rumors or trashed a dude who deserves trashing.

I can do this.

"Do you have ID?"

"Oh, yeah." I fumble through my bag to get it out. "Sorry. My brain's not working yet. I'm supposed to report to the key production assistant. I think his name is Patrick. Do you know where he is?"

The burly security guard checks my ID against his list and passes me a lanyard that proclaims me to be crew. He sits back and yawns as he points down a long hallway. "That way, I think. I don't know. This place is weird. There are actual tunnels they're using. Apparently whoever used to own this place made his money smuggling booze or something. Don't wander down there, though. I would bet it floods."

I promise not to wander and then immediately break the promise because he's right and this place is huge. It's been years since I was here, and I hadn't exactly walked in the front door. The production crew has also taken over the building next to the mansion as its primary studio, and that's the building I'm wandering through now. I likely won't see a ton of the mansion since that's where the "contestants" are going to live. I'll primarily be running between sets.

I walk down one hall and find hair and makeup, and it looks like they're wrapping up. A stunning woman is sitting in one of the chairs, having her natural curls worked on. Her makeup is flawless, and she could be a model.

The real filming begins this evening when the first cocktail party with the king will take place, and His Majesty will dash the dreams of three women right then and there.

When I think about it, it's kind of brutal.

But the good news is I'll likely be wandering around this place trying to find coffee or the right lightbulbs or whatever the directing crew requires. I won't have to watch the drama that will play out this evening.

I turn around from that dead end and find myself walking toward the smell of coffee. I'm a couple of minutes early, right? I can get my own coffee before I get everyone else's.

"Hey," a voice says as I pass an open door. "Hey, are you the new PA?"

I want to cry because I have to say yes. I stop and back up because he hasn't come out of the room, merely expects me to hear him and return. That's the nature of what I'm going into. I'm the lowest of the low. The assistant to all assistants. I flash a bright smile as I take in the room. "Hi. I'm Anika Fox."

The man is standing in the middle of a room filled with comms equipment. He's not the only one, but he's the only one who seems to care about me. The rest of the guys don't bother to look up from where they're organizing what is likely everything they need for the day's filming.

"I'm Patrick Dennings. This is my set and you're late." Patrick is probably twenty-five and looks like he could be talent. He's extremely handsome, with blond hair and a face that could be on a magazine cover. He's dressed down, but I would bet the man is fashionable as hell in his daily life. He's what we call the key production assistant, which means he's in charge of all the production assistants and is likely very territorial over his position.

He's also super irritated with me. I check my watch again. "I'm here ten minutes before my call time."

"You're here twenty minutes after everyone else arrived. Look, I get that you're some kind of nepo hire, but I don't care who your mother or father or uncle is. I don't care if you're someone's side piece."

"Hey." I wasn't about to take that from him. "And I don't care that you're some asshole who thinks because he's slightly higher than me on the staff, that it's okay to harass me."

Now all the boys are looking my way.

Patrick frowns. "Harass you?"

I need them all to understand I'm not going to put up with their toxic crap. Oftentimes I have to introduce myself. "Yeah, look, you can dress me down all you like, but if you call me a whore again, I'll have you wrapped up in a lawsuit. I am new to this set. I am not new to life, and despite my short stature and blonde hair, I'm not going to allow anyone to push me around, and that includes you."

His eyes narrow. "You're not going to last long here."

He's not the first bully I've dealt with. "We'll see about that. Now I would like to be the nice version of myself, but I can introduce you to the other side of me. If you want me here thirty minutes before the call sheet says, tell me. I have gotten neither call nor text. I assume you have access to my paperwork and therefore you have my phone number."

He puts down the comm he's been inspecting. "We have a meeting before every shift. I update the crew on what's being filmed that day and what will be required of you. Now you know, and I'll expect you here on time."

He's not exactly polite, but he's also not screaming so I count it as a win. "I'll be here for the meeting tomorrow. Where do you need me tonight?"

He seems to calm, going back to his equipment check. "We've gotten hit with a curve ball. Completely out of nowhere, the director has decided to do some viral marketing. He's going to live stream some of the meetings and do some candid shots with the contestants. It's going to be live on the network's website. He's hoping it turns into one of those break-the-Internet things."

"Live?" It's kind of my nightmare. I know they used to do live shows back in the day, but you know what we have now? Editing. Editing is an important part of life. It is the eraser on the pencil we call entertainment. "Is he sure he wants to do that? What if one of the contestants says something awful?"

Patrick's shoulder shrugs. "Well, then he's absolutely sure to go viral. I don't think he cares. I think he knows what's on the line, and he's willing to do pretty much anything to make this show a success. That means he's going to pull out all the stops."

Which means Joseph Helms will be relying on the crew to make his vision come true. I am suddenly happy I'm going to be the coffee girl. Though Patrick isn't responsible for filming, he will feel the burden of the live segments. Everyone will.

"Where do you want me?" I ask. I don't like the man, but he's obviously under pressure.

He sighs and picks up a comm unit. "Take this to the west side of the building. We've managed to get the city to let us shut down the side street so we can film the horse-drawn carriages delivering the future queen to her king." He gags a little. "Pass this off to Joe's assistant. Her comm wasn't working earlier. And then you can help the cleanup crew."

One of the other men snorts.

"Cleanup?" It feels like a trap.

He gives me an asshole smirk. "Yeah, can't have the horse crap showing up in the shot, can we? Good luck with that, new girl."

I'm back to hating him, but I can't exactly walk out in protest. I take the comm. At least I'll get to meet the woman closest to Helms on set. She's been his assistant for years, and it will be good for me to get close to her. "Will do, boss."

I start to turn.

"New girl," he says, causing me to stop.

I turn, waiting for some more of his vitriol.

Instead he frowns, and his tone is softer. "I didn't mean to call you a whore. I apologize. My boyfriend and I broke up a couple of weeks ago and I'm still cranky about it. If you think the horse poop is punishment, it's not. I had you on horse detail long before you annoyed me. You're the low man for now, and you'll get the crappiest assignments. Literally. Do your job and we'll get along."

I nod. "All right."

"The lockers are two doors down. Drop your stuff off and get that comm to the set. They're about to start," he says.

I hustle out because it looks like this job is just beginning.

The "studio" is a maze of rooms, and it takes me a while to figure out how to maneuver my way to the other side of the building where I can get to the set. Everyone is buzzing with energy, and I hear them talking about the live shoot.

Most of them think the idea is risky. Some of them are excited to work live.

Everyone thinks Helms is a genius who's slumming.

"I have no idea what he's going to do now," a woman with a headset on says as she walks through the door. "That woman is insane. The king is gorgeous. I would give up a job to have a shot at that hunk of a man."

I step through the door as she heads for the elevator.

"Yes, the director lost his shit when he found out," she says as the door closes behind me, and I find myself in a romantic paradise.

Okay, I know it's cheesy, but I'm a hearts and flowers girlie. I like the romantic crap, and they've done a fabulous job. They've brought in thousands of flowers. They decorated the street and the buildings. There's a red carpet that leads from where the carriage stops to where the king will greet the contestants. The sun is setting and the lights are about to come on, and the whole place feels magical to me. Sometimes I think I can't see the flaws, the falseness of a set. All I see is a different world, a place we made as a space for the story we want to tell.

This is something of a story, I think. Surely there's a story somewhere in here that will entertain…whoever happens to watch a show like this.

They've closed the narrow side street down at both ends, and I can see we've got help keeping crowds away. There's an NYPD cruiser at either end and two elaborate carriages fit for a future queen. I step down and the horses are right there with two trainers and two men who are dressed like they're picking up a Bridgerton for a ball.

I can already smell the horse poop, so fantasy over.

"Is that my comm?" a woman asks. She's wearing jeans and a T-shirt that shows off her toned body. She's stunningly gorgeous, and she gives me a smile as I hand over the comm.

"Yes. Patrick told me to bring it to the director's assistant, who I assume is you," I reply. "I'm going to be on set tonight working with the horses. If there's anything you need, let me know."

She settles the unit over her head, adjusting the microphone so it's away from her mouth. "I'm Christy, and yes, I'm Joe's assistant." She looks me over. "If you hadn't been holding that comm, I would have thought you were wayward talent. You're a pretty girl."

That got weird fast. "Uh, thanks."

She snorts. "I'm not hitting on you. I have a problem, and you might be the solution. Come with me. You're off poop duty." She touches the comm. "Yeah, Joe, I found someone who'll work. She's a PA, but she'll fit right in. You wanted a shortie, so maybe this works out." She starts to walk inside the studio, looking back at me, an expectant expression on her face. "Are you coming or not?"

Definitely a trap. Still, I'm almost certain I'm about to meet the man I'm supposed to be investigating, so I follow her. A couple of winding staircases later and I'm ushered into a luxurious space that's made up like a lush mancave. There's a bar on one end of the room and a massive screen that takes up a whole wall.

It's nearly impossible to have a trailer on a city set, so this is what passes for the director's trailer. His hideaway and workspace.

There's a desk with pictures of Joseph Helms and his wife. Mrs. Helms is a beautiful blonde who looks slightly younger than her middle-aged husband.

I know Jess can't stand the woman, but I hope I don't have to be the one to tell her if her husband is cheating.

"I can't do it with twelve," Joe says into his cell as he walks in from another room. "The whole thing is timed. I need thirteen contestants. No, I can't have him cut one less. You are not understanding the situation."

"Neither am I," I whisper under my breath.

"Okay, I'll give you the cheap-seats version." Christy is also a blonde. She's tall and willowy and weirdly reminds me of the woman in the picture, though they're obviously not the same. Christy is older.

The man seems to have a type, and I realize why I'm here.

Blonde, cute, young-looking.

Jessica knows exactly what she's doing. She found her bait, and apparently it is me.

"So we have thirteen contestants," Christy says, her voice low so she doesn't disturb the currently pacing director. "There are ten episodes we're planning to film. One of the women who was set to compete got a call from her agent who got her a job on a TV show. The trouble is she has to be on set tomorrow. I've begged her to stay on tonight and the king can simply cut her at the first elimination ceremony, but she claims she needs her beauty sleep. So I've lost our sales rep from Nevada and everyone is freaking out."

"I thought she was an actress."

"They're all actresses. Well, almost all. I think the midwestern girl is really an accountant," Christy says. "But it's better we talk about what else they do for a living. None of them are solid working actors, of course, but almost all of them want to be in the industry."

I'm not following fully. "I don't understand. If he's scheduled to cut three women, why not simply cut two? It shouldn't cause a disruption with the shooting. You'll still have ten episodes."

"But he's obsessed with this live event he's got going. It's set up for thirteen women," Christy says as her eyes follow her boss. "I've tried to get him to see it's okay, but he insists on the original thirteen. I guess he's worried people will ask questions if he doesn't have the thirteen that were promised."

"Why would he worry about that? It's not in his control." Things go wrong all the time. No one blames the director. Nope. That's a PA's job.

"He's had a couple of rumors circulate that he's hard to work with. He's not. He's the sweetest man," Christy assures me. "But he's in the running for a big franchise, and he wants everything to be in line with his vision. Thirteen is apparently his perfect number. And that is where you come in... What was your name?"

"Anika."

She brings her fingers to her lips in a chef's kiss. "Oh, you are perfect. And you're the right size. You're a six?"

I nod. "Why do you need to know my dress size? Am I going to be working in a costume?" It isn't completely unheard of. If they need a crowd for a scene, they sometimes hire actors or shove crew into the appropriate attire and let them shuffle around. "You need a walk-on one?"

A *one* meant I wouldn't have any lines and wouldn't be asked to do anything more specific than walk in a direction. I would be set décor. A two and three were basically small part roles often with a dash of dialogue.

"Nope. I need a lot more from you." Christy waves a hand to get Joe's attention as he places his cell phone on the bar. There's no booze there. Just a bunch of soda and water bottles, reminding me he's sober and seems to want to stay that way. "I have the solution."

Joe turns and his eyes widen. "Oh, yes. She'll do nicely."

"I'll do what?" Terror is kind of flowing through my veins at this point because I've got an inkling of what they need from me.

The director gives me a wide smile. "Compete for the crown."

Yep. I want to be back with the horses.

Chapter Five

Somehow I find myself sitting in a makeup chair, a man tsking over me as Christy and Joe explain the turn my life has taken.

"Don't frown so much," the makeup guys says. He's the last one left. At one point I'd had three people hovering around me, fixing my hair, my nails, my everything. It's enough to make a girl nervous. "The makeup settles in and gives you ghastly shadows."

"I don't think I should be doing this at all. I'm a production assistant," I point out. I like to play around with makeup when we go out to clubs and stuff, but I don't wear a lot of it in my normal life.

"You *were* a production assistant and now you're a contestant." Joe seems perfectly content now that he believes he's got girl number thirteen on the hook. "Tomorrow you can go right back to assisting. Think of yourself as a stand-in. This is going to be easy. I won't even make you do an introduction video. Normally there would be several hours spent getting a contestant's life story."

I know what he's talking about. It's what they'd been doing for weeks. Interviewing all the contestants. Not that most of the footage will reach the airwaves. Some of the contestants will get three minutes on air before they're cut.

"Hours for a few minutes of tape," Christy says with a shake of her head. "It's mind numbing. When are we getting back to real film?"

I agree with her, though movie shoots can also have take after take after take for that one perfect moment of film. "I don't know that it's ethical for me to take a contestant's spot. Maybe if I call her…"

Joe frowns. He's a handsome man in his early sixties. Despite his well-documented substance abuse problems, he looks healthy and fit, with salt and pepper hair and bushy eyebrows that seem to be a vehicle for his every emotion. Those brows are in a deep *V* now. "Absolutely not. She's dead to me. You, however, are very much alive, and I think you're going to be spectacular. And by spectacular I mean you'll blend in and no one will notice you until you're standing in the elimination room without a flower." He looks back at Christy. "Are we sure we have to go with the daisy? Roses look better on camera."

"His Majesty insists it must be oxeye daisies, and they have to come from Ralavia," Christy says as the makeup guy hovers over me with a massive eyelash in tweezers between his fingers. He studies me like a problem he needs to solve. "So now we have a couple thousand of them in cold storage. We need to use the daisies."

Joe shrugs, obviously giving in. "The guy's been more than easy to work with, so I'll give on the flowers. Anyway, you'll be standing there without a flower, and I'll need you to look heartbroken. Can you do that for me, Anika?"

I'm pretty sure the only expression I'm going to be able to muster is deer in the headlights. Makeup guy zeroes in, placing the giant lash on my eye. I swear I can see the thing when I blink. I'm a little worried I might be able to fly with it. "What about the ethical aspect of this situation? You know that I signed an agreement that as an employee of Pinnacle Entertainment, I'm not allowed to try out for any of our reality or game shows."

"You didn't try out," Joe points out. "You were recruited. And I already called legal. They're waiving that clause. They're viewing it as nothing more than a favor to your director. You'll be helping me out, and I want you to know I'll remember that. I remember the nice things people do for me, and I like to repay them with kindness."

And jobs. That's what he's talking about. He's offering to give me a leg up. Working on his next film could be a huge deal. He really wants this.

The problem is the thought of being in front of the camera gives me hives. Not real ones. Real ones might get me out of this situation, but my skin stays a creamy neutral with some sparkly undertones thanks to the magic the makeup man has worked. He's kind of an ass, but the man knows what he's doing. My hair is in a blonde halo around my head, and my neck seems graceful and long. I look like a very modern princess.

I still don't want to go on camera. "Mr. Helms, I think there has to be someone better. I am not any kind of actress. I'm weird, and being nervous kind of turns me into a walking cautionary tale."

"You won't have to talk much," he promises. "And we'll edit out anything that doesn't look good. You can trust me. I won't make you look like a fool. Only a little of what we film tonight is going to be live. The rest is normal production. There's no problem we can't clean up in post. I'll even let you sit in on the editing."

It's unheard of. Editing on a show like this is everything. Heroes and villains are made in the editing room. I would love to sit in on the editing just for the experience. And yet I can't make myself say yes. Saying yes seems like a slope I don't want to slip down. I can make a mess of things, and I'm supposed to be flying under the radar here. "Have you called a casting company? I'm sure they can have someone here soon."

His expression tightens, but the words that come out of his mouth are patient. "Not soon enough."

"We need to get the introductions filmed in the next two hours. The live elimination ceremony is scheduled for eleven," Christy points out. "We can't be late."

"It's going to be tight as it is," Joe agrees. "But the live stream is going to have millions of viewers. It's going to whet their appetite for the show. And it's going to make our premiere numbers skyrocket."

"I think I'm too nervous. I'm going to be terrible at this. I'm the girl who threw up on stage in fifth grade when they wanted me to say one line. One." I never lived that down, and there are still people out there who call me Vomitting Ani. It's not something I want to do on national TV. I'm a behind-the-scenes person.

"Can we have the room for a moment?" Joe asks.

My nerves shoot up because I'm not sure I want to be alone with this man. He's been nice so far, but I get the feeling I'm about to meet his ruthless side.

The makeup guy shakes his head as he leaves, as though he's done what he can and can't help me anymore. Christy puts a hand on Joe's arm as though offering him support and then she leaves, too.

I'm left alone with the very man I'm supposed to be investigating. He stares at me for a moment. An awkward, long moment.

"Anika, this show is important. I know everyone thinks it's all bullshit, but I have a different point of view." He keeps a respectful distance, his tone still calm and soothing.

I know it's important to him. That's part of the problem. "I'm sure it is, and that's why I don't want to mess things up for you."

He seems to consider my words, those brows of his furrowed in concentration. "Ah, you've heard the rumors and think this is all about me proving to Jessica Wallace that I'm in control and I won't go off on a bender."

I feel my skin flush. "I don't think that."

His expression gentles. "Then you're the only one. I understand what I did made everyone question my capabilities. I'm an artist, but I still have to be insured, and she can't pass me that gorgeous franchise if I can't get insurance to cover me. But that's not why I think this project is important. There's more at stake here than my career."

"I know it's a massive production and it employs so many people," I begin.

He holds out a hand. "Again, this isn't about me or anyone in the crew. This is about our bachelor. I'm friendly with the king. I shot part of a movie in his country."

"I'm sure he's nice," I allow.

"It's not about him being nice. The king is a great guy, but more importantly he's a magnificent king," Joe says. "Reg is a very modern monarch. He's out there with his people every day. Look, don't tell anyone because we have an illusion to create, but there's not a ton of money in Ralavia right now. After the floods a couple of years back, the king used an enormous amount of his own money to rebuild the capitol city. He's doing this because he thinks if people see how beautiful the country is, they'll come back. Tourism was wiped out by the floods, but the country is ready to welcome them again. They need those tourist dollars or they'll have to default on their debts soon."

I'd heard about the tragedy that had taken place in that part of the world. "So this is like a tourist ad?"

He nods as though happy I've caught onto the idea. "Yes. The ski season is coming up right after this airs, and we're going global with this one, so we're hoping Europeans remember Ralavia exists and bring their money back to the country. Put some food on the country's table, so to speak. Reg isn't doing this because he wants true love. He's doing it to keep his people from starving."

My heart hurts for him, but it also hurts for the contestants. "But what about the women who are here for the right reasons?"

Damn. I just said it. Told you there would be a lot of that phrase.

Joe chuckles. "I assure you they're all here for the same reason. Fame. How many of these things end up working out? One in a thousand? No one expects them to genuinely get married. The winner of the show will do some press with the king, wave from the palace a couple of times, and then they'll quietly break it off and no one will be all that surprised."

"That feels cynical." Even as I say the words, I know I'm being naïve. This is why I like to work on the fictional side of the entertainment industry. It's all characters, and the actors don't have to risk their hearts or their mental health.

"Or he could find the love of his life here," Joe says, a plea in his tone. "You never know what can happen when you put people together. There will be some excellent opportunities to get to know the king. Why can't two people fall in love here? They fall in love at work all the time. All I'm saying is I need you, Anika. The people of Ralavia need you. It's one night and then you're out, and you will have helped a whole nation."

Or they could do it with twelve contestants. I want to say that, but I doubt it will move the man.

He's figured out exactly the path to take with me, and I realize how dangerous this man could be if he doesn't want to do the right thing. He's charming and smooth and didn't take *no* from me. He has me right where he wants me, and I can't wriggle out of the trap. "All right. One night. I'll blend into the background. Maybe I can be that girl who smiles and looks relieved that I didn't get picked because I didn't feel the connection either."

Joe opens the door, and I realize Christy and the makeup guy have been waiting right outside. They hadn't been making alternate plans in case he failed. They know he'll get what he wants.

"Tears would be so much better," Joe replies as they all move back in. "If you could look crestfallen, maybe have a couple of tears clinging to your cheeks, that would be perfect."

"Don't sob." Christy is rummaging through the rows of clothes they have set up. For the most part the contestants will wear their own clothes, but a good selection is kept in case production doesn't like a contestant's fashion sense. "It looks terrible on camera. Unless you're going to flip a table. That makes for great TV."

Joe shakes his head. "Absolutely not on the first night, though I think we've got at least one girl who will cause some serious drama tonight."

"All of the makeup is waterproof." Makeup guy finally gets the second lash on my lid and stares down at me. "There's plenty of makeup remover in the mansion. Takes a while to get it off, so whatever your skin care routine before bed is, add a half an hour. You're as good as you're going to get."

"But I'm not going to be in the mansion," I say, worried I'm going to have the makeup clinging to me for the next year. "Should we tone this down?"

"You look perfect," Joe insists. "You look like you could be the queen of a small, impoverished European country."

That makes me laugh. He's a charming man. I view him as something of a fatherly figure, but I would bet a lot of women fall for his humor and his ability to figure out a person quickly. When fame hadn't worked, he'd gone straight for my heartstrings. They are always there, waiting to be plucked. Waiting to get me in trouble.

If it helps feed a nation, I suppose I can make it through one whole cocktail party and pretend to be upset I'm not picked out of a group of random women.

There's a brief knock and then Patrick is walking through. He's got a headset on and a clipboard in his hands. "Mr. Helms, we're ready for you. I've got a missing PA, but we'll work it out. I'll fire her as soon as I… What the hell are you doing here, Fox?"

I'm just making the boss love everything about me today. "I got sidetracked."

His face flushes, and it's obvious he's ready to do that firing right here and now.

"Anika is doing me a very large favor, Patrick," Joe says, putting a hand on Patrick's shoulder. I notice the way Patrick stiffens but doesn't move away. "We've lost a contestant, and she's going to take her place. It's one night. The king will reject her and she'll be back on your team in the morning."

"I want to work with the horses," I say because it slips out. See. Nerves make me say stupid things.

Patrick shifts away from Joe, straightening his shoulders and making for the door. "There won't be any horses tomorrow, but I'm sure I can find something suitable for you. Like I said, we're ready to start. The talent is dressed and awaiting their carriage rides. I've got craft services set up at the end of the block since it's going to be a night shoot and I doubt anyone will be able to stop for a real dinner."

"Somehow I think they'll manage," Joe says. "We're making history tonight."

"People still want to take breaks," Patrick insists.

Joe puts an arm around his shoulder as they start to walk out the door. It's a fraternal thing, but Patrick looks uncomfortable. Not a huggy guy.

"That's why I have you to deal with all the union drivel," Joe is saying.

The door closes and Christy holds up what I can only describe as if a sunbeam was a dress. A way-too-short dress. It's gold and made of sequins and glitter.

"Perfect," she says. "And I hope you can walk in five-inch stilettos because I've got a pair of Louboutins that match this dress perfectly. You're an eight, right?"

I'm not, but it won't be the first time I give up comfort for style.

I sigh and pray I make it through the night.

Chapter Six

"He's the most gorgeous man I've ever seen," a brunette says as she sips on the champagne production has so helpfully provided. "I can't wait to see him in person. I've never met a king before. Well, I met the king of our local corn parade, but Dennis Dully doesn't count. He's not like historic or anything. His dad's just rich. I'm Hannah. I like your dress."

I stand in what's serving as a green room. I'm last on the list to make my "entrance." One by one each gorgeous woman has had her name called, makeup hurry around her to ensure she's sheer perfection, and then she's led out to meet her doom/possible true love. I'm feeling the doom vibe heavily. Hannah is the first person to talk to me. She's maybe twenty-two and on at least her second glass of champagne.

"Thanks. I didn't exactly pick it out, but it's nice," I admit. When I'd first walked in, about half of the contestants had been inside, each wearing some version of formal wear. One woman had obviously taken her cue from Kate Middleton's wedding dress, complete with tiara. It was a whole bag of elegantly dressed cats. "Can I get you a water? I suspect there's going to be a lot of booze at the cocktail party. They do that on reality shows to heighten emotions."

It's predatory, and the sober ones are usually the first ones to leave the show. Despite the true love aspect of the production I'm on, the king won't be making all the decisions alone. The producers will "advise" him. They're not about to let go of a scene-chomping villain before they absolutely have to.

"She should keep drinking because it's the only fun she's going to have tonight. There's no way she makes it through."

Yes, the villain is in the house.

"That's Shelby," another voice whispers. "She's super mean. Ignore her. I'm Ashley. There are two other Ashleys, so I'm Ashley F. Did you take Brittany's place? I heard she got the call to be a corpse on the new *Law and Order* and grabbed it with both hands. I would have, too. I heard the corpse is a sex worker. It's the best corpse you can possibly play."

I'm torn between asking why sex workers make the best corpses— sounds a little serial killer to me—and introducing myself to Shelby. I can probably fit my painful stiletto all the way up her ass.

But I've vowed to fly under the radar. "Hannah, why don't you come over here? You've got a stray hair."

She looks like she's on the verge of tears, and that will send hair and makeup into a tizzy.

Patrick opens the door, pointedly ignoring me. "Shelby, we're ready for you on set."

The obvious villain of the group straightens up to her impressive height. She's supermodel tall, with long dark hair and a patrician face. She could be a member of royalty and she knows it. There's something cold about her blue eyes. "Time to meet my future husband. Good luck, girls."

It is plain to see she thinks we'll need it.

"Wow, she's a lot," I say because I can be charitable. When I'm working as an assistant again, I'm going to weaponize some incompetence when it comes to her. Also, I'll be in the editing room if the director keeps his promise. I'll find every time she looks constipated and make that her still shot of the day.

"Don't mind her," Hannah says, giving me a watery smile. She sips her champagne like a champ. "She's nothing more than another mean girl."

Ashley F shakes her head. "Nah. She's like all the mean girls rolled into one skinny designer bag with supermodel legs. Everyone thinks she's going to win. She's nice to all the men on the production crew. She'll be sweet to the king, and he won't see what a massive bitch she is until it's far too late. It's a tale as old as time. She's practically got the tiara on her head."

"Like you care," Hannah shoots back.

"I do," Ashley insists. "Look, I won't turn the guy down. He's gorgeous and all, but I'm more of a rock star kind of girl. I'm mostly here because my agent told me it's a good way to get on people's radars. Hannah here is a true love kind of girl. How about you? Sorry, I didn't hear your name when they brought you in."

Because Christy had shoved me into this dress and dropped me off here without a word beyond "don't fuck up."

The trouble is I can fuck up easily. I'd almost snatched Shelby's sure-to-be-fake hair off her head. No real hair sits that perfectly. "I'm Anika." I realize I'm not sure how to explain my presence. Although, unless they're going to fire me, the women will figure it out very quickly. "I'm a production assistant. When the other girl decided to be a corpse, they pulled me in because I fit into her dress. Except I don't. I won't be bending over anytime soon, if you know what I mean."

"That dress is perfect on you," Ashley F promises. Her dark skin contrasts beautifully with the yellow of her cocktail dress. She's stunning, with close cropped hair that shows off the definition of her face. She's slender and tall.

In comparison, Hannah is maybe five foot four and looks like she just came out of the cornfield. Not that she's not pretty. She's lovely, but she's got an air of middle America about her, from her staid, almost matronly dress to the somber bun at the back of her head.

"Did production pick out that dress for you?" I ask.

Hannah smooths down the black dress. "My original dress had a big stain on it. I never noticed it before. They said this will be better anyway. It will show up better on camera or something."

"Colors show up better," Ashley F replies. "Not that black doesn't look good on you, but I would put you in jewel tones, and definitely a shorter skirt. When you have short legs there are ways to cheat the camera. Why wouldn't they let her wear what she wants? Sorry, this is my first show like this."

"They're playing to stereotypes. I would bet Hannah here is from the Midwest. With a degree in something like business or marketing." I turn to Ashley F. "You're in the business. They'll give you some leeway. She's not, so they'll mold her image to better fit the character they want her to play."

"But I'm me," Hannah says. "I'm not a character."

"You are to them." And likely to most people who would watch the show. On a show like this, they don't see you as a human being. You're a character on a show. Some people can handle that. I would bet it's not going to bother Shelby at all. But I'm worried about Hannah, and I've only recently met her. "They want to put a bunch of different people into a room and see what chaos they can create. You'll be an excellent target for someone like Shelby. So here's the key. Don't let her push you around."

"I'm scared of her," Hannah admits. "I think I'll stay out of her way."

"Good luck with that," Ashley F replies.

The door opens again. "Ashley F," Patrick calls out.

Ashley straightens her skirt and walks for the door. "See you out there, ladies. When I get to the cocktail party, I'll save you a place to sit."

The door closes behind her, and Hannah takes another long drag off her glass. "She's nice. There are a couple of others that are too, but a lot of them are super bitchy. We have to share rooms in the mansion, and I got kicked out twice before I found someone who would let me stay with her. I thought I looked good in this dress."

I turn to my new friend. "You look spectacular in that dress, but maybe the next time they try to put you in black, insist on jewel tones. You're not a doll for them to dress. You're Hannah, and you're here to meet a king and fall in love in a very short period of time. While he's dating a whole bunch of other women."

Her laugh spills through the now almost empty room. "Put like that it does sound crazy." She sets her glass down and sighs. "I think I might be the only person here who thinks it really might work. I thought everyone else sent in an application like I did, but from what I can tell everyone's got an agent or someone they know who got them on the show."

I don't want to burst her bubble, but I also don't want her to think this is a fantasy come true. "You have to remember that this is a television show. It's for entertainment, and sometimes the production team will manipulate things to create drama. Don't worry about it. I'll be around after tonight."

"You'll be at the mansion?" Hannah asks.

I'll be doing whatever job Patrick decides is the worst, most humiliating he can find. "Probably not, but I'll be around."

Hannah looks confused. "Well, how can you say that? What if he picks you?"

That is my biggest fear. If I ever see Luca again, I'll have to let him know that getting picked by this dude totally outranks turning into my mom.

It's not going to happen though. I'm going to walk out there, shake hands with that handsome king, and try not to make a fool of myself. I'm going to then stay away from him so he has the reasonable excuse of "I didn't get good time with you, you glowing ball of sunshine. Goodbye." Then we'll part and Cinderella can go back to mucking the stables. Yes. That's how the night is going to go. When this airs, Harper and Ivy are going to make so much fun of me, but I might look pathetic enough that Heath's grandma makes me a lasagna all of my own, and I will not share that sucker. That can be my prize for getting through all of this. "He won't."

"You can't know that," Hannah says sagely, then frowns. "You know what? I like my hair down."

I nod. "Then go for it."

She seems to brace herself. "I am not their doll."

"You are your own doll." If I can impart a bit of feminist wisdom before I fade into the background, I'm going to do it. Tonight I'm a shiny fairy here to help those in need.

Her hands go to the back of her head and suddenly the neat bun tumbles around her shoulders, softening her face. Her dark hair is slightly wavy and the tiniest bit messy, and it makes all the difference.

"Are you in love with that jacket?" I ask. It's a sparkly bolero, but it's a little too long on her short frame and hides her waist. I have to wonder if production is trying to point a big old finger at who to kick off. If that man lets her go, I'll take her straight back to my place and we will order Thai and talk about our narrow escape.

I won't let her be alone because she seems to believe this is real. So I want to give her the best chance I can. I am Katniss, and the belt around my waist is my bow and arrow.

"I hate it," she admits, "but the whole thing is a bit big on me so I thought it balanced the dress out."

I slide the gold, glittery belt from around my waist. This dress doesn't need a belt. It's plastered to my body and not coming off anytime soon. On me that belt is a decoration. On her it's going to change the whole shape of her outfit. I bring it around her waist and fluff it up so it shows off her hourglass figure. With her hair down and that fussy jacket off, she looks sexy and sweet. She only needs one more thing. I pull the necklace from around my neck. Christy had told me I needed some bling, but the dress itself is one big ball of bling. I have too much and Hannah not enough. Together, we can balance each other out and be better versions of ourselves.

"I can't take your necklace. It's beautiful."

I shake my head. "Honey, this is not mine. If it was mine, it would turn your neck green. I could never afford this. If I'm right this in an actual emerald, and it's going to look so good against your skin. It should draw his eyes exactly where we want them. You have nice breasts."

She flushes but lets me clasp the necklace around her.

The door opens as I'm fixing her hair.

"Hannah." Patrick frowns my way. I'm fairly certain he thinks I'm causing trouble. And then he smiles my friend's way. "We're ready for you. You look perfect."

So he isn't the worst. It appears to be only me he doesn't like.

She takes a deep breath. "I'm so nervous."

I give her my brightest smile. This is the part I'm good at. I'm an excellent wingman and will always have all the right words for my friends. "You have nothing to be nervous about. You look gorgeous, and he would be lucky to have you. Now go out there and show the world how amazing you are."

Her shoulders are thrown back as she walks away with Patrick.

And I'm left alone.

I wish there was something beyond booze here because I could use one of those breaks the director apparently isn't fond of. I walk over to the bar and sure enough, there is only expensive vodka and fairly cheap champagne, the two ingredients almost guaranteed to lead to someone crying in the bathroom or flipping the aforementioned table. Now that's a tale as old as time. Put a group of women who don't necessarily eat in an orderly way in a room with vodka and a man for them to fight over. Who wouldn't want to watch that?

I stare at the mirror over the bar, and I have to admit, I look surprisingly cute. But in an entirely relatable way. In a best friend of the main character way. Attractive. Non-threatening.

I need more cool scars. People don't take me seriously. They see me and think "Hello, girl next door. You won't mind being a doormat."

I'm going to have to do something about the Shelby situation. She's going to make everyone miserable. I can only hope that she gets cut tonight, but history tells me that one will hold on to the end. The producers will likely want her to stay around for the drama of it all. Unfortunately, no one wants to watch a bunch of women happily dating one guy. It's not like that would happen, but if it did it would likely bring in super-low ratings and not make it to a second season. However, there are ways to create drama that don't hurt the people around you. Shelby went for the easy target, so I needed to find a way to make Hannah harder.

Not that I will be there or have any power to fix the problem since I'll be picking up the poo of any animal we have on set. Patrick will likely find a couple if we're petless.

My brain is frazzled. It was easier to not panic when I had someone else to focus on.

What the hell am I going to say to this dude who's just trying to save his country?

That's it. Concentrate, Anika. This is a performance, so practice.

I draw myself up to my full height and try my friendliest expression. "Good evening, King Reginald. Welcome to America. I hope you find a lovely, if temporary, bride here."

No.

"Hi, I'm Anika. I'm here because playing a dead hooker was more interesting to the last girl than meeting you."

Too harsh.

"Such a pleasure to meet you, Your Majesty." I try a deep curtsey that nearly sends me rolling on the floor. Seriously. Don't try that in heels.

"Well, that'll flash your boobs his way." Patrick is standing in the doorway. "I suppose that's a choice."

I frown at the man. We have not gotten off on the right foot, but that hadn't been my fault. I've found in my business—in all businesses, I suppose—that if you start apologizing for things you didn't do, some jerk will try to pin everything on you. "Are we ready?"

"Yes. Hannah's carriage left two minutes ago. They'll check her lighting and then do a quick live stream. Please don't forget this is live. Don't make small talk with the king. All you need to do is introduce yourself. Tell him how happy you are to meet him, and then hustle into the mansion for the cocktail party where you'll hide in the corner until it's time for the king to cut you." Patrick holds the door open for me, and I walk down the short hallway and onto the street.

If we were in LA, there would be crowds of people where the police had blocked off the street. It's one good thing about filming in New York. No one cares. Like no one. New York City is a place where celebrities come to be utterly ignored by normal people who are simply trying to get through a damn day. Sure enough, I can see people walking at the end of the street, but none of them are gawking.

"Do you understand the plan, Fox?" Patrick is looking at me like I'm an idiot.

"Blend into the wall, get cut on live TV, try to cry on cue and look pathetic." I manage to make it down the steps without tripping and mentally add *don't let the shoes kill you* to my list.

The carriage is like something out of Cinderella. To the viewer it will look like we're at a distance from where the dark-haired man stands, his hand out to shake Hannah's. We're roughly a block away. I can see them standing, bathed in golden light, but I can't make out more than he's got dark hair and is really tall. He's got a good half foot on Hannah in her ridiculously high heels.

I hope he's being nice to her.

"Time to go." Patrick holds a hand out to help me up in the carriage.

I'm a bit worried he's going to do something to make me fall, but he's a steady balance, and I manage to get myself into the luxurious-looking seat. I say *looking* because it's actually stiff and uncomfortable, but that's the way it goes.

"Sit up straight, Fox. You look like a glitterfied Marie Antoinette being driven to her execution," Patrick grouses.

Well, that sums up how I feel except no one offered me cake.

There are production assistants and hair and makeup people all over, like a swarm of productive bees, ensuring everything—including me—looks perfect. The horse handler offers the gorgeous white horse who will pull my carriage a carrot.

No one offers me a carrot. If I'd been nothing more than a production assistant, I could have raided craft services by now. My friend Ivy knows where all the good food carts are. I could use one of her favorite cheap tacos right now. I wonder how His Majesty would feel if I showed up two-fisting tacos. Or hot dogs. Falafels.

I'm extremely hungry and doing this thing where I let my brain float while my body does something it doesn't want to do. Like when I used to have to jog to prove I wasn't unhealthy in high school gym class. Or when I had to hold a light in place for three straight hours on my second film set.

In this moment, I don't want to have someone putting blush on my face and making my lips look poutier. I don't pout.

Three hours tops and I'll be able to chuck the shoes and become Patrick's bitch again.

See, that doesn't sound appealing either.

"Are you in there?" Patrick is standing on the railing.

I flash him my fakest smile. "I'm right here, boss."

He studies me for a moment. "You disassociate like a freaking champ. You're going to have to teach me how to do that." He frowns like he's said something he didn't mean to and steps back down, shutting the carriage door. He hoists his thumb up. "She's ready to go. Fox, remember that when you're done with this, you're on my time again, and I won't care that you got to play princess for a day. You're going to be a commoner like the rest of us."

I give him a jaunty salute as the liveried driver takes his place.

"But what you did for Hannah was cool," he says as the lights turn on and suddenly all attention is on me. "I won't forget that."

"All right, folks. We're live in five." The director has a megaphone. He sits in a crane chair about ten feet off the ground. "Four, three…"

The last two numbers are counted down on his fingers, and then the coach begins to move. I'm jostled and kind of tilt to the side. There's a good five seconds when I'm absolutely sure I'm going to tip over, and with this dress being as short as it is, I will be flashing everyone watching Pinnacle's streaming app. I barely manage to not make myself a forever meme by staying upright, but now my heart is pounding.

It's not pounding like in anticipation of meeting my true love. Nope. It's pounding because I'm going to fall out of the carriage or say something ridiculous or not be able to say anything at all.

The carriage moves slowly, and I remember to smile. That's what I'm supposed to do. Smile and look like I want to be here.

From the look on the director's face as I pass him, I am not succeeding. Christy stands beside him, smiling like a maniac and letting me know I should, too. *More smiles* she says silently.

So I do. I barely see anything as the carriage moves and I struggle to stay upright.

And then I'm there and some dude wearing a costume that reminds me of *Downton Abbey* is offering me a hand.

I look over to where the king stands.

Where the familiar-looking king stands.

It's Luca.

The same guy I spent one of the best nights of my life with that involved absolutely no sexual contact.

Well, he told me he has a high-powered job.

I feel my jaw drop, and then those red-soled shoes hit the railing and I'm the one dropping.

I'm falling, and the guy who should catch me steps back in horror.

I'm certain I'm about to faceplant on the concrete when strong arms go around me and I'm eased to the sidewalk.

Luca's face lights up with what I can only think of as amusement. "Hello, gorgeous."

I'm in so much trouble.

Chapter Seven

"Keep filming," the director yells, and everyone goes back to their places.

Luca makes sure I'm steady on my feet before he steps back. "I'm King Reginald Lucannon St. Marten, at your service, my lady."

That freaking accent. It's super British. I thought the man was English, not Ralavian. Ralavious. Ralavan. I don't know. Of course I don't know anything. If this had been a regular job, I would have studied everything I could about it and the people involved, but I'm not truly here to help the production. I'm here to spy, so all my research has been on Joseph Helms.

There's the sound of a throat clearing. You know what I mean. It's that sound that tells you you're taking too long.

I'm sorry my panic attack is going on too long. I thought I was on one show, but it turns out I'm Meredith Grey meeting my boss after I slept with him the night before. Except for the sleeping with him bit. Even that feels important. Like maybe our body parts had been separate, but I swear there was some soul touching in there.

I'm going to have to force myself to get through this. I'm here to film my thirty-second spot and then get rejected.

By the sweetest, loveliest man I've ever met.

This suddenly sucks. Hard.

"Your Majesty, I'm Anika. I'm an executive assistant from New

York." I sound like a pageant contestant. All I need is to throw in an *I love America* and I'll be Miss USA. I'm also merely parroting what I've been told to say. They don't want it to sound like I work in the entertainment field. Not relatable or something. Apparently I'm more relatable if the person I'm grabbing coffee for is a billionaire CEO and not a Hollywood director.

He gives me a grin that I feel in my freaking womb. I don't intend to use that particular body part for a long time, so it's not welcome. "It's lovely to meet you, Anika."

Awesome. We've done the hard part, and I can go blend into a wall at the cocktail party. If I can find one that's made of gold glitter. If I can't, I might stand out. Though if I stand next to Tiara Kate, no one will notice me because of her flashing diamonds.

I start to pull away, but his hand holds mine fast.

"Are you from the city?" he asks. "Or did you mean the state?"

He knows exactly where I'm from, but he seems to know how this game is played. I don't want to play with him. He's the only man in years I've met who seemed real to me. It hurts to find out the truth. "Born and raised in Hell's Kitchen."

He looks me up and down, though somehow manages to make it not feel like he's leering. Rather he looks at me like I'm a work of art and he appreciates me. "A Manhattan Princess. Intriguing."

"I'm no princess, Lu...Your Majesty." I don't care that the cameras are rolling. I need him to understand. "I'm just a person."

"You think a king can't be a person?"

"I think a king has obligations I can't imagine." I can't help but think about what he'd said to me that night. He couldn't kiss me, couldn't stay with me because he had something he had to do. I'd honestly thought he hadn't found me attractive and had a charming way to get out of doing something he didn't want to do.

What if he'd been honest with me? He'd known he had to be right here for the next few weeks, and then he would have to show his fiancée off to the world so his plans could work. It could be a year or so before he and whoever won his "heart" could be free.

His hand shifts on mine, and he's bringing it to his lips. "But suddenly obligations don't seem so terrible." His eyes hold mine, and then he releases my hand. "After all, I'm surrounded by beautiful women."

"Thirteen of them." My mouth is running of its own accord now because the carefully laid plan is blown. I'm already supposed to be in that mansion, wolfing down whatever's passed for appetizers and counting down the time to when I can get out of these shoes. "You know it takes thirteen to make a coven. Now that would be fun. If you were dating thirteen witches and they could hex each other and send you love spells."

His eyes have widened, and I know I'm having one of those Anika moments. Right on the Internet.

"I think I'll stick to women like you." He's smiling at me like he finds me perfectly charming and not weirdly quirky in a "she might lose her shit and kill me" way.

I do have that look about me sometimes. Or so I've been told. "Well, I should go and join the others."

He reaches over and smooths back a lock of hair that's escaped the rest. He tucks it behind my ear in a sweetly affectionate way. "I'll see you in there, Anika."

And I'm released. I practically run away, fleeing up the steps as I hear the host of the show step in.

"Well, she was interesting," the host says in a jokey way that lets me know he would cut me right now.

"She was indeed intriguing, Tom," I hear Luca say.

"So is your queen here?"

"Oh, I definitely think my queen is here this evening," Luca assures him as one of the assistants opens the door for me.

He says more, but the door closes quietly behind me.

And I get ready to face the music.

"What the hell, Ani?" Ivy's voice comes over the line. "I'm sitting here making fun of women who think it's a good idea to date a dude on camera and suddenly one of my best friends is there. Trying to date a dude on live TV."

I've spent the last hour moving from whatever room Luca was in to one he wasn't in, watching most of the women snag him for some one-on-one time.

It's maddening.

When I'd felt my cell buzz in my bra, I'd snuck away.

"And is that the same guy from the bar?"

Ivy hadn't talked much to Luca beyond threatening his life if he murdered me. When we'd gotten to the café, she and Heath had been in a deep discussion of how to fix their AI's sarcastic bent. I thought maybe not be around her so much. It was obvious to me the AI was learning from its source material.

I'm huddled in the corner of the luxurious mansion that is being used to house the potential queens. I can hear the ladies partying in the other room. I'm holed up in what passes for the kitchen. I say passes because there's no food here. Just bottles of wine and booze and diet soda. I know there's some canapés being walked around, but when my cell phone had buzzed, I'd realized I hadn't locked the sucker up the way I should have. At least I'd turned off the ringer.

I'm going to get in trouble, but what's the worst that can happen? They fire me and then I don't have to watch the man I've been crushing on date a whole bunch of gorgeous women? Go into fantasy suites with them? I'm an assistant here, so I could be the one he calls to get him a box of condoms.

"Yes, and I didn't know," I say into the phone, keeping my voice down because they're filming. This part isn't live, so it feels more normal to me.

Not that anything feels normal.

"But didn't you spend the night with him?" Ivy's voice has gone low, too. "Wait. Hold on. Harper's calling in. I knew she was going to watch it. She acts so pretentious. Like she only watches PBS or something. Hah. She slums with the rest of us."

There's a pause and then Harper's voice comes over the line. "Holy shit. Ivy, are you watching this? Why is Anika falling out of a Central Park carriage dressed like a slutty Academy Award?"

I wince, but the description is accurate. "I'm not used to these heels."

"Ani? I thought you would be...well, I don't know," Harper admits. "What the hell is going on? Was that Luca? That looked like Luca. He did not mention he rules over a small European country. That feels like something he should have talked about."

If I'm panicking, at least I have my girlies freaking out with me. "I know, right?"

"Or he could have wanted one normal night before he had to start this show." Ivy plays a part she doesn't normally play. The voice of reason. She's usually better at being the voice of rage. "I know I'm not like a king or anything, but as the only one of us who has been on the cover of a magazine, it can be nice to meet someone who doesn't know who you are. Who doesn't have any expectations of you."

Who doesn't know how brutal your fall from grace had been. Ivy is well on the way to climbing back up the hill, but she took the hard way down once.

I can see what she's saying. "I told him I'm a production assistant. He should have told me he was about to be involved in a production."

"Sure. He was supposed to think that in a city of eight point five million with hundreds of production studios, that you would be working on his."

Ivy is starting to annoy me. "He could have asked. But no. He was too busy playing that stupid game Heath gave us." I'd thought it made us go deep, but we should have spent some time in the shallows, too. This whole thing could have been avoided if we'd made normal small talk.

Me: Yeah, I work as a production assistant.

Luca: Oh, hey. I'm about to start a production. It's a reality show.

Me: Same. Wait. Is it the same?

And then we would have known, and I could have told the director to find another assistant to take corpse girl's place, and I would likely still have to grab his condoms from Duane Reade.

"Hey, he was only trying to help. Honestly, it was kind of my idea," Ivy says. "Also, uhm, burn those cards. They're annoying. He keeps asking me questions. He says he has to know everything about me before he formally proposes. He's a nosy bastard."

Oh, I'm going to buy him part two of that game and hope it has some blank cards so I can fill out a couple of questions of my own.

"I still have not heard why you were on my computer screen." Harper tries to bring us back to the problem at hand. "And why were you talking about covens? That was weird, you know. The Internet now thinks you're some kind of Wiccan."

"They do?"

"Oh, yeah," Ivy replies. "There are already fun threads on your vid. Some of them think you're going to try to enchant the king. Most of them think you're a cute weirdo. And there's talk that you faked that pratfall."

That's horrifying. "I did not. Why would I do that?"

"Hey, a wardrobe malfunction can jumpstart a girl's career," Ivy continues. "But they don't know you. We know you can trip over air."

"Thank god he caught you. That dress... Tell me you're wearing underwear." Harper sounds like my mom.

I don't want to lie to her. There's a reason I haven't sat down even once. I'm not sure that would end well. "Well, my granny panties made lines, and I didn't bring a thong."

Harper groans.

"Look, one of the other girls dropped out, and the director needed thirteen for timing or something." Though now that I think about it, maybe it is a dark ritual. It feels like one. "It doesn't matter. Luca is going to reject me at the live elimination. Tell me no one's watching."

I know I should be pulling for this thing to be successful, but I'm being selfish.

"Yeah, absolutely no one's watching." Ivy is usually an excellent liar. I feel like she's not even trying here.

"It's late. No one cares. It was a stupid idea." Harper makes a better attempt.

I still don't buy it. "How many?"

Ivy laughs. "Oh, man, it's got a million plus views already. Ani, people love you. I mean they're totally making fun of you, but they love you. And there is zero way that man is going to reject you."

"He looked at you like he could eat you up," Harper agrees. "They're talking about that on the Internet too. You two are hot together."

I knew something they didn't know. "Doesn't matter because he's going to cut me loose."

The door slams open and my nemesis is standing there, his face a glowering red. "Are you fucking kidding me? You are not supposed to have a cell phone."

I wince. "I forgot about it. I'm also not supposed to be a contestant on a reality show, but here we are."

"They're looking for you. We need you for the welcome champagne shot. Get your ass out here," Patrick barks.

"I have to go," I say into the phone. "It's going to be okay. By tomorrow everyone will forget tonight. I'm just one more girl in a short dress who should watch where she's walking. Talk to you tomorrow."

I hang up before they can argue with me.

Patrick holds out his hand.

I stare at him.

"Phone." He looks even more irritated than usual as he shifts his attention from me back to the living room and then back to me as though I'm keeping him from his real job but I'm also dangerous, so it's not like he can take his eyes off me.

All contestants give up their phones. They're allowed to talk to loved ones but under some kind of supervision. Contestants can't spend all their time mooning over a man and fighting each other for him if they're on their phones.

I stride to him, wincing because my feet hurt, and drop my precious phone into his hands. "I'll expect that back in a couple of hours."

He slides it into his pocket. "You have an odd sense of time, Fox. The elimination ceremony goes live in fifteen minutes. The director is upset that you didn't do one of the live shots from the cocktail party. You know all the other women snagged the king to get some one-on-one time. You're supposed to be pretending to be a contestant, not an ornately dressed hermit."

So my plan has worked. I'll deal with Joseph being irritated with me. It might be helpful because I'll see how he handles being annoyed by his subordinates. I walk through the French doors because this is almost over. I'll be locked into my postage-stamp apartment, curled in a fetal position on my Murphy bed in mere hours. I will nurse a bottle of wine and try not to Google myself.

I might stay off the Internet forever.

Patrick moves ahead of me, disappearing onto the set.

As I turn the corner to join the other women, I wonder how I would look with red hair. And a new face.

And I bump straight into a big hunk of man.

Luca reaches out to steady me, and a grin lights his gorgeous face. "Ah, Anika. I've been looking for you."

The kitchen hadn't been enough. I should have hidden in the pantry.

Chapter Eight

I try not to think about the fact that his hands are on my elbows, cradling them and holding me up so I don't topple over. I seem to fall a lot around this guy. "Sorry. I'm struggling with the heels. I usually wear sneakers."

"We only have a moment," he says. "They think I'm in the bathroom. What are you doing here? I never thought I would see you again. Why didn't you tell me you were on the show?"

"I didn't know." Though even if I had known, I wouldn't have been allowed to tell anyone. Not my mom or my friends. Certainly not some random dude I'd met in a bar, no matter how gorgeous and charming he was. Because I'd been "cast" so late in the process they hadn't shoved an NDA in my face, but I'm sure it's coming.

His eyes have narrowed, and it's easy to see the suspicion there. "You didn't know you were going to be competing on the show? I find that hard to believe since the casting went on months ago."

I don't like the way he's looking at me. There had been a sense of surprise before, but I had thought he was happy to see me. Now he's had time to think, and he's obviously come to some wrong conclusions. "I started the afternoon as a production assistant. How have they not told you this? One of the women dropped out and they shoved me in this golden tube, placed these godforsaken shoes on my feet, and plopped me in a carriage."

An elegant brow arches over suspicious eyes. "So you're trying to tell me that you had no idea who I was the other night when you approached me."

How quickly he forgets. "I didn't approach you at all. Darnell did."

"But you were the one who talked to me." He manages to make the words sound almost accusatory.

"Because I liked you. I thought you were cute. I didn't realize you were some royal dude looking for a wife on reality TV." I know why he's doing this and I feel for him, but in the moment while he's staring down at me like I'm some kind of gold digger, I'm not feeling fair. "I'm not sure how you think I would know who you are. I would expect a king to have some security around him."

"Oh, I have security. They're simply discreet. There wasn't a moment when we were truly alone," he admits.

"Okay, that feels creepy. So if you'd come upstairs with me that night, someone would have been watching us?"

"Someone would have stood outside and made sure I didn't get into trouble," Luca admits. "How are you working on this show and you have never seen my face? I know I'm not British royalty, but I've been in the press, and I've done a lot of publicity for this show. We've already filmed quite a bit. How did I miss you?"

"Because I wasn't there. I was only hired to work with the primary crew starting the first day of the basic shoot." I need to put some distance between us. I try to step back, but his hands tighten around my arms.

"I'm supposed to believe you had no idea, that you weren't trying to get a leg up on the other contestants. Let me tell you something, Anika. You might be looking for an easy life, but it won't be with me."

Asshole. I pull back. "I don't care what you think, Luca. Or Reg, or whatever the hell you want to call yourself. According to Patrick, you've only got another fifteen minutes or so and then you can get rid of me. But you should smile when I come down to shake your hand because that particular expression you have right now is not doing you any favors. Now let me go."

"That's the problem. I don't want to," he mutters under his breath, but he steps away, his hands coming up. "It's hard for me to believe you didn't know. The other night... It was special to me. I should have known it wasn't real."

"It was real to me. Look, I thought you were a lonely tourist, and I enjoyed spending time with you. I would have slept with you. The truth of the matter is I saw you and thought I could have some hot sex before I started this job and I'm consumed with it for months. You were a treat I was giving myself. That's what I meant to do, but by the end of the night I was already thinking about how to get your number. I'm sorry I don't keep up with European royalty." I actually do, but like the British ones. I mean if a Swedish royal gets involved with a sex scandal I won't ignore that, but past that I am clueless. "Look, Luca, I need this job. All you have to do is cut me and everything will go back to normal. I'll be professional around you, and you can get what you need out of this process." I wince because I was given the rules. "Journey. We're not supposed to call it a process. Apparently that's too clinical, but I mean it really is a process…"

"Ani." He stops me, getting back in my space. He looms over me, and I can't help the way my heart races. He's in a ridiculously well-cut tuxedo, his hair perfectly slicked back. "I want to believe you."

I shake my head because it's time to move this along. I've got a date to be humiliated on camera soon, and I'd like to get through it. "You don't have to. It's all going to be over in a couple of hours. I'm sorry about that. Filming takes longer than you think."

It might go faster since Joe is determined to keep up his live marketing idea, but normally these things take hour after hour because they constantly have to reposition the cameras to get the right shots.

Hours that the women spend in their heels.

"It won't be over for me." There's something plaintive in his tone.

I do feel for him. So many things, but I latch on to sympathy because the other things are painful. "You're going to be great, Luca. You'll find what you need. At least I hope you do."

"Your Majesty, you're needed on set." Christy is standing in the doorway, wearing her radio and carrying a clipboard. "And the producers would like to have a word with you about how tonight's ceremony needs to go."

He's still staring down at me like he's not sure whether to be angry or to eat me alive in the most decadent way possible. "All right."

He steps away and turns to go, straightening his jacket and flashing Christy a confident smile. He's back to being the perfect royal superhero.

I wonder how many women he's kissed tonight. Usually they take it a little slow, but I would bet Shelby at least tried to get her perfectly done lips on him.

I don't want to think about all the times this evening some woman dragged him into what seemed to be a private alcove for an intimate—if you consider four cameras on you intimate—chat with the man I'd spent hours getting to know.

Except I hadn't.

Had I?

"Fox, I'm serious. Get your ass in that living room." Patrick is back and he points the way he wants me to go.

Like I don't remember. I totally knew it was that way. I think. It's a gorgeous place, though it's not in the best of shape. It doesn't matter. It will look great on camera, but I can see where this mansion could use a real live, not-cheated-for-prime-time-TV glow up.

I'm going to have to learn how to get around here. It will help me to better avoid Luca at all costs.

Did the guard say there were tunnels? Because I can hide in tunnels. I can maybe become a mole person and happily live out my life underground and not have to go through with this.

"There you are." Hannah has the biggest grin on her face. She's followed by Ashley F, who sips on her cocktail. "We've been looking everywhere for you. Did you get any private time with him?"

Again, that is a wide definition of the word *private*. Still, I kind of had. "Yep."

"Isn't he amazing?" Hannah puts a hand to her heart and sighs, looking like a Disney princess who's finally found true love.

I can't tell her that he's not exactly here to truly fall for one of them. I mean I kind of think she should already know. I'm still surprised when people think professional wrestling is real, and that's what this is except with a lot of moisturizer and passive aggressiveness taking the place of fake violence. "He seems nice."

"Ladies, I need you all in the main living area." Patrick is the slightest bit less chilly than he is with me. He must like Hannah. Or she's just not me. "We're going to begin the king's choice in a moment."

"The king's choice? Is that what we're calling it?" I ask.

"Elimination seems cold, and the rose ceremony is trademarked. Also, the daisy ceremony seems incredibly derivative," Patrick says, sounding awfully prim.

"Well, we wouldn't want anyone to think we got this idea from somewhere else," I shoot back.

He shakes his head and moves on. "I hope I don't see this attitude tomorrow or you're going to have a rough time, Fox."

He touches his headset and begins to speak, leaving us behind.

"What does that mean?" Ashley F asks. "I thought they wanted us to have attitude."

"It means I'll be back in the trenches tomorrow," I explain as we start toward the room where the cocktail party seems to have moved. Our steps echo along the parquet floors. "They pulled me out of the production assistant pool. The king is going to cut me along with two others this evening. Excuse me. The king is going to decline to choose me, and this Cinderella is going back to sweeping the chimney."

Ashley F hustles to keep up with me. I'm short, but I can power walk when I want to, and I want to now. I want to get this over with. Seeing Luca like that completely unsettled me. I don't like being unsettled. Settled is better.

A deep sense of disappointment coats my whole soul. At least I'd had that night. It hadn't ended the way I'd wanted it to, but I had the memory of walking through the city, talking to him, holding his hand and getting ice cream.

Now that ice cream is ash because it had been lying to me. Lying.

He isn't some nice guy. He's a guy like all the rest. He is cynical and wouldn't believe a word I said, and that was that.

No. It's better this way. It's better that I see who he truly is. I won't be mooning over the man anymore. I'll throw the condoms at his face when he asks for them, and I'll buy the cheapest ones and the smallest size. Nothing will be lubed for her pleasure. Nothing.

"Wait. So you're going to have to go back to work?" Hannah asks. "I thought we went to a hotel until after the shooting's over."

"They usually let the ones who are eliminated very early go home," I say as we approach the right doors. I know they're right because there's a whole army of entertainment professionals hanging around this particular hallway. Also, I see Luca disappear behind the ornate doors. "They're not allowed to talk about what happened, but the first few aren't sequestered like the later contestants will be. In my case, I'll rejoin the production crew."

"That's going to be weird." Hannah stops in the middle of the hall. "I don't think I like that. You haven't really had a chance with him."

I can't tell her how much of a chance I've had with the man and how completely screwed up it had been.

It hadn't seemed screwed up at the time. It had seemed magical.

"Yeah, I don't think you got time with him all night," Ashley is saying as we approach the table where craft services is set up. "Everyone has pulled him aside at least once. Of course then Janice comes and steals him away. She did it three times tonight. It was rude. Not even Shelby did that, though I'm pretty sure she already kissed him."

That's a kick to the gut. I don't want to think about the fact that he'd declined to kiss me but he's been all over Shelby.

I focus on the table in front of me so I won't show anyone that I have stupid tears in my eyes.

It is mean that they set up all the real food away from where the contestants could sneak a chicken tender or shove some fries down their throats. No. We're supposed to have canapés and carrot sticks because we have to fit into dresses like the one I'm wearing.

I'm seriously considering slipping a couple of sandwiches down my golden tube dress because I know how long this is going to take and I need some fuel. I'm about to snatch one when a familiar face appears.

"Hey, baby. You look real good. I think it was stupid smart of you to fall like that. You want a cookie?"

My mom. My mother is standing at the craft services table, and my day is complete.

"What are you doing here?" I stand there, sure my jaw is hanging open.

"I could use a cookie," Hannah says. "I'm not all that into vegetables. I was hoping for mini burgers."

Ashley F snorts. "Girl, you are going to have a rough couple of weeks."

"I'm working, baby," my mom says, offering Hannah a chocolate chip cookie. "And you, young lady, are welcome to come to my table and grab some real food. I'm afraid if you're in that mansion you have to cook for yourself, and I caught sight of the way they stocked the refrigerator. It's very healthy, if you know what I mean. Why are so many of you vegan?"

I do not have time for my mom's antics. "You didn't mention you got the contract for this production."

She shrugs. "You didn't mention you were going on a reality show so you could marry a king. He's hot."

"He's too pretty." My mother's best friend and longtime business partner, Tonya, walks up with a big batch of what I suspect is her pasta salad. It's a recipe she's perfected over the many long years she and my mom have been in the business. "Ani, I thought you were dating that lawyer."

"That was last year," my mom says. "I thought she was giving matchmaking a try. You know she recently became a client of Lydia

Marino's. I know. I was shocked, too. I thought she only took Italian Catholics. Maybe if I'd known she would match up Swedish Lutherans, I wouldn't have wasted all that time with Bill."

My dad. Sure. That's great to hear. That divorce is the gift that keeps on giving.

This is a problem I will have to deal with later. But I will take a cookie. It's better than nothing. "We have to be on set. If we're not, Patrick might kill me. Mom, I will talk to you tomorrow when I'm back to my real job."

"What does that mean?" Mom asks with a frown.

My mother being here is a wrinkle I certainly haven't counted on, but it's meaningless in the grand scheme of things. I love my mom. She's wonderful, but she can be a lot. However, she also feeds the crew, and she's done it well for years. Everyone loves my mom and Tonya.

Maybe if she feeds Patrick well enough, I won't get fired.

"It means I'll talk to you tomorrow." I turn and walk away, only wobbling slightly. It's not that I never wear heels. I'm a woman of a certain youthful age. We love our heels, but I'm more of a chunky heel girl. I love a good wedge because that feels solid to me.

I'm balancing on a knife's edge in these, and not doing it well.

I stride in, munching on my cookie, and stop because that is a wall of gorgeous women.

They're all in their places, standing on risers in two rows, perfectly positioned. Every one of them is flawless. Not a hair out of place. No lipstick on their teeth. These women know how to walk in any heel you give them.

I am so out of place.

"Ladies," Patrick barks. He points to the beautifully decorated space that forms the set of the elimination ceremony.

Luca stands to the side with Joe and another two men in suits I recognize as producers. They're high level so they won't remember my face, but I've worked on projects with both of them before. They're sharks, and they seem to be looking over a list. They point to the paper and Luca shakes his head.

"We should hurry." Hannah smooths down her dress. "Do I have anything in my teeth?"

Ashley F shakes her head. "No. You look great, and I think he liked you."

Hannah smiles. "I think he liked you, too. He was grinning when he brought you back. I think we're going to make it." She looks at me, her face falling into a forlorn expression. "I wish you'd had some time with him. If he could get to know you…"

"I'm great. This is perfect for me." I cross the distance between us and the rest of the contestants as Patrick places me right beside the king stealer known as Janice. She's probably one ten soaking wet and looks like she could have been plucked out of a Barbie box and placed right here on the show. She wouldn't be the Barbie who had a career. She would be trophy-wife Barbie. I would bet she follows a bunch of trad wife streamers.

"Stay," Patrick orders like I'm a puppy who might run off.

I would if they hadn't made me wear these heels.

"Seems like you were smart enough to know you don't have a shot," Janice says out of the side of her perfectly painted mouth.

I hate a mean girl. "At least I didn't make a spectacle of myself by ruining everyone else's time alone with the guy."

"I had things I needed to say to him," she whispers back.

"Then you should have said them during your own time," another woman hisses.

I will be out of here soon. Just a couple of hours of repositioning cameras and getting the right lighting and I'll be back in my tiny apartment. It's what I tell myself while Patrick calls for quiet and the assistant director gives us all instructions.

Be aware the camera is on us at all times.

Don't forget some of this will be live streamed.

Be ladies. No fighting, but a few tears and some righteous indignation is more than welcome.

Then Luca is standing there, and I'm wondering if he'll drop me first and get this over with. I send him what I hope is a pleading look as the host does the whole rigamarole about the journey, and how hard it is finding a soulmate, and Luca's queen is right here in this room, yada yada.

"Ladies, it's been my greatest honor getting to know each of you this evening," Luca says in that sexy British accent of his. Also a lie. "I hope you understand that if it was my choice, I would keep all of you." A chuckle goes through the crowd like they think it's amusing he would keep a bunch of women, most of whom obviously don't like each other. "But I'm looking for more than a wife. I'm looking for someone who can help me with the responsibilities of my country. With that in mind, I'd like to make my first decision." He picks up one of the flowers a PA has set on the table beside him. "Hannah, will you continue on this journey with me?"

Well, at least he has some sense. I can hear a gasp go through the woman next to me. Janice obviously didn't think Hannah would get through.

I smile—what might be my only genuine expression all night—as Hannah nearly trips on her way to the king. She handles it all with a shrug, and it's easy to see Luca finds her amusing.

"What could he want with that country bumpkin?" Janice asks, though her lips don't move.

I'm going to make sure Janice gets absolutely nothing she wants. "We're not supposed to talk."

"Fox." My name is hissed from Patrick's mouth.

I shrug his way as Hannah takes the first place on the bus to queendom. Fake queendom. I don't know what to call it.

Maybe I can get a takeaway bowl of pasta salad on my way out the door.

Although Patrick will likely rip the borrowed dress off me, shove me into overalls, and tell me to start cleaning up.

I hate this life.

"Emily," the king announces and a stunning woman on the opposite side of the platform starts to make her way to him.

"Ashley W."

I'm disappointed *W* got called before *F*, but I'm still certain my new friend will get one of those daisies.

My feet hurt and the cookie I'd downed is long gone as we move into the second hour. Joe has gotten two live streams in, and I'd stayed frozen through both.

"I heard the live stream already has over three million views," someone on the second row says.

"I know. It's super exciting. I just hope I don't get cut on the live stream. That would be brutal," someone else says.

It will be liberating.

At least that's what I tell myself. This is nothing but a funny story to tell my friends. Or as a two truths, one lie. I bet I can get a lot of people with *I was once rejected on a live stream by the king of a small European country.*

"Reset. This time we're going to eliminate a contestant since he'll be letting go of several of you and I want you each to have some time onscreen." Joe doesn't look like he feels how late the night has become. He's fresh as a daisy, and I'm trying not to yawn. I wonder how bad my eyeliner looks. After midnight I become a raccoon with smudgy eyes and a desperate need to eat some trash.

I can hear my stomach growl.

It's not cute.

I look over and the women who will move on are standing there. It's time for Luca to cut one of the remaining contestants.

Me. Let it be me.

"So if you hear your name this time, I'm sorry, but you're not a good match," Joe says and manages to sound sympathetic. He nods Luca's way, and then we're rolling again.

This is my moment. I can feel it. I'm going to give him my brightest smile and tell him I understand and wish him all the best, and then I'm going to use the bathroom.

I never knew how nice it was to simply be able to go whenever you want to. I'm going to throw these shoes at Christy, run to the bathroom, and then find my comfy clothes, elude Patrick, steal some of my mom's food and eat it huddled on a subway seat. I'll hiss at anyone who gets close, and New Yorkers know when a girl's having a day. I'll only have to worry about tourists, who will be unnerved at my state of unwellness...

"Chloe, I'm sorry. We didn't have enough of a connection," Luca says.

Bastard. He's going to make me stand here. He's a good king. If you like medieval torture kings.

Chloe cries and tells him he's making a huge mistake. Some of the girls aren't here for the right reasons but she was and... I stop listening to her. I'm focused on him.

He's got a blank look on his face. Oh, he's still handsome, and he's making all the right moves. He holds her hand and nods as though he understands. He tells her he's sorry.

This has to be crappy for him, too.

"I knew he would get rid of the fat chick," Janice says.

"Oh, I suspect he'll get rid of the bitch soon," I shoot back as quietly as I can.

The woman in front of me turns slightly. "I like you, new girl. Janice is a straight-out bitch, and I hate using that word. It's the only one to describe her, though."

Janice rolls her eyes. "Sure. Tell yourself that, Riley."

So she's great with a comeback. I would say that to her but we're moving on. The next hour passes and I'm thrilled that Ashley F gets picked and sad that Shelby does, too.

Another woman is cut, and she cries and asks him to reconsider. It's painful to watch until she looks over at Joe and asks if that was good.

Luca looks tired.

And then it's down to me and Janice.

"All right, this is it," Joe instructs us. "We're live in five, four..." Three, two, and one.

Luca stands there in his perfect tux, and I know he's making this hard on me. He's decided I did him dirty, and I can only hope he doesn't need to go over all the reasons he's cutting me.

"This is a difficult decision, ladies. You're both beautiful and charming, and I'm sure you're both queens in your own right. But I'm looking for something specific. I have to think beyond myself. My queen has to have more than grace. She must have kindness and a selfless streak."

That asshole. I *am* kind and selfless. When do I think of me? Certainly not doing this job. I'm everyone's assistant. I'm the one all people rely on.

It hits me hard that I don't have anyone to rely on. Not in a soul-deep way. I have my friends, but they have lives. Have I ever had someone I shared every moment with?

I feel my singularness in this moment in a way that brings tears to my eyes again. I feel vulnerable and exposed, and it's not fair. This is going to hurt more than I thought it would, and cameras will chronicle every moment of my pain.

"Anika, will you continue this journey with me?"

I smile and nod, brushing away those stupid tears. "I understand."

Luca is holding out a daisy.

"Are you fucking kidding me?" Janice proves she knows how to get the villain edit. There are a couple of shocked gasps from the crew, but they don't stop taping. "Her? She's pathetic."

Wait. What had he said?

"And this attitude is why I couldn't pick you," Luca replies with a frown. "You were selfish tonight. All the women respected the needs of their fellow contestants. All except you. I'm sorry it can't work. But I think Anika and I have an excellent connection."

I feel my eyes go wide as Hannah unleashes a squeal of delight.

"We do?" I ask.

His eyes warm visibly as he looks my way. "We do."

He holds a hand out and helps me down the steps. He didn't do that with anyone else. I'm the only one who needs help. He presses the daisy in my hand and leans over to brush his lips against my cheek.

"If I have to stay, so do you," he whispers. "Welcome to my hell, Persephone."

It takes everything I have to smile and accept the flower. I manage to say something about trusting the journey. Then I join my fellow contestants.

They bring out the champagne and no one even thinks to order pizza.

Confessionals

Hannah

What a magical night. The king is amazing, and I love all these ladies. Anika was so nice to me, and I really like one of my roommates. Her name is Riley, and we clicked. I'm so excited to be here. So ready for this journey. I know it's going to change my life.

Ashley W

I'm surprised at the amount of Ashleys here. I hope he cuts them. I want to be the only Ashley.

Tiara Kate

I know. It looks good on me. I brought one for every day I'm going to be here. My mom always told me to dress for the job I want and not the one I have. The king will see how good I look with a crown, and he won't be able to resist.

Chloe

I can't believe he cut me. We had such a great connection until that b**** Janice ruined it. If only I'd had another few minutes with him, I know he would have seen the real me. He's made a huge mistake. I think he's my soul mate.

Shelby

He's shy. I like that. Or maybe he's playing a little hard to get. I tried to kiss him but I think he's afraid of our chemistry. He's kept a couple of mousy women who absolutely don't have any connection to him at all, so I know he's trying to make this easy on himself. I expect I'll get the first one-on-one date with him.

Janice

What a joke this is. I feel sorry for all those poor people in his country because they could have had a real queen. You know if he can't handle an actual woman who knows what she wants, then I'll leave him to the sheep.

Anika

Yeah, I was shocked. Uhm, do you know if there are any sandwiches? I looked in the fridge and it's all vegetables. Uncooked vegetables.

His Majesty

I think she's here. I'm excited to start this journey, and what an amazing group of women to be joining me. Who surprised me the most? Anika. I definitely didn't expect I would meet someone like her. She's intriguing. And I think she's hungry. Someone should feed her. But then, I like a woman with a good appetite.

Chapter Nine

"Get some sleep, new girl. The dates start tomorrow. I don't know if anyone gave you the schedule. Sierra must have packed hers up when she left and I didn't see the producers talking to you, so I expect you have some questions." Riley stands in the doorway dressed in silk pajamas that look every bit as stylish as her cocktail gown had. Riley is the woman who'd practically high-fived me for taking down Janice.

Who is gone. Everyone is relieved, but I'm confused.

I have so many questions. But I don't think Riley is going to be the one to answer them. Nope. That will require one royal highness of a man. "A schedule would be great. I'll ask the production assistants for one tomorrow. When is breakfast?"

"When one of our asses gets up and makes it," Riley admits. "I don't know that any of these women are big cooks, but there are a bunch of protein bars and shakes and yogurts. Our call time is ten. We're supposed to be in casual clothes or pajamas for the illusion that we've recently woken up, and then the host is going to come in and announce who's going on the group dates and who gets the king all to herself."

I sit on a single bed in a room that apparently had once been occupied by Janice and Chloe. I was sort of moved into the mansion. If one can call moving my purse up here moving in.

Patrick had told me someone would bring me my things in the morning, but as a contestant, I wasn't allowed to leave.

I am a princess in a Gilded Age castle, and it's all Luca's fault.

Luca—who had practically run after the director got his champagne shot. I'd been ready to hunt him down, but they'd moved the herd back to the mansion for sleep. Hannah had too much champagne and I'd put her to bed before realizing I had one saving grace.

A room to myself because the girl who's place I was taking had been rooming with two people Luca had cut. I'm not sure if it makes me feel lonely or if I'm enjoying the idea I don't have two roommates.

"Let me know if you need anything," Riley says. "This is my third show, so I know the ropes. I did this social media game show in England, and I was the third out in Best Home Chefs. I think that one was fixed because my duck breast was not dry. I heard you're a PA."

"I was. I think I'm probably fired now."

She smiles, her even white teeth a gorgeous contrast to her dark skin. "I doubt that. I heard the director talking things over with the producers, and they were saying people on the live stream loved you. That girl next door thing really works."

"I wasn't trying to play a part," I admit. "I was only supposed to fill in. They promised me I would be eliminated."

She nods. "Yeah, well, there's your first lesson. They lie. I think this is a fun thing to do, but I never forget that we're not human to the producers. We're a commodity. But it's not like we're angels. Half of us are actors looking for a gig, and most of the rest will end up heading to LA because this kind of attention is addictive."

It isn't to me. "Thanks for telling me. It was probably the pratfall that did it."

"You fell coming out of the carriage?" Her eyes have gone wide. "Why didn't I think of that? It's so relatable. I've got my eye on you, Ani. You're cool. Watch out for Shelby and Katy. I suspect they did something to Hannah's dress. That wasn't her original dress. She thinks it got messed up during travel, but I sense a sabotage."

"We should tell production." It's good to have something to focus on.

"So they can do what?" She's looking at me like I'm naïve. "Give them a featured spot? Like I said, I understand things from this side of the camera. If you need anything, I'm right down the hall. I'm rooming with Hannah and Emily. I know this isn't *Survivor*, but you'll find we still have tribes and alliances, and a knife in the back still hurts even when it's covered in glitter. 'Night, Newbie."

She turns and walks down the hallway, closing the door behind her.

I've been assured I'll likely have a roommate tomorrow, so I should enjoy tonight.

How can I enjoy anything when I have no idea what's going on?

Why did he keep me? He made it sound like he was freaking Hades, but he doesn't even start to have that bad boy vibe about him. Luca is more like Captain America, except with a British accent, and where did he get that? Ralavia is nestled in between a corner of Germany and France.

I have to find a way to talk to the man, to let him know he doesn't have to punish me.

I don't have my phone. I feel naked without my phone. I can't even call Harper and Ivy to tell them I'm trapped in our favorite mansion with nine other women, most of whom want to murder me, and I have to share the most beautiful man in the world with them.

And figure out if my director is a big old asshole. Luckily I haven't seen anything suspicious from Joe Helms yet.

Yet being the operative word.

I'm sitting up in bed wearing one of Ashley F's T-shirts and Hannah's PJ pants, watching the lights outside, when I hear a knock and a panel slides open revealing a hidden door.

So I do what comes naturally. I throw myself bodily at the intruder, ready to defend my life and honor. Though that's a ridiculous word. I wouldn't be losing my honor. However, I'm not letting it happen.

"Anika, it's me," a familiar voice says as he wraps his arms around me, holding me close. "It's just me."

I take a long breath. Just him? Luca is the bane of my existence. I know that's hyperbole, but it's late and I'm tired, and he snuck into my bedroom via the wall that is supposed to be a freaking wall and not some kind of doorway to wherever he's come from. And he's holding me like I'm precious. Like he doesn't want me to get hurt. I can smell the soap he used. I would bet he's recently showered because he smells like bergamot.

What am I doing? If I stand here another minute, I'll tilt my head up and basically beg the man to kiss me. The man? The king. He's a literal king, and this is ridiculous.

"What do you want?" I'm well aware of how bratty I sound.

"A truce?" He offers me a medium-sized paper bag.

I stare at him for a moment. There are snacks downstairs. Well, if one can call fruit a snack. There are an enormous amount of rice cakes, for some reason. Nothing in that pantry had sounded good, but I could think of one thing I wanted. "Is it a cheeseburger?"

His lips curl up in the sexiest grin. "And fries. Cheddar cheese, mustard and ketchup, no onions, double pickles."

He's my hero again. I take the bag and open it, inhaling the heavenly scent as I move over to the bed, sitting down. "Where did you come from?"

He sits on the bed across from mine. He's ditched the tux for sweatpants and a T-shirt that shows off the fact that the king likes to stay fit. "There are tunnels between here and the hotel I'm staying at across the street. They lead up to the basement of each building. I suspect it had something to do with bootlegging during Prohibition. Though I don't know why this building has so many secret doors. There are at least four. This one leads to a hidden stairwell that goes down to the basement. So I can get here without anyone seeing. I asked to make sure you were in here alone."

I have that burger halfway down my throat when it sinks in. "This was Janice and Chloe's room."

He grins. "Yes, it was. So sad I had to let them go."

Okay, maybe there's another side to this man. I'd viewed him as this wholesome hero, but there are some underworld, manipulative asshole vibes coming off him now. I wish it didn't do something for me. I should probably be in therapy. "You let them go so I would be alone in here?"

He shakes his head, and his expression changes in what I assume is an attempt to look innocent. It doesn't work. "Not at all. We didn't connect in the same way I did with... *Ich kann das nicht machen.* Anika, I'm sorry about earlier. I was surprised to see you and I didn't handle it well. I'm afraid my suspicious nature took over. I thought perhaps you had tried to get an advantage on the other women."

"I didn't." What language had he just spoken? Because it was hot. I hate how hot this man is. Even at two in the morning he's gorgeous, and I'm worried I look like I survived a dumpster fire. Barely.

"I know that," he agrees. "I talked to Joseph. He cleared everything up."

That's surprising. I'd gotten the feeling he wanted to keep it a secret. "You told him we met?"

He nods. "I told him everything. He said it was one night, and we didn't know each other. It doesn't disqualify you."

That didn't explain everything. "He was supposed to tell you to cut me."

"He did," Luca replies casually. "I chose not to. The producers agree with my decision."

"Because of the live stream stuff?"

He shrugs. "Apparently we have chemistry. Joe wanted to honor his deal with you. It wasn't his fault. It was my choice. I was being selfish. Even thinking you might have manipulated our first meeting, I still wanted you here. From the moment I saw you falling out of that carriage, I knew I wouldn't cut you."

I down a couple of the fries, well aware that I'm probably not making a great impression, but I'm so hungry. "Because you wanted to punish me."

He frowns, an expression that does nothing to mar his gorgeousness. "Punish?"

"Well, you said it yourself. You called me Persephone."

That frown curls into a grin I can only describe as intimate. "I thought it apropos. This feels like hell to me, and I kidnapped a beautiful woman to make my time here less terrible."

"Most men would consider this heaven. You've got ten women vying for your attention."

His nose wrinkles as though he's smelled something noxious. "I have plenty of attention. I don't need more."

I don't understand him at all. "Then why are you here?"

"I suspect you know. Isn't that how Joe managed to convince you to do the job?" He shifts back on the bed, stretching his long legs out and leaning against the headboard. Like he's settling in for a nice long chat.

When did the room get so warm?

"He said something about tourism."

"My country took a hit a couple of years ago. We're known for our ski resorts and our casinos. Consider us a lesser-known Monaco. Ralavia was considered a playground for the wealthy. Then we had a vicious disaster." His tone is even, but there's something about it that lets me know this is hard for him.

"A flood."

"It was more than a mere flood," he corrects with a sigh. "We had torrential rains for over a week, and the dam that we depended on for most of the capital's power couldn't handle it. Apparently the department that was supposed to ensure the dam was kept up hadn't done their job. It burst without warning and killed six hundred and seventy-four people."

My heart hurts for him and his country. "That's terrible, Luca. I'm so sorry."

"We're a country of less than a hundred thousand people. In an instant we lost almost one percent of our population. Because I didn't check on things. Because I was busy helping plan a polo event."

I can hear the guilt in his voice, and it threatens to tear me up. "Luca, you're not an engineer."

His jaw goes tight. "I am, though. I'm an engineer and a doctor and a taxi driver and a croupier. I'm a mother and a father. I'm a banker and a schoolteacher. And that day I was a gravedigger, too."

I hadn't thought about how hard it was to be the king. "I understand that you feel responsibility to your people, but no one can be all things to all people. It wasn't your fault."

His head falls back, and he sighs. "My advisers would disagree."

"I don't get all the king stuff. Are you like the Brits? No one would think King Charles should have checked up on a dam."

His head shakes. "I am much more hands-on than that. I am the functional head of the country. We have a simple parliament, but they are there to advise me. I make the decisions when it comes to Ralavia. I offered democracy to the country. They voted to go on as we have. So now it is written into the constitution that they must vote to uphold the monarchy every five years."

"That seems like a generous thing to do." I don't know a lot of people in government who would give up power.

"It's the only thing to do," he insists. "I wouldn't leave my people saddled with a bad king."

Sneaky king. "So you basically manipulated them into a kind of democracy. They elect leaders to advise you, and they can kick you out if they don't like what you're doing."

"My father thought it was a ridiculous idea, but I've wanted to propose it since I was a child," he admits. "I'm worried they might do it this time, and I fear the chaos that will come. We're not in a good position financially, but there is a faction of the population who blame me for what happened, so I don't know how the vote is going to go. I have two years to turn things around."

So he's on a timeline. "And you thought a reality dating show would do it?"

His jaw tightens. "I thought a reality dating show would allow the world to see that Ralavia is coming back. We've spent years rebuilding. We've put everything we have into it. Everything I have into it."

"What does that mean? Like your own money?"

He nods. "Oh, yes. I sold most of the property the crown owns around the world. I'm obligated by the constitution to keep up the palace and certain other historical residences, but if I could sell it, I did, and I put that money into rebuilding."

"Why didn't you go to investors?" It seems like the simplest way to get what he needs. "If it's as beautiful as you say, then I'm sure there are hotel groups that would love to build there."

He dismisses the idea with a regal shake of his head. "So they can pay my people a pittance and keep the money for themselves? No. We've always kept out the big companies. We're small. If we allow them in, we'll disappear. We'll be nothing more than a part of France or Germany. We would lose our unique identity, and there have been times when that was all we had. Times like now. We rebuilt the chalets and hotels and restaurants. The bistros and cafés and resorts are ready. But tourism is still down over fifty percent. I don't have the funds to do an advertising campaign, so I thought of this."

"This was your idea?" Somehow I have a hard time believing that.

He shrugs. "Well, I tried to get film crews to come in, but there was a pandemic and then a strike. I called Joe because he'd filmed in our country a few years ago. We talked and this is what we came up with. People love shows like this. They talk about shows like this. I need them talking about Ralavia. The final episodes will be filmed there. I can show off my country, and hopefully that will bring the tourists back."

All in all, it's not a terrible plan, though I still have real problems with it. "The director seems to like you a lot."

"I like him, too. I know he's had some troubles, but don't we all go through that? Anyway, that's why I'm here. He convinced me most of the women wouldn't truly be here to find a husband. I don't like the idea of hurting them. But if fame is what they're seeking, then they'll get what they came for."

This is where he's wrong and where I have problems. "Some of them are here for you."

A brow rises over his deep brown eyes. "How? They don't know me."

"They're here for the idea of you, and I worry they'll get their hearts broken," I explain.

He seems to think this over for a moment, his eyes closing as though he's weary. "I'm sorry for that. If you'll tell me who you're worried about, I'll let them leave early."

"Wow, that feels cold. You're not going to give this thing a chance at all?" I know I'm being naïve, but it doesn't feel fair to me.

His eyes come open, staring at me as though coming to some inner decision. "Perhaps I could be persuaded to."

"What is that supposed to mean?"

Luca's gaze is laser focused on me. "It means I'll go through the whole process with an open mind as long as you go through it with me. Ani, we fit together well. Even the bloody Internet can see that. They loved you. They loved us together. I read the comments."

That's so not fair. "They let you on a computer? That's against the rules."

"The rules for you," he concedes. "Not for me. I still have a country to run. I have a unique contract with the production company. I'm allowed to make decisions others wouldn't be able to. I like you, Anika."

"You don't know me." I want to give his words back to him because I do like him. I like him way more than I should. Nothing he's said this evening has thrown me off. He cares about his people. He sacrifices for them. That's what this is. A sacrifice. He's not some young prince out to party around the world and sleep with as many women as possible. He already seems weary at the prospect.

"I know you better than any woman I've dated in the last few years," he says with a ghost of a smile. "I know that you had an imaginary friend named Daisy, and that you smile when you think about your mom's chocolate chip cookies. I know you love your friends, but you want something more. You want something more than friendship. What if I could offer you that?"

I feel my heart constrict. "Are you offering to love me, Luca?"

A hand waves off the thought. "Nothing so ordinary. That's something you should know up front. I want to be honest with you. I don't believe in the whole love thing. Not in a romantic fashion. I've always known that marriage would be a duty for me. I've never dated a woman without marriage in mind. When my parents were alive, there was a list of suitable women."

That's a kick in the gut. I've been dreaming about this man and he's on the "love is a social construct" train. So much for romance. "Well, they would be shocked at where you are now."

"Things change," Luca says. "Responsibilities change. This marriage—if there is one—will be out of duty as well."

I can't help the bitterness that wells up. He's like so many of the men I know. "So let's go over what you're offering this mystery woman. You admit you don't have the cash everyone here thinks you have. You work all the time, so she won't be getting a doting husband, and you don't believe in love."

If he's bothered by my accusations, he doesn't show it. "I have some lovely jewelry. Don't discount that. The crown jewels are spectacular. I wasn't allowed to sell those, either, so they're waiting for my wife."

I don't understand how he can be so cavalier about something as serious as a marriage. "You would truly marry one of us?"

"The wedding would take place in Ralavia at the expense of the production studio. A royal wedding would bring an enormous amount of money into the country. There are all sorts of industries associated with it that could juice the economy."

And that's the only thing that matters to Luca. "It feels cold."

He moves to the edge of the bed, leaning toward me. "Only if we make it cold. Or we could go into it knowing we're going to be good friends who have excellent sex and work together for our people. That's what I bring to this marriage, Anika. I bring a whole country who will love you, who will look up to you. I bring what I think you need. Purpose."

"I have purpose," I reply. "I'm building something of my own. A career."

"You could build a country," he offers. "You could change the lives of all my people."

I shake my head. He's got the wrong girl. "No. Whoever you end up picking could do that. You are going to dump me at the next elimination ceremony. In fact, pick me for the one-on-one date and you can dump me right there."

He groans, a frustrated sound. "Why would I do that? You're the only one I want. If it weren't for the money, I would say let's go right now. I would whisk you away to Ralavia and end this silliness."

He's forgotten some important details. "If you didn't need the money and attention from the show, you wouldn't know who I am. I wouldn't be on that list your parents left you."

"Then perhaps something good could come from this," he says quietly.

I can't believe he's serious. This has to be some sick joke. "Luca, I'm not going to be your fake fiancée."

"It doesn't have to be fake," he counters like he's being the reasonable one. "I need to get married. You'll look good at my side."

"That is not a reason to get married."

"All right." He nods and seems to switch tactics. "How about this one? I like you. I like you far more than anyone I've met in years. I haven't been able to stop thinking about you. I wanted to kiss you that night. I wanted to go up to your flat and spend the night with you, and we wouldn't have been playing chess."

No. We would have been all over each other because he's right about one thing. We have insane chemistry. I'd felt it that night. I feel his pull now.

But he's wrong about everything else. "I understand why you're doing this, and I even get why it makes sense for you to find someone like me and offer her a bargain. You want to make a deal with a practical, reasonable woman."

"So no one gets hurt," he agrees.

"Except I would." I have to be honest with him. It's the only thing that might save me. "I will. I guess we didn't go as deep as I thought we had because otherwise you would know that I'm a hopeless romantic. What you're offering me... It would be awful. I would fall in love with you and you would tolerate me."

He reaches out as though he wants to take my hand, but I shift away. He sighs. "Why do you say that? I told you I like you. We could have fun together, do good work together."

"It's not enough."

"It has to be."

I groan because I'm not getting through to him. "Luca, I'm not going to marry you."

He takes a long breath and then seems oddly upbeat. "We'll see about that. I've been told this is a process. A journey. I have a whole journey to convince you."

"You want me to have to watch you date nine other women, and you think that will change my mind? How many women did you kiss tonight?"

"Kiss?" He manages to make the word slightly distasteful. "I met them tonight. I wouldn't kiss them. That Janice person did have many hands. I had to be quick. I think Shelby might have tried to kiss me, but I turned away at the precise right time. Men from my country have excellent instincts about these things."

What planet is he on? It is certainly not planet reality dating show. "Luca, you have to kiss the women. Like all of them."

I have finally flummoxed the man.

"Have you ever seen a show like this?" I ask, though I'm almost certain I know the answer. "Have you watched a couple of seasons of *The Bachelor*? Or even something like *Love is Blind*?"

"No," he admits. "I don't watch shows like that. This seemed simpler on paper. It's more difficult now that I'm here. I'll be honest, I didn't like how some of the women looked at me. Like they could eat me alive. It was disconcerting."

"Welcome to womanhood."

"But it doesn't matter because now I have you. I should think about the kissing thing. There's got to be a way around it. It's not seemly for the king to kiss multiple women. I'll make a law," he assures me. "So there. Problem solved. You won't have to watch me kiss anyone at all."

I feel like a cage door is starting to swing closed, and if I don't get out, something terrible will happen. "Come on, Luca. You have to honor my wishes. You have to let me go. I have a job to do."

"From what I can tell no one treats the production assistants well." He seems to be mulling the problem over in his head, and I don't think I'll like what he comes up with. "You'll have more fun this way." His expression turns serious. "I can't make you say yes to me in the final ceremony, but I can make it difficult for you to not give us a chance. How about we make a deal. One chance to get out of my web. If you can honestly say you're not interested in me after I do one thing, I'll cut you tomorrow."

Oh, I can say some words. I'm not interested. I can absolutely say those words. I don't have to mean them. "Do your worst, Your Majesty."

He shakes his head. "Luca. The rest of them can call me Reg or Your Majesty. I'm Luca to you. Reg is a king. Luca is just a man."

He reaches out and takes my hand. Without thinking about it, I respond by rising gracefully. Well, rising. I nearly dump the bag of food all over my bed.

"What are you doing?" I have to tilt my head back because he's so tall and so very close. His body brushes against mine, and there's that insane chemistry I wish I had with someone who didn't have a whole country depending on him.

"Showing you how it can be," he whispers before he leans over and his lips find mine.

I want to stand there, to be utterly unmoved. It's a kiss. I've been kissed before. It's lips on lips, with maybe a little tongue somewhere in there. When you think about it, it's kind of gross. Except I feel sparks. They shoot along my skin in the sweetest way as his hands find the back of my neck and he cradles my face. Warmth shoots through me, and I swear I can feel my uterus contract when his tongue drags over my bottom lip.

I have no idea how long we stand there, his mouth on mine, my hands wrapping around his body so I can get as close to him as possible. The world seems endless in that moment, and I want to do nothing more than stay here with him.

He pulls away, and there's a light in his eyes as he looks down at me. "And that is why I won't let you go." He steps away and moves toward the slightly open hidden door. "I don't suppose you want me to stay with you tonight. Like I said, I don't need some process to tell me what I already know. But we will have to pretend for the cameras."

Pretend like we're falling in love. The problem is I wouldn't be pretending. "Cut me tomorrow. Please, Luca."

A forlorn look crosses his face. "That I can't do, *Schatz*. In this I will be selfish. One thing I will be selfish about."

"I thought you were a nice guy."

"I'm a king. I can't afford to be nice."

"What did that mean? That thing you called me?"

"*Schatz*? It's German," he explains. "We speak English and German in Ralavia. It means treasure. Good night, Anika. I will see you in the morning."

He disappears behind the wall, and I'm alone.

God, he's going to break my heart.

Chapter Ten

Group Date #1

I'm feeling more like fighting this morning as I sit with the others chosen for the first group date. I don't want to admit that there was a piece of me that was surprised—and disappointed—that Luca hadn't chosen me for the one-on-one date. Instead, I was selected to go with five other women to Central Park to play touch football.

The other four get to go to a special exhibit at MOMA.

Guess which one I would prefer.

"So your clothes haven't shown up yet?" Ashley F sits down beside me.

We're sitting on the vast green of the North Meadow. Production has blocked off most of the space which I could have told them will piss off so many locals since this is one of the places in Central Park where you don't need a permit to play a spontaneous game of football or soccer.

There is nothing spontaneous about what's happening on this field now.

"What do you mean? I got two suitcases delivered early this morning." I'd been told Ivy and Harper had run by my place to pack everything I would need. They'd been thorough. I'm pretty sure every piece of clothing I own is in those cases. They kind of exploded when

I'd opened them up.

I wish they'd hung around so I could talk to them. I wish it had been one of them delivering all my makeup and hair supplies instead of Patrick, who'd rolled his eyes and questioned my choice of suitcase.

Ashley's smile wavers. "Oh. Okay. So we should maybe talk about how to dress for a date."

Ah. Yeah, so everyone else is in super-cute outfits. They look like Sports Barbie, with their micro shorts and tank tops that cling to their every curve.

I'm in sweats and a T-shirt that declares *I'm done adulting.* I'm not. I'm absolutely adulting in a way that I hope gets my dressed-down backside booted from the show.

I know the producers are already upset as one of them asked if I needed more time to get ready and I'd smiled and said no.

"I'm dressed to play football. I don't know about the rest of you. You're going to go down hard. I wonder if I can get some knee pads." See, typically this is where someone asks me for a crazy request, and I go off into the city to fulfill it. I'm betting Patrick won't be doing that for me.

"It's not about football and you know it," Ashley F says.

"It's about looking cute while you play." Ashley W is a bouncy ball of fun. She's a twenty-something social media influencer from Chicago. She sits on my opposite side, so I'm surrounded by Ashleys. I wonder where the third one is.

"It's about looking good for the camera," Ashley F corrects.

"I thought it was about looking good for the king." I can't help but glance over to where Luca's sitting on a picnic blanket with Shelby, laughing at something she says as the camera films their one-on-one time.

"If I look good for the camera, I look good for the king," Ashley F informs me. "But, girl, you need to let us dress you because this is not cute."

I know it's not cute. I meant for it to not be cute, but I'm still a little sad about that.

"Is there a reason you're not wearing makeup?" Ashley W asks with wide eyes. "Are you poor and you can't afford any? I get all mine from sponsors. I can loan you some."

I've been surprised at how nice most of the women in the house are. With the exception of Shelby's bitchiness and Katy's cattiness, the ladies are cool. They helped each other get ready for their dates, cheered when Hannah received the one-on-one date, and took chores either cooking or cleaning up after breakfast.

"I have some makeup," I reply. "I was going for a natural look."

Ashley W shakes her head. "Oh, no, sweetie. There's no natural look on film. I mean there is, but it's accomplished by putting on a lot of makeup. I'll help you before the next king's choice ceremony. I'm practically a makeup artist. You should watch one of my tutorials. Well, if we could have access to the Internet. What did people do before TikTok?"

"Talked to each other. Read books." I could go for a book. Maybe one where the heroine finds herself lost in a faery realm and gets railed hard by the prince.

Or maybe not.

"Eww. That sounds terrible." Ashley W shudders delicately.

Ashley F leans over. "They do it so we get bored and cause unnecessary drama."

She's right about part of what she's saying. "It's totally necessary drama. No one watches if everyone loves each other and shares the dude without a single complaint. Who's the guy pacing on the sidelines? He's not a producer."

There's a tall man wearing a suit and aviators pacing the outer edges of the shoot. He looks completely out of place because everyone is casual today. Not this guy. He looks like a man on a mission, and he has to have something to do with Luca since every couple of minutes his attention refocuses on the king.

Ashley W squints behind her designer sunglasses. She obviously hasn't started the Botox some of the other women have. "Oh, I think that's the bodyguard. He's hot, too."

He is, though in a tough guy, I can kill a whole bunch of people and not blink an eye way. If you like that kind of thing. I'm more about the dude who looks like a nice guy but is really an asshole who's lasered in on me. But oh, hey, I don't believe in love.

Get some therapy.

The more I think about it, the more I want to be anywhere but here.

"They say the king doesn't go anywhere without him," Ashley F whispers, looking around to see if anyone's watching. "I think your mom is trying to get your attention."

I bet she is. I bet she has some questions about my current attire. "I don't want to bother her while she's working. If she puts out sliders, you should stock up. They're delicious. And she does perfect French fries."

I wave over to my mom, who sends me a what-the-hell look, but I'm "working" so I do not have to deal with a lecture from my mom on why my hair is in a messy bun when everyone else is sheer perfection.

"Anika," a familiar voice says. "For some reason the king wants to shoot some one-on-one time with you. I don't suppose I can convince you to brush your hair."

Patrick. The bane of my existence. Or is that Luca? What happens when there are multiple banes? I get to my feet, ignoring the grass stains on my sweats. I got them from playing the game instead of giggling inanely while pretending not to know what to do with the ball.

It's not fair. The other women are doing exactly what they should do. I'm being the bitch here, but I can't stop thinking about what Luca said the night before.

He doesn't believe in love and even if he did, what am I supposed to do? Give up everything I have to become the queen of a postage-stamp country in Europe? I'm not royalty. I have a career I love. A career I can lose because Luca wants me to be his safety choice.

I'm a bit bitter, and I hate the fact that now I wish I'd been more careful with my appearance because he looks like a Greek god over there and I'm about to sit beside him.

"My hair is fine," I grouse as I get to my feet.

"It's on the messy side." Ashley F follows me, pulling a small comb out of her back pocket. Before I can stop her, she's smoothing my hair back.

"And you could use some blush."

I don't know where Ashley W kept that blush compact in those skin-tight, tiny shorts of hers, but she's brushing it on my cheeks in no time.

Both Ashleys step back, eying me critically.

"She'll do," Ashley F says.

"She has to, but I'm going to tie her to a makeup chair tomorrow before filming," Ashley W vows. "And we have to do something with all that hair. It's gorgeous. It's a crime to keep it up like that. It should be blowing in the wind so you can look like the sun goddess you are."

"And then it would have whipped right into Shelby's face," Ashley F says with a firm nod. Then she smiles. "Oh, I take it back. That's what she deserves. She just tried to go in for a kiss and the king denied her. Wow. That's embarrassing."

I look over and Luca's got big, sympathetic eyes going as he explains something to Shelby. Shelby's lips purse and she nods, but when she's helped up, her eyes roll. She's flushed a deep red as she stomps away. The woman wore platform heels to play football. It's ridiculous. Even more ridiculous is how fast she is in those suckers. Like if the zombie apocalypse comes, Shelby's good. Even if she's in a designer dress at a cocktail party, she'll zip right out of there.

Oh, if the zombie apocalypse happens right now, I might not have to go and sit with Luca and pretend to fawn all over him.

See, everything has a silver lining.

"Those girls are being kind to you," Patrick says as he marches me across the verdant battlefield. "You could at least try."

"I don't want to be here. I want to be working," I say under my breath.

"Well, strap in, Fox, because I've seen how people on the web reacted to you. I have no idea why because you seem boring as hell to me, but they love you. There's zero way the producers are letting you go. You're getting the hero edit, but you're going to make it hard on everyone, aren't you? If they can't make you look good from the way you act..."

I know where he's going. "They'll do it by making the rest of them look bad."

Patrick nods. "Some of them won't care. Shelby's already determined she's going for the villain edit. I don't think Katy will give a crap. But it'll bother Hannah when they make her look dumb."

And they could. Even if she isn't. It's all about the edit on a show like this. I'm screwing things up for everyone else, and I don't mean to. All I want is to go home and pretend like I haven't caught big old feelings for the gorgeous, smart, funny, can't-ever-love-me king.

"Okay." I can't argue with him about it. "I'll try harder tomorrow. I promise. I don't suppose you could let me have my phone for a couple of minutes. I need to ask my friends to grab some things for me."

"Hey, kiddo." Tonya waves my way as we pass the craft services table. "Don't tell anyone but there's a container of your mom's meatballs in the cooler for you. I'll slide it your way before you head out. Patrick, don't give me that look. I can cut you off."

"Like I care," he calls out, not looking back. He keeps moving. "You better not forget those meatballs. Sneak them in, and don't let anyone see you. I do care. That table is my only source of nutrition, and your freaking moms make these individual chicken pot pies that I'm obsessed with. I do not want to know how many calories are in them."

Crew usually don't worry about calories. They are always on their feet, always working. They will burn the calories. "Moms? Huh. I guess they are. I mean Tonya's been around since before I was born. She's my mom's best friend. When I think about it, she's my mom's most serious and long-lasting relationship."

I might not have learned how to have a healthy marriage from my parents, but I did learn longtime friendship from those two. Tonya and my mom have been there for each other through broken marriages and terrible dates. Tonya didn't have kids, so she served as a backup parent to me.

Patrick touches his earpiece. "Yes, she's here. We'll be ready to shoot in five. And the coffee is on its way." He looks back at me. "Give me a list of what you need and I'll call your friends. They're cool. Your friends that is. Not you."

"Never me," I agree and sigh as Luca walks up to us, a bright smile on his face.

"Have I told you how lovely you are today?" Luca asks like I'm not wearing grass-stained sweats and a snarky shirt.

Patrick touches his earpiece again. "We're going to need to schedule a medic to look at the king's eyes."

He walks off, grumbling.

That is a deeply unhappy man.

I turn to Luca. "Are you going to cut me today?"

He simply smiles, an expression that literally makes my body tighten. I'm pretty sure I just spit out an egg. "Why would I do that when you look so good?"

"I look like crap."

"You look real. Don't get me wrong. You look perfect when you're beautifully made up, but you also look perfect like this. You looked adorable when you caught that ball I threw to you," he says. "Out of all the women, you're the only one who took the game seriously. That's what I'm looking for in a bride. Oooo, that's the perfect thing to say in those… What did they call them?"

I can see clearly now all the mistakes I've made. "Confessionals."

Known in the scripted world as the talking head. This is where the contestant speaks directly to the camera and confesses all their feelings about what's happened. On a show like this, the word *falling* will be in heavy rotation.

He nods. "Yes, confessionals. I will confess that of all the women today, you are the one who I will remember. We looked at each other across a crowded field and I knew I had to get the ball to you."

"I was playing on the opposite team. It was an interception," I point out.

His perfectly coiffed head shakes. "Not how I remember it." He moves into my space, his voice going low. "You should know that I've told the producers about the laws in my country concerning public displays of affection when it comes to the royal family. It's sad, but we must maintain standards. Shelby didn't take it well."

"You told them you wouldn't kiss anyone the whole time we're filming?" I have to wonder how that had gone over.

"I explained to them that when I'm properly engaged, I can kiss my fiancée. Until then, I can't kiss women."

Then I'm safe. "So you won't try kissing me again."

"Oh, I'm going to sneak into your room again for a make-out session as soon as possible. I said women. Plural. I can kiss one in private. Lucky you."

"No, not lucky me. Luca, this isn't fair."

"It feels fair to me. Come on. I got us ice cream."

He leads me back to a sitting area the production assistants have put together. Patrick fluffs the pillows on the bench, and I can see the assistant who's waiting with two cones in hands. One chocolate and one…

"You remembered I love strawberry," I say, my heart clenching slightly.

"I also remembered that you love it from the cart near the zoo, not the one closer to here. I had an assistant get it. He kept it in a cold bag. I hope it's acceptable."

I nod.

I'm so often the forgotten one. It's not that my friends don't love me. Or that my mom doesn't care. They do, but they're busy. They're all big personalities, and I can get lost in the shuffle. The truth is I'm excellent at helping people. I'm not sure how good I am at anything on my own. Being part of a team has always been my strong suit. But it doesn't get me noticed often.

Luca notices me. He sees me.

That might be the nastiest trick the universe could play on me.

"Are you ready?" Joe is suddenly there, and he's frowning. "You trying to stand out, Anika? That's not the way to do it."

I'm supposed to stay in his good graces. How can I do that if I'm pissing him off? "I got my clothes late. Sorry. I'll be better tomorrow."

"She looks fine," Luca argues. "We're playing sports. I can't believe the women who are wearing heels. You should thank her for not being a medical hazard. Come, Ani. Let's get our ice cream before it melts. What shall we talk about?"

He's taken my hand, and I can't help but curl my fingers around his.

"Patrick!" Joe yells, sounding more annoyed than I've ever heard him before.

I watch Joe and Patrick walking toward the one trailer we have set up as the assistant director moves in on me and Luca. He takes over the filming with the competence of a long-term professional.

"We're rolling in three," the assistant director tells us.

I lean in because once they start rolling, I won't be able to be real with him. "Thanks for picking Hannah. She's excited about the one-on-one date. She's an excellent choice."

He frowns. "Ani, I picked her so I can cut her. I don't want to hurt her. Despite what you think of me, I didn't come here to break hearts. I thought it would be kinder this way."

I can't let this happen. She'll be devastated. I can work on her, can make her see how amazing she is and that she doesn't need to marry a king to do great things, but only if she's here. "You can't let her go this early."

"You said it yourself," Luca points out.

I shake my head. "She's going to get hurt either way. Give her some screentime. Don't dump her on the second day. She's a sweet kid."

He's silent for a moment, and I should be worried. Very worried. "I could be persuaded to keep her."

My teeth clench. "I suppose if I don't block the door tonight, you'll consider it."

One broad shoulder shrugs. "My darling, if you block the door, I'll climb in through the vents. I've already thought of all of this. You'll find I'm an excellent planner. No. I was hoping you would pretend to like me for the camera."

He knows exactly how to get to me. "Liking you isn't the problem."

But it is. I like him a lot. Despite everything, I want to be around him. There's a part of me that is satisfied by the fact that he seems to be ruthlessly pursuing me.

I have to remember where I am and that nothing is real here. He's pursuing me because he's in an impossible position and I'm the easy way out.

He looms over me, and it's hard to remember all those truths when he's standing there looking gorgeous. He stares down at me like I'm the only person in the world for him.

"I'm glad because I like you quite a bit," he says.

"We're ready, Your Majesty." Christy is standing to the side of the picnic blanket, a frown on her face. "That ice cream you insisted on is going to melt if we don't get going."

Ah, there it is. That's what I need to hear.

"We couldn't have that." Luca winks down and takes my hand, leading me back to the blanket.

And all those cameras that will be on us as we film our "scene."

Still, when the ice cream comes, it tastes perfect. It tastes real, and I'm flooded with sweet memories.

As the cameras start to roll, I wonder if this will be a good memory. Or something I regret for the rest of my life.

Chapter Eleven

I walk back to the group feeling weird. Like I'm caught between joy and despair. That's probably dramatic, but that's how I feel. I almost managed to forget there were cameras on me when Luca was talking about what it was like to grow up in Ralavia. Even though he's royal, he'd still been a grubby boy who liked to dig in the mud, and he knows a surprising amount about bugs. It's a reminder that he's human, that despite who he has to be in public, he's also the man I spent one of the best nights of my life with.

And then it's over and Ashley F takes my place while I head back to the group.

Shelby is standing there when I join the rest of them, who are checking their hair and makeup at a small stand placed there for exactly such a reason. I know it's hard to film in a park, but it feels like they could have done more than one small mirror and a bar-height table for five women to ensure they're TV ready. Well, four women and me, who is now thinking I could have put on some lip gloss.

The fact that Luca didn't mention my lack of makeup is a point in his favor, but I suspect he knows that. The man does seem to instinctively understand how to deal with me.

"I'm only saying you could hide the cellulite better if you wore long pants." Shelby sounds syrupy sweet as she gives Emily "advice." I haven't talked much to anyone since I joined the group. I'd spent time the night before with two of the Ashleys and Hannah, but I'd avoided the rest since I was supposed to be eliminated.

Emily looks to be around twenty nothing, with long, dark hair and wide eyes. Like she walked off an anime screen. She wouldn't be the badass. She would be the princess everyone fought over.

"I thought I looked good. These are my favorite shorts." Emily kind of stammers as she looks down at her legs, checking for cellulite that obviously doesn't exist.

She's on the midnight train to body dysmorphia.

"The shorts are fine." Shelby manages to smile in a way that a psychopath probably thinks is friendly. "But on a less…curvy girl."

Emily isn't curvy at all. She's a tiny stick, and that would be great if it's her natural state. There are women out there blessed with a magnificent metabolism that keeps them model thin, but most of us carry a little weight naturally.

And we shouldn't feel bad about that.

I would bet Shelby's never had a real problem with weight in her life, and empathy isn't her strength.

"You look fine," I tell Emily. "Better than fine. Shelby's a jealous hag, and she's doing what I like to call game playing. I know most of the women here are nice and you're going to make friends for life, but not with her. She's the one we'll still be rolling our eyes about when she's on her fourth divorce and the only show they'll cast her on is one about botched plastic surgeries. I'm not sure if it will be she went too hard at the lipo or the fillers. I'm thinking fillers."

Shelby's jaw drops, and I'm going to be honest, some subtle filler might help. Her lips are as thin as the rest of her. "How dare you."

Emily giggles behind her hands.

I've shocked her. I get it. I do not look like the kind of woman who can throw down verbally and doesn't mind getting in a word knife fight. It's the whole assistant thing, but I've learned how to defend myself and others. I learned it from Ivy, who is a badass, and Harper, who runs her own construction crew. When we were kids, they protected me, and taught me how to do the same for others.

It might be easier to stand back and hope that Shelby doesn't look my way.

But it's way less fun.

"I dare because I do not care what you think," I reply. "Now if you want to adjust your attitude, we can be friends. The cameras aren't on you right now. You don't have to be this person. I get that you want a lot of screen time, and being the bitch of the free world is a great way to do it, but you don't have to cut up everyone when the cameras are off."

"I didn't come here to make friends," she replies, her eyes narrow.

"You also didn't come here to get married," I shoot back.

"That's where you're wrong. I did come here for Reg," Shelby vows. "You might not know who that man is. You might be some nothing from off the streets who barely knows American history, much less what goes on in the rest of the world, but I do know a thing or two. I know Reginald Lucannon St. Marten's family. They're related to most of Europe's royalty. But you wouldn't know that because you're small, Anika."

"I'm small because I don't worship a monarchical system that went out of style a hundred years ago? Come on. You can do better than that," I shoot back.

Emily's head turns from me to Shelby like she's watching a tennis match.

"I don't have to. You see if you don't care what I think, I really don't care about you." Shelby's arms cross over her chest. "You can make friends all you like. They're only keeping you around because some people on the Internet are amused by you. You can't believe for a second that a man as powerful and wealthy as Reg is going to pick you for a bride."

Oh, crap. She doesn't know what she thinks she knows. I suppose that's part of Luca's plan. He can't exactly go around talking about how he put his own money into rebuilding his country. Not if he wants to keep up the mystique of royalty.

I wonder why he feels like he needs to. I like the idea of a king who puts his people before his own comfort, but it probably doesn't make for exciting television.

"You know I'm not here for that, but you also have to know that being a massive bitch won't play well when you get out of here. We're not back in the days when a queen could do whatever she wants. I might not know as much about the king's royal line as you do, but I do know that like every other modern monarchy in the Western world, his relies on the goodwill of his people. If they don't like you, he can't marry you. What you don't get is that if you take this seriously, you're not auditioning merely for him. He can't think about himself. He has to think about a whole country, and half of them will be women who won't want a nasty, jealous hag as their queen. Think about that the next time you open your mouth."

"Shelby, production would like a private moment with you," Christy says, as she frowns my way. "And don't listen to a word she says. She doesn't know what she's talking about. You're doing great. You are making some great television."

Shelby gives me a death stare as she walks away, Christy's hand on her arm.

"You're doing so well," Christy assures her.

I'm almost certain I hear her telling Shelby that I'm the jealous one. Which I am not. So not.

"Thanks," Emily says. "I'm starting to realize not everyone here is nice. Thank you for sticking up for me." She frowns suddenly. "And these shorts look good on me."

"They do. They make your legs look a mile long. Though we should talk about how to play football." I think girls should take sports seriously if we're going to play them. I personally was a beast on the volleyball team at my college, and it taught me a lot. It taught me I can get overly aggressive about a few things, hold a mean grudge, and how to gently turn down a chick who could potentially behead me with her biceps.

A low sigh comes from behind me. "That's going to have to wait, Anika. We need to talk."

I turn, and Joe is standing there.

"Emily, if I could have a moment with your friend," he says with what appears to be a weary smile.

"Of course." Emily gives me a wave and runs off.

"Anika, you can't talk to the other contestants that way." Joe looks all paternal as he stares down at me. "I understand that Shelby is a lot to handle, but you know why she's here."

"I thought I did. I thought she was probably here to get famous," I admit. "Turns out she's really here to transform her life from everyday American girl to world-famous rich queen. She's going to be surprised."

"You can't talk about that, either." His voice has gone low, and he looks around as though trying to make sure no one can overhear us. "We have to maintain the illusion of wealth and glamour, and honestly, it's not like the king is broke. I assure you he can still keep a wife in style. But we have to pretend like whoever wins his heart is going to be the next Princess Di."

"Well, we all know how that worked out for her." The world doesn't treat women who demand respect kindly. We're supposed to take the scraps they're willing to give us with a smile and never complain.

"Ani, come on. You know how this works. I'm not the bad guy here. The show needs a couple of Shelbys to move the drama along," Joe explains. "Don't make it harder. He can cut her at four, but we need her until then since he already got rid of Janice. I was against that, but he picked you instead."

"Because the producers forced him to." I know I'm ignoring the truth, but I don't want to admit it.

Joe snorts. "I assure you no one makes the king do anything he doesn't want to. Or doesn't feel is necessary. The producers gave him their opinion. Up until the moment he sent Janice home, I was under the impression he was going to do as I'd asked and eliminate you."

I can't help but think about the fact that Luca told me he'd known he would keep me from the minute I fell out of that carriage. "I told him I wanted to go."

"You always have the option of eliminating yourself. I think it would be a mistake, but I certainly can't keep you here."

I'm not sure why I didn't think of that myself. Probably because my dumb girl heart is already thinking about the fact that I'll have to stay away from him. I'll have to watch him go through all of this, and he won't sneak into my room at night. Which I totally do not want him to do. I'll have to watch him pick some other woman's heart to break. Which should sound like an excellent idea to me, but it doesn't.

"I'll think about it. Maybe I can make an announcement tonight or something. I can be back at work in the morning."

"No. I think it's better if you leave, that you don't come back. Patrick's already hired someone. I think you would be a distraction. I'll call some friends and see if I can get you on another set," he offers. "It shouldn't take me more than a day or two."

My gut clenches because I realize what an awful bind he's just put me in. "You told me I could move back to my job."

"Yes, and it would have worked if you had been eliminated and almost no one knew you. You've made an impression now, Anika, and I don't think you're going to be able to gently shift back into an assistant role," Joe tells me. "I also don't think it would be particularly good for your mental health to have to basically serve these women."

"I can handle that." What I can't do is leave this set until I have a report for Jessica.

What I don't want to admit is that the idea of never seeing Luca again disturbs me.

"I'm sorry, Anika. I like you. You seem like a great PA, but I'm not going to fire the one we had to hire in," he says. "So it's your decision. The producers will be thrilled if you stay. Your numbers are great. The audience we've tested the first night tapes with are most excited about seeing you with the king. The only person they're as invested in is…"

I know what he's going to say. "Shelby, because everyone loves a great villain."

I doubt that's how Shelby sees herself. I'm sure she thinks she's being forthright and assertive. Both great things—and things women aren't allowed to be. But there's a line between forthright and mean, and she's crossing it. Production will use it all to make her the one the audience loves to hate.

"Yes," he agrees. "She's giving us everything we need. You, on the other hand, are not. Anika, please understand that you are lovely no matter what you wear and the whole hair thing looks comfortable."

He seems to be tiptoeing around the point.

"I look like hell." I don't have to. I can be honest.

"I wouldn't say that. I would say you look like a woman who doesn't want to be here," he argues with a gentleness I wouldn't have expected from him. "That's not going to hurt you. It's going to end up hurting Luca. He has more at stake here than any of us."

So I should leave.

But I can't leave.

If I'm honest, I don't want to leave.

"I'll take more care with my appearance tomorrow," I promise. "I have nicer clothes."

"So you're going to stay?" He asks the question with a wary expectation.

"I'll stay until Luca lets me go." I'm not sure how I'm going to convince him to keep me until I figure out if his friend is a sexual predator, and when I'm sure then let me go immediately so I don't get my heart broken when he asks me to marry him on national television and I have to say no. But that is a problem for another day.

"Good." He puts a hand on my shoulder. "I'm glad because you and Luca have real chemistry. If you two were actors, I would cast you as a couple."

"Sir, we're ready for you." Patrick is standing behind me. His perpetual glower is there, too.

"Excellent." Joe starts to walk toward our temporary set.

Patrick frowns my way. "You had a chance to leave. Staying is a mistake, but you clearly have issues with judgment."

He follows the director.

I sigh and look in the mirror. Yep. I could definitely use some gloss.

And those meatballs Tonya promised me. I glance over to the craft services table where my mom is setting out a big tray of sandwiches.

"Have you decided to join the rest of us in makeup land? Or are you planning on staying all-natural Barbie, complete with mom hair?" Ashley F asks.

I don't have mom hair. Except I realize my mom is literally wearing her hair exactly like mine. I pull the ponytail holder out. "I'd like to freshen up a little. Now that the game's done."

Ashley F opens her makeup bag. "Oh, honey, the game has barely begun, but I think it's going to be interesting to have you as a real player."

I sit in the makeup chair and let Ashley start to make me look like I care.

Confessionals

Hannah

He's the most handsome man I've ever met. I can't believe he picked me for the first one-on-one date. I'm over the moon. I just know I'm going to absolutely fall in love with him.

Shelby

Reg is everything a woman could possibly want in a man. I'm going to be the one who marries him. These other women shouldn't even try.

Riley

I didn't notice the works of art. Not when the real work of art was standing right in front of us. Reg is so amazing.

Tiara Kate

I've already won the crown. See. I have a real crown. I mean it's not real. But once I marry the king, it will be. I was born to be a queen, and Reg is the perfect king for me. Renvalia won't know what hit it. What? Regalia? Renlava?

Ashley F

The group date was amazing. It was so wonderful to see Reg in a more casual setting. He's so funny and down to earth. I'm definitely falling for him.

Ashley W

I really wanted that one-on-one date, but I like Hannah. I can see where he would pick her. She's lovely, but I don't think she's ready to be a queen. I am. I've become royalty on social media. I can bring the kingdom into the modern age.

Emily

I'm a lawyer, and I think that man is guilty. Guilty of stealing my heart.

Katy

Did you see what that Anika girl was wearing? Eww. I don't know why he called her over. She looked like a suburban mom or something. Are we sure she's not? And it was sad the way she dropped that ice cream all over her shirt.

Anika

Did I? Huh. I didn't notice. No. I didn't miss the fact that I dripped a little ice cream. But it wasn't because I got lost in his eyes. I just wasn't looking. The ice cream was good. Do you know what isn't? Protein bars. They're gross and taste like cardboard, but that's what everyone around here eats. If they eat. Have we considered we're teaching eating disorders? Throw in a burger every now and then. What? Oh, I guess the date was fine. He's nice. Yep. That's all I have to say. Except I'm serious about the burgers.

Chapter Twelve

It's late when we return to the mansion. Luca's already on his one-on-one date with Hannah, and I can't help but be a little relieved that I missed helping her get ready. It's not nice or fair, but I have to acknowledge that it's weird getting another woman ready to go on a date with the guy you just had a date with. Even after someone helped me with my makeup while we were on a date with the same dude.

"I'm going to take a shower," Shelby announces as though anyone cares.

"I'll start dinner." Emily sets her bag down. "Is chicken okay with everyone? I saw some chicken breasts in there."

"I'm sure it's not okay for the chicken," one of the vegan girls pipes up. "Have you thought of the chicken?"

"Well, the chicken's already dead, so I'm thinking he would probably not want to be wasted," Emily shoots back.

I am not hanging around for that showdown. I've got a tray of meatballs I do not want to be forced to defend either physically or morally. I simply want to eat them while I stare out the window and wish I was home, thinking about anything but that man.

"Hey, you're Anika, right?" A short girl with glasses and a headset on stops me before I climb the stairs.

Ah, the new production assistant. The one who took my place. I'm not going to tell her I tried to get her fired earlier. I didn't really, but it would have been helpful. "Yes. And you are…"

She stops, surprise in her expression. "I'm the PA assigned to the house."

I feel for her. I've been her. She should know I'm not going to treat her like a servant who should grovel for scraps. "That is a weird name, but one oddly suited for your job."

She snorts. "Patrick said you were sarcastic. I'm Lily. No one's asked my name. They usually call me PA. Which is funny because Pat's middle name is Arthur, so his initials are PA. He's the one with the oddly suitable name."

I'm surprised she's already so comfortable with her new boss. "You've gotten to know him very quickly. He wasn't that friendly with me."

She shakes her head. "No. I've worked with him many times. This is like our tenth shoot together. I've known him for years. We were interns together."

So that's how they replaced me so quickly. He'd likely been upset he couldn't hire his friend in the first place. "Has he always been so irritable?"

She shrugs. "Heavy is the head that wears the crown. Or so they tell me. He's always been a wee bit taciturn, but he's a good guy. I think this job is getting to him, though. He's definitely more difficult than he usually is since I would say he's an excellent boss."

"Well, you should understand he doesn't like me."

"I'm not sure he likes anything about being here, though he's on his way up. I was surprised that the director's spending an awful lot of time with him," Lily confesses. "Usually we don't get a lot of face time with a director of that caliber. They have their own assistants. It's probably why he's anxious. He knows if this shoot goes well, he'll get asked to oversee the assistants on Helms's next film. That would be a big jump for Pat."

I don't mention that Helms's already offered me that job. "Well, I wish him all the best. It's good to meet you. Let me know if there's anything I can do to help."

"Oh, I was told you would say that, and I'm supposed to tell you to spend your time trying to… Well, he thinks you should brush your hair more. Sorry. I guess he can be a dick. I appreciate the offer," she says with a sunny smile. "I needed to let you know that someone from construction brought in another suitcase of yours. I guess one of your friends dropped it off earlier today. The construction chick is working in your room. Something about the electricity. I don't know. She sounded super competent, so I left her. I didn't want you walking in and getting surprised."

So Ivy or Harper had been by, and I wasn't able to see them again. And I hadn't noticed anything wrong with my electricity. Of course I'd been way too busy the night before worrying about my chemistry with a certain royal to explore the room.

It is one more reminder that my life is not currently my own. I get privacy when it's convenient for everyone else.

"Thanks." I start up the stairs as Lily tries to referee the dinner argument.

We have the night off. At least some of us do until Hannah returns from her date, and then we're supposed to do some shots of us talking to her about how the date went. She's specifically asked if Ashley F and I would join her for those scenes. You know the ones where she swoons and we smile like we're not all trying to marry the same dude.

Pure fantasy.

I trudge up the stairs, hopeful that the construction person will finish the job soon because I could use some alone time. It's been a long day, and I still have cameras to smile for. I'm starting to think I'm on a wild-goose chase when it comes to Joseph Helms, but I have to find a way to investigate, and that means not fighting this whole process thing.

But I don't intend to be an entirely good girl since they want us to all hang out together, and I'm going to hide in my room until I have to giggle with Hannah. I hope I have cute PJs. Ivy thinks a lot about comfort. She might only send me the overly large nightgowns that make me look like I'm ready to go to bed in 1897. I stand by them, though. They are warm and comfy.

But I'm all about the camera now.

I walk into my room, and my heart threatens to stop. I didn't realize until this moment how lonely I've been. Oh, I'm surrounded by people. So many people, but not a one of them knows me. The only one who it feels like knows me is Luca, which is probably why I want to be around him so much.

But the woman currently standing on a stepladder working on the chandelier in the center of the ceiling knows me. She's known me since we were six years old.

"Harper." I put down the meatballs, and the world gets kind of watery.

"Hey. You're back." She sets down the small pliers she's been using and hops off the ladder. "Ani, we've been so worried about you. They wouldn't let us in to see you when we brought your clothes and makeup. Ivy even pulled out her cast-iron bitch routine and that man was not moving. Sweetie, are you okay?"

I take this moment to burst into tears. It feels good. It feels freeing to be able to cry and not worry that there's a camera picking up my every emotion and logging it for later drama. Harper's arms close around me, and I feel like I can breathe for the first time in days.

Half an hour later, we're sitting on the bed, all of Ashley F's good work drowned in my crying jag.

"So you went on the group date this morning and now he's on a date with the other women?" Harper isn't a big follower of this kind of reality TV. She prefers watching home reno shows where she nitpicks absolutely everything the hosts do. I've seen her throw popcorn at the screen because the host used the wrong wrench. In her opinion. I won't even go into the laughing fits she has when they start talking budgets.

"No. He's on a one-on-one with Hannah. That means they're alone. I mean as alone as you can be with five cameras on you," I explain. "At the end of the night he's supposed to decide to keep her around or send her packing."

Harper looks horrified. "So she will have to come back here and tell you the date went so badly she's getting the boot? That seems harsh."

It's kind of worse than that. "Oh, no. If he sends her home, someone will come and pick up her stuff, and that will be how we find out she's not coming back. No good-byes. Just the long limo ride to the hotel where they'll sequester her so the press can't figure out the elimination order. I know it sounds weird, but it's a big deal. There are whole sites out there dedicated to spoiling every show."

"So that's why I had to sign that contract and turn over my cell phone," Harper muses. "I didn't read it. I know I should have, but it's not like I'm trying to get a new job. I had to set eyes on you physically, and Ivy hasn't managed to hack Pinnacle's system to give us access to credentials."

That sends a thrill of pure horror through me. Ivy has skills. "She did what?"

Harper shrugs. "She failed. Said they've got a surprisingly good firewall, and Heath said a whole bunch of stuff about how he would visit her all the time in prison and maybe try to sneak a file into one of

Lydia's lasagnas. Then Ivy didn't know what kind of file he was talking about, and it got weird. It always gets weird around them. It's the whole mad-in-love thing. So that's why I went to your mom, and she got me this temp job. This place is even more amazing than I remembered. Of course, it's also falling apart. I've already had to work on plumbing and the HVAC unit, which was not installed properly and is going to ruin the crown molding. I'm ninety-nine percent convinced it's original. When are you coming home?"

Mom hadn't mentioned she'd gotten Harper a job, but then we'd all been in a hurry to get out of the park when the filming was over. "What did my mom tell you? She was there for the elimination ceremony. Did she tell you that Luca went back on the agreement the director made and kept me?"

"Oh, she did not put it like that," Harper explains with a grin. "She said you were so beautiful that the king couldn't help himself. He had to keep you. She also said it came down to you and some ho-bag moron who complained about gluten in tortilla chips. Her words, not mine."

My mother takes allergies seriously, but she would think someone with a serious gluten problem would know corn contained none of it. Not that it matters. Janice had so many other problems. "The man didn't take one look at me and fall all over himself. That was me. He's keeping me around because he knows me. I'm like his emotional support contestant."

"I don't know," Harper hedges. "Your mom told us he stares at you like she stares at Tonya's coconut cream pie."

I shake off the visual that hits me. Luca doesn't know my mom. And my mom has no idea what's going on with me. "I think I'm the only person he knows. He's not some crazy player, from what I can tell. He's not doing this because he's trying to find love."

"Then why would he do it? Is he looking to hook up with a bunch of women?"

I shake my head. "Not in any way. He's even instituted a rule that he won't kiss anyone on camera until he picks the one."

"On camera? What about off?" Harper asks.

I can feel myself flush. "That's none of my business. What he does off camera."

Intelligent eyes narrow. Harper has the scent now. Sometimes she's like a predatory cat scenting blood. "You told me he didn't kiss you the other night."

"That is true." Let it go. Let it go. I sing the song in my head like a mantra.

"Ani, has he kissed you since then?"

I'm a terrible liar. I'm really bad at it. Ivy can lie like a champ. She can make up the craziest story, and never once wavered when our parents would get mad that we missed curfew or got caught with a bottle of purloined booze. Harper was a cool customer. She would back Ivy, and we would almost be there. We would be so close to getting away with whatever we'd done. Then whichever parent was interrogating us would find the weak link.

Me.

"He did." She doesn't even wait for me to confirm. She knows because I'm sure I've gone super pink. Like bubble gum. It's the curse of my Nordic skin. "He kissed you. Oh my god. Did he even wait until the elimination ceremony thing? Or did he kiss you immediately after the cameras turned off? How did the other women handle that? They must hate you."

Only the truly heinous ones. I'm not normally hateable. "They don't know."

"He found a private place?" Harper is relentless. "It doesn't seem like there's a lot of privacy. I thought they filmed everything.'"

"Well, uhm, you're going to find this interesting from an architectural standpoint." She is going to take this way too seriously. "There are tunnels that connect the hotel across the street to this mansion."

Her jaw drops. "It's from Prohibition. I've seen it in some of the older buildings, but I never imagined it would be here. This place was owned at one point by the George family, and there were absolutely rumors about them running booze during the 20s. And the hotel was a speakeasy."

Excellent. I've got her on historical buildings. I'll take that for a thousand, Alex. If she's telling me about the history of the mansion, she's not probing for more information. "That's fascinating. I bet they'll let you walk in the tunnels if you tell them you need to fix things."

"There is so much to fix. I could take this whole place back to its Gilded Age…" She stops and frowns. "What do the tunnels have… He's at the hotel. That's the same hotel we found him at. He came over here after the filming was done? How did he get from the basement?" She snaps her fingers. "Servant stairs. Where's the hidden door? No, wait. Let me see if I can find it myself."

I'm glad she's having fun. She's up on her feet, running her hands over the walls.

"He wanted to tell me a couple of things and get our stories straight since it's not great that we met before the show. Technically that's against the rules, but the producers decided since we hadn't planned the meeting, it's okay to move forward. Lucky me."

"It's here." She knocks on the wall and nods. "Hollow. Where's the mechanism? Ah, there it is." She pushes lightly, and the door swings open. Harper turns my way, her eyes wide. "Anika, are you telling me an actual king showed up in your room last night via secret passageway and he kissed you? Like how was this not the lead story? You're crazy about this guy. Did he turn out to be a douchebag? Ivy thinks he's got big douche vibes, but Heath thinks he's cool. Lydia is already looking into him. We had a meeting and everything."

The last thing Luca needed was to have Lydia get interested in him. "I don't think Luca's going to be filling out any of her shockingly invasive forms."

Lydia says she's found a couple of matches she would like to explore with me, but I'm unsure. What if there isn't a man out there for me? Isn't that the real fear? That there's no one out there. No soul mate. No magical one. Just a life spent wishing for someone to share time with, to build something with.

Harper studies the doorframe. "I wouldn't count her out. Lydia can be persuasive. And Ivy says she's working on a way to get on set. She's real pissed I found a way but wouldn't smuggle in a laptop so she could Facetime us. Where the hell would I shove a laptop? Also, it's a good way to get my ass fired, and it looks like you're here for a while."

"Don't you have a job?" It's not a question I need the answer to. Harper inherited her father's construction company when he passed. She's been working crazy hours for years.

"I already stopped by. We have three jobs going here in Manhattan, and all three are running perfectly," she assures me. "I check in with my foreperson every day. Don't worry about that. So Luca sneaks all the way over here to kiss you?"

"No, he snuck over to talk to me."

"How did he know you would be in this room?" Harper can be an extremely logical person. I know what she's doing. She's looking at the situation from every angle. "Also, how did you manage to snag a room of your own? From what I can tell, they're not using any of the rooms on the third or fourth floor. They've got you all crammed in on two. It looks like this one is set up for three of you."

"Forcing us to live together makes for better drama. I'm surprised they haven't moved someone in here. Luca figured out where they would put me and then eliminated my would-be roommates at the first elimi…" If I'm staying, I need to get on board with production protocols. "…king's choice ceremony."

Harper's nose wrinkles. "That's terrible. But so interesting. He knew about the tunnels, knew he could get here, and he made sure you were alone."

"Like I said, it doesn't look good if everyone thinks the show is rigged. I haven't told anyone but Joe and Christy that we know each other. That's the director and his assistant. The producers know, but they said it's fine and I'm supposed to keep my mouth shut about it." I'm supposed to do that about a lot of things, but it occurs to me that Harper might be helpful. Since I've been displaced from the PA pool, I can't trust that Joe's going to treat me the same way. So far he's been very much a gentleman around me. Even today, he didn't berate me for my clothes, nor did he give me the whole "you could be so pretty if you would only show some skin and smile more" vibe. But that might be different with someone he would consider far below him on the power ranking. Like someone in construction. Harper's a gorgeous woman and my opposite when it comes to looks. I'm short and curvy. She's tall and athletic. I'm blonde. She's got raven dark hair. She might be his type. "So you're going to hang out for a while?"

She sits back. "Yeah. I convinced the head of construction that I'm an actual expert on restoring buildings of this time period. He's worried because of the deal they have with the owner. They're not allowed to screw anything up or they'll have some heavy penalties, and his expert is only around part time. I'll fill in where they need me, so I'll be here in the mansion most of the time."

"If you get a chance, watch the director for me. If you hear any rumors about him, I'd like to know."

Harper snaps her fingers. "This is why you took this dumbass job."

"I can't…" I begin.

She holds up a hand. "Talk about it. NDA. All right. I'll help out. If there's dirt to be dug, I shall dig it. But we need to talk about Luca because he's not acting like a man who's not interested. Was the kiss bad? Did you find out you don't have chemistry?"

Why am I holding back on her? Probably because I'm having to talk about Luca all the time, but no matter how much I like some of these women, I won't admit to them about how I really feel. "We have insane chemistry."

"Yeah, I kind of got that from the other night. I think it's sweet that he knew what he was going into and so he didn't kiss you then. Now you're in it with him and he's all over you. Have you thought about the fact that this could be a good thing?"

Only every minute of the day. "It doesn't feel good. It feels like the worst mistake I can make, and I'll be making it with everyone watching."

"Who cares?" Harper asks.

"Uhm, everyone watching."

She sighs and looks slightly disappointed in me. "Who cares about them? Ani, what the rest of the world thinks isn't important."

"But it is." I know I shouldn't talk about this, but it's not like Harper is going to be calling up Spoiler Steve to tell him Luca's secrets. "He's a king. He's trying to get attention for his country. They need to bring tourist money back. That's why he's doing this."

"And he's a horrible multitasker? He can't fall in love along the way?"

"He doesn't believe in love."

Harper groans. "That's something dumbass guys say until the minute they actually fall in love. I would bet his parents had a marriage of convenience, and they didn't teach him how a functional couple works. So he's afraid of being a part of a real couple."

"I think he would make a deal with me in a heartbeat if I would say yes," I admit. "He would love to know exactly who he's going to pick so he can start planning the wedding, which probably won't happen."

"Did he say that?" Harper asks.

"He doesn't have to. I know how these things work."

"You know how these things work for other people." She gestures my way. "You're Ani. You're a sparkly sweet unicorn who sometimes uses her horn to skewer the bad guys. You're special, and I think he sees that. All I'm saying is if you like this guy, why not take the opportunity to find out if it can work."

She's forgotten a few important points. One in particular. "Because he's a freaking king."

"He didn't seem like one the other night," Harper muses. "He seemed cool. I think the whole king thing is a distraction for you."

I would think a kingdom would distract anyone. "I can't be a queen."

Harper shrugs like it's not a big deal. "Of course you can. You would look good with a tiara, and you have to admit you love some bling. And honestly, you're way bossier than you think you are. You might follow Ivy and I sometimes, but when you put your foot down, it's down. Remember when Ivy wanted to give that eggs benedict street vendor a shot?"

Just because I won't allow my best friends to get food poisoning isn't a reason to put on a crown. "You can't be serious. I'm a girl from Hell's Kitchen. I'm not going to rule over a country."

"I don't see why not," Harper counters. "I doubt there will be a whole lot of ruling going on. I suspect you can wave with the best of them. And you might be exactly what that country needs."

"Or I could be a disaster." This is silly. I'm not here to fall in love with a guy who is so far out of my league, he has medals dedicated to reminding me of his place in the world. I know. I heard Tiara Kate talking about them.

"You're never a disaster. Well, maybe that once." She grins my way. "When we accidently went to the wrong club, and it was an underground fight club."

I have to laugh. We'd thought it was a dance club, and it was. Only not the way we'd thought. It was one massive mosh pit. "I was very good. No one suspected I would be so mean as to knee that guy in the groin. They always underestimate me. If he didn't want to get hurt, he shouldn't have been in the mosh pit."

"Yep, they always underestimate you." She drops her head to my shoulder. "Don't underestimate yourself. Now, are those your mom's meatballs? Also, what's up with the bear?"

I glance over, and there's a pink teddy bear sitting on the dresser. It's a sweet-looking thing with a red ribbon around its throat. It looks soft and cuddly. "Must be set décor. Which means they probably want to shoot here at some point. Ugh. This is the only place where I can be alone."

"Then I should fix that chandelier." She's on her feet again.

At least one of us is happy with her work.

Chapter Thirteen

It's after midnight when I hear the snick of the hidden door moving and feel the rush of cool air that comes when it swings open. And annoyance that he thought I would be waiting up for him. I'm not. Mostly. I just can't sleep.

I'm in the same pajamas I wore for my side scene with Hannah. She'd come back from her date with a dreamy look on her face and stories about how amazing Luca—sorry, she calls him Reg—is. She's maybe more than half in love with him, and I can't help but wonder if I'm making a mistake asking him to keep her.

"Hey." I'm not surprised he's here. I would be more shocked if he hadn't shown up. "How did the date go?"

It's the weirdest question. Almost like *honey, how was work today?* That's how comfortable I feel with him walking into my bedroom. Most relationships feel awkward for months until you find a nice routine, but Luca and I fell into something soothing from the moment we met. Like something settled into place, and the world made more sense.

I say we. I mean me.

He's obviously changed clothes. I doubt he wore track pants and a T-shirt to the fancy restaurant he took Hannah to. I'd heard about all the details, the camera catching my reactions to everything, including the daisy she'd shown off. They'd met with the chef and taken what sounded like a flirty, cute, cooking class before sitting down to the meal they prepared and talking about their futures as they looked out over the city skyline.

"It was fine," he replies. "She was a good choice because she knows how to cook. I'm mostly useless in the kitchen."

He'd been described as adorably inept. "She said she had to help you a lot, but she didn't seem to mind."

"It didn't mean anything, Anika." He closes the door behind him with a quiet click.

I stare up at him because he needs to hear some truth. "It meant something to Hannah."

"It didn't mean anything to me beyond I enjoyed talking to her. Not in a romantic fashion. Merely as humans stuck in the same place getting to know a little about each other." He moves in and sits on the bed beside me. "You should have let me cut her, *Schatz*. I can do it gently. I wouldn't hurt her willingly. She seems like a nice young lady, but she's not the one I'm interested in."

Now I feel like a jealous bitch. I give him what I hope is a sunny smile. "It's nothing personal. I was just asking."

He stares at me for a moment, a soulful look in his eyes. "Anika, I would let them all go if I could. If I could, I would be that man you met in the bar. I would be normal."

"There's no such thing." I meant to tell him I'm tired and he needs to keep his distance. I have all the right instincts and intentions when he's somewhere else. When he's standing in front of me, my only instinct is to touch him, to talk to him. "I'm sorry. I'm being jealous."

He picks up my hand and brings it to his lips, sending a spark through me. "You have nothing to be jealous of. I told you. I'm not going to touch any of them. Even though I got a hearty lecture from the producers. Did you know they expected me to…what's the American word…hook up with most of the contestants? They asked me what I would be doing when we made it to the overnight dates. I didn't know there were overnight dates."

He sounds so sweetly prim, I almost laugh. And then I realize this man who keeps talking about intimacy like he's a 19th century virgin is staring at my chest. It's a good reminder that he's a man.

A man who seems to only want me. The problem is can I trust him?

"That's how these shows go, Luca."

"Perhaps for regular people, but I have to have higher standards. So I explained to them that these intimacies will not happen." He sighs and puts my hand down before moving to the bed across from mine. He sits and stares at me for a moment. "It's for the best. I don't think I could play the Casanova role. I know most men like me have reputations, but I, for one, did not earn it. I've only had a couple of girlfriends, and I'm not much for finding a woman for the night."

I can't help but think about the fact that I could have been that woman for the night. He could have come upstairs with me, and then we wouldn't have this terrible sexual tension between us. Would we? Or would it have made it so much worse knowing? "No, when you get one on your hook, you let her go. You're a catch and release guy."

"I'm not," he argues. "That's what you don't understand. What happened the other night was out of character for me. I don't even know why I went down to the bar. I could have ordered room service, but something made me want to sit in the bar and pretend to be normal for a while. And then your friend pointed you out and I wanted to be the kind of man who could drop everything and join a bunch of strangers for an impromptu dinner. It made Hans a little crazy."

"Your bodyguard? The one who did perimeter sweeps all day?" He'd looked totally out of place on our laid-back set. The women might be dressed to the nines—unless they were wearing perfectly appropriate for sports clothing—but the crew are typically jeans and T-shirts people. Hans looked like he was in the secret service. Which I suppose he kind of is, in a Ralavian way.

"Yes. He takes his job seriously. I tried to explain to him that no one is going to want to assassinate me, but he pointed out I'm technically dating ten women, so I should watch my back. He should have joined the comedy circuit when he left the army."

I'm with Hans on that one. I get the feeling Shelby might try to take him out when he cuts her. "You have an army?"

"A small one. It's mostly ceremonial, though we do some serious training."

I'm so curious. "We? You didn't mention military service."

"Everyone in Ralavia serves two years in the military," Luca explains. "Typically right after what you would call high school and before university."

I don't want to be curious, and I don't want to remember all the things he's told me, but I can't help myself. "You said you went to boarding school in England. Is that why you have a British accent when you speak English?"

His jaw firms as he nods. I'm starting to learn his tells, and this one is all about being uncomfortable. Not necessarily with talking, but with the incident we're discussing. "Oh, yes. I learned quickly to adopt an accent that helped me to fit in. British schoolboy culture isn't what I would call inclusive. Not at that level. I went to Eton. I wasn't the only royal there at the time, but I was the only one who sounded German."

I remember my own slightly chaotic high school experience. "Why should that matter? I went to a school where everyone seemed to be from somewhere else. I would have thought your accent was cool."

"*Ich bin sicher, das würdest du, Liebling,*" he murmurs. "Unfortunately, you were not there, and so when I speak English I sound like a Windsor. And like those famous men, I went into the military when the time came. That's where I met Hans and learned how serious he is about his job."

"Was he in the same unit?" I ask.

Luca's head shakes. "No. He's a few years older than me and I suspect he was planning a long career in the military before he got pulled out of his team and assigned to royal duty. He was going into the horse guards, an elite unit. They're the only unit we send when NATO or the EU or other allies request assistance. But no. Hans got stuck babysitting, as he calls it."

I try to imagine him in a military uniform. It wouldn't make him less hot. "So you weren't allowed to be a normal soldier?"

"Oh, no," Luca says with a wave of his hand. "I was only allowed to serve because it was expected, but I had a guard on me twenty-four seven, and I would never have been allowed into combat. I did learn a few things, however. I love flying now. I can fly almost anything, including a jumbo jet. And I love helicopters. It's fun to make Hans go the lightest shade of green."

"So he was following us all night?"

"He never let us out of his sight. And I had the cab stop a block away to pick him up. He was very irritated with me over that. He had to jog."

I would give it to the man. He's good. I hadn't seen him at all. Or maybe I'd been too wrapped up in Luca to notice anything around me. "What does he think of this plan of yours? Is he vetting the contestants? You should tell him I was a juvenile, and I don't know how that cotton candy got in my mouth."

His lips curl up. "He thinks I'm insane, but as his parents are close to losing their home because their business dried up, he understands. If Joe is serious and he's willing to shoot part of his next film in my country, then this whole gamble will be worth it."

Because a shoot like that can bring millions into the local economy. And if one production goes well, word gets around. "You need to think about infrastructure."

"Already done," he says with obvious satisfaction. "We put a good deal of money into a production studio. We are a small country with a business-forward government. Despite how small we are, we can stand in for any number of European countries, and we're cheaper than they are. We're ready for business. Once we get tourism going and our reputation as a good place to film is established, I can relax a bit."

He sounds like he knows what he's doing, and I shouldn't forget that he has an agenda. "What does relaxing look like, Luca?"

"I don't know. I think I forgot how to when my parents died."

"You were young. I knew that when you told me, but I didn't have certain important context. That's a lot of pressure for a twenty-six-year-old." I can't help but think about what Harper said earlier. She'd talked about Luca not having a role model relationship. "What were they like? I kind of got the feeling you had a complex relationship with them."

That gorgeous mouth of his becomes a stubborn line. "I didn't come here to talk about my parents."

"Why did you come here then?" I ask. "To tell me you kept your word about keeping Hannah? I realized that when she showed up and we spent an hour and a half talking on camera about how the date went."

"And you're jealous." He sighs and moves his big body so his legs are in front of him and he's sitting back against the headboard. "I would be, too. It's an odd situation and one I did not expect to find myself in."

"You had to know it would be awkward to date so many women," I point out. "It'll get weirder as you get to know them all."

"I didn't think any of them would move me," he admits. "I thought I would come in and find a woman who could play the part for a few months. That's how the producers sold me on it. They said I only had to get engaged. I didn't have to actually have a wedding. It would be good for tourism, but I don't have to go that far if I don't want to. I think they would prefer it since it's written into my contract that if I marry one of the women, they have to pay seven million toward a wedding in Ralavia."

I smile at the thought. They were banking on this show going the way of so many others. There are only a handful of couples who meet like this who are still together a year later, much less married. If you want to get married, go on *Big Brother* or *Survivor*. "Now that would get you some tourist dollars."

He turns my way with a wolfish smile. "Excellent. Let's do it."

"Luca," I say with a sigh.

He twists his body again so he's facing me. "I'm not joking, Anika. Why not? I like you. You like me. There are some nice jewels that come with the job. Are you seeing anyone?"

He's annoying me again. "That's not the point. And the fact that we like each other isn't a reason to get married."

"It's the best reason I can think of," he confesses. "Honestly, it's the best outcome for me. I never expected to like the woman I marry."

"What does that mean?"

"It means my parents expected me to marry someone from another royal family, and they didn't give a damn if the marriage satisfied something in my soul. Marriage for them wasn't about love or happiness or being content. It was about the crown. Always about the crown. My mother was connected to Danish royalty. She married my father when she was eighteen and was expected to immediately produce an heir. It took her fifteen years and painful fertility treatments to finally give birth to me. To say their marriage was unhappy would be denial. From what I can tell it was hell, but they did it."

"Not for you." I can see plainly where this is going. "They did it because royals don't divorce. But Luca, you can't expect a modern woman to stay in an unhappy marriage."

"No. I don't. I would never put my wife through that," he promises. "I don't care about children. If I marry and the name dies with me, then at least I will have brought real democracy to my country. But it's hard to change. Our history is all we have. Our rituals and traditions are part of that, but I assure you I wouldn't hold a woman hostage to the crown. We could have a prenup that allows you to leave if you're unhappy."

"We're not in the same situation at all. I didn't come here to find a husband." He's overwhelming me, and he's not saying the words that will make me say yes. I honestly don't know that there are words that will make me say yes.

I love you.

He could say that, but I wouldn't believe him. Not now.

He seems to think about that for a moment. "Well, it's good I have a few weeks to change your mind then. Scoot over. I thought you could watch one of those shows with me. You know, the one this one is based on. We can watch and talk about it and then I'll know better how to act."

I roll my eyes. "There's no TV in here. They don't allow us contact with the outside world."

"Then it's good I came prepared." He opens the door and says something in German and then an iPad is being pressed into his hand.

"Luca, is Hans sitting in the stairwell?"

Luca shrugs. "I told him there wouldn't be an assassin in the tunnels."

"*Immer gibt es Attentäter in den Tunneln,*" I hear a low voice say.

"*Du bist ein paranoider Mistkerl,*" Luca shoots back.

Some things are clear from context. "He's right. There could be assassins in the tunnels, but more likely an unhoused person looking for shelter in the subway tunnels and finding their way here."

He closes the door. "I can handle it. Now, I have all the streaming things. Where do I start?"

He climbs onto the bed next to me, though I'm under the covers and he stays on top. I'm excited to see a device. I haven't seen my phone in days, and I miss it. The truth of the matter is I'm doing us all a favor by teaching Luca how to act like a man who wants to find love by driving through a handpicked selection of women deemed "right" by a group of wealthy producers.

Wow. It's really a little like a royal marriage when you think about it. He's got a limited quantity to pick from, and he's got to get it done or the production/crown fails.

He logs in and I find a show to start with.

"This one is closest to what we're doing, ie, this is the one we're ripping off," I explain.

"Ripping off?" Luca asks, that elegant brow rising.

I wave away that worry. "If one show is successful, there will be one hundred and fifty variations out the next season. You've got your generic pretty people finding love *Bachelor/Bachelorette,* group dating shows where they throw a bunch of pretty people on a beach and watch them fight. Watching your ex date is a thing. Oh, and then there are the ones that are profession based. Like farmers."

There's a pained expression on his face. "I should have known what I was getting into, shouldn't I?"

I shrug as I start season one, episode one. "That's why you need an agent, buddy. Now hush. You might learn something."

He settles in beside me. "This is nothing I ever thought I would need to know. They didn't cover this at Oxford."

I roll my eyes his way. "Show off."

His lips curl into a sweet smile. "You are an incorrigible brat."

"I thought I was a treasure."

His hand comes out to cup my cheek, and he leans over, brushing his lips over my forehead. "It's all about perspective. You can be both. I like the fact that you're both, Anika. You can be everything."

I am not going to cry. I force myself to pay attention to the show. "All right. So here are the introductions. They're important."

Sometime around episode three I fall asleep, my head on his shoulder.

When I wake up in the morning, someone's tucked the covers around me.

I feel warm and cared for.

I steel myself for the day ahead because it's time to go back to work.

Confessionals

Tiara Kate

I don't get what Reg sees in Anika. I mean I guess I don't want to vomit looking at her, but she's not the most fashionable among us. Have you seen that granny gown she wears to bed? There's comfort and then there's the Middle Ages.

Hannah

I'm happy for all of us to get to spend time with such an extraordinary man. What would I do if I was queen of Regalia? Relavia? What would I do if I became queen? I guess the first thing would be to learn how to pronounce the country's name right.

Ashley K

I can't believe he cut me. I thought that date was going great. Then I told him I don't drink beer because it's nasty and he cut me. How was I supposed to know a dude from wherever he's from takes beer so seriously? I thought he would be into wine.

Shelby

Everything is going wonderfully. Reg and I are already making excellent decisions together. But I have to wonder if he's as eager to kiss me as I am to kiss him. That rule is antiquated. What are we going to do on the overnights? Talk? That sounds terrible.

Ashley W

I thought he liked me. I thought he was going to pick me because we had a moment tonight. We were standing over the buffet and I told him I like sauerkraut and then he said he liked it too. I don't think anyone else ate the sauerkraut, so I don't know why he would cut me. He's going to find out all those other women hate his cultural food and then what's he going to do?

Emily

What's the hardest thing about being in this house? It's old and drafty, and some weird chick keeps walking around the mansion going on and on about the original crown molding. Is that a codeword or something? That's annoying, but the real awful part is how nasty Shelby is. She's not here for the right reasons. I don't know why Reg keeps her.

Ashley F

Oh, dealing with Shelby is the worst. She's not a girl's girl, if you know what I mean. Like if she had a squad, it would be made of Cruella de Vil, Regina George, Bellatrix Lestrange and that woman who made JoJo Siwa cry when she was twelve. I don't know what the king is thinking because if she becomes his queen, that country is going to be ripe for a revolution.

Anika

Everything's good. Yep. All good. Looking forward to my next group date. Fun. Do I want private time with L…Reg? Uhm, I think we can get to know each other in a group setting. I wouldn't want to take time away from the other women. They're all so lovely and smart. He can't make a wrong choice. Except for Shelby. That would be a disastrous choice. Not sure what he's thinking.

Riley

I think Hannah is wonderful. She's become my best friend in the house. I can tell her anything. Since we lost our roommate, it's been me and her sitting up every night talking. Telling each other everything. In our pajamas. Yeah, of course we talk about Reg. I mean what else would we talk about? That's why we're here.

Katy

I was cool with Shelby at first. I'll be honest, I like a mean girl. You can trust that they will always tell you the brutal truth. I think it's meaner to not tell someone they have lipstick on their teeth or to fail to mention that they shouldn't leave the house in that micro mini because it makes you look like a whale. I was surprised when she turned on me. I thought we were close. But I overheard her saying that I'm just here for the fame. Bitch has to go.

Chapter Fourteen

Two weeks into this godforsaken process and I am ready to strangle someone.

And that someone has a name, and her name is Shelby.

"One of us has to talk to him," Ashley F says as we're sitting on the couch in the mansion. It's early afternoon and everyone with the exception of Shelby has the day "off." *Off* is a euphemism for we don't get to leave the house or see the king. There's a one-on-one date today, and the rest of us are filming confessionals and this house meeting scene.

I can tell where the director thinks the real drama is because Joe is right here and not across town filming Luca and Shelby and their magical day on the Upper East Side.

"Can you say that with a bit more feeling?" Joe interrupts. "The sentiment is exactly what we're going for, but there's no place for subtlety. You're mad at Shelby, and this house meeting is going to steer the ship when it comes to her. You're fed up and you can't take anymore."

Ashley F nods and closes her eyes like she's prepping for a scene.

Which she is.

Is it real? Do we all hate Shelby for how awful she is? Yes. But apparently we're not hating her in a film-ready way.

"We're still rolling." Joe adjusts his glasses, sitting back in his chair while Patrick hands him a travel mug of coffee.

I haven't had to deal with Patrick unless I was on one of the group dates and at the elimination ceremonies, of which there have been two. Two of the Ashleys have left in what I like to call the limo of doom, and it was all very dramatic and tearful and there was something about sauerkraut that I didn't fully understand. I feel like I'm floating through these days.

But the nights...the nights are when I feel solid ground beneath my feet. The nights are when I feel alive.

Every night without fail Luca sneaks into my room and we watch shows. He gets surprisingly emotionally invested. I've started asking my mom to sneak me extra food for our midnight binge fests.

Last night she made me a small but lovely charcuterie box, with grapes and gouda and salami and crackers. Luca made me taste the grapes because apparently they don't have cotton candy grapes in Ralavia. They also don't have men who make poor choices. At least that's what he tells me.

And I've also started getting a little snack for Hans. I'm not sure if he eats it, though. He's serious about poison, too.

"Enough is enough. We can't let her get away with this," Ashley F says with a fierce look in her eyes. "Reg is having the wool pulled over his eyes by her. She's so sweet with him. He doesn't see the other side."

"What can we do?" Emily asks, her eyes wide. "I've tried talking to her and it ends up with her telling me... Well, I can't say it here. It's not ladylike."

Says the girl who can fart the alphabet. I'm not joking. It's a real skill. She's super feminine on camera and kind of a bro off it. I like her.

"Ladylike is going to hurt the man we all care about," Tiara Kate says.

He's kissed me several times, and there was one hot make-out session that was only interrupted because I was sure I heard someone coming down the hall toward my room. I don't think Luca is used to being shoved out the door like he's a teen boy and my dad came home unexpectedly.

I fall asleep most nights resting against his shoulder and I wake up and wish he was there.

I'm in serious trouble because I don't think he's going to cut me, and I don't know what I'm going to do if he asks me to marry him.

"Ani?"

I shake my head and look around, trying to figure out who's talking to me. "Yeah?"

Katy frowns my way. Even though it's after dinner and we're supposed to be relaxing, she's in designer wear, Chanel earrings swinging as she shows her displeasure. "We asked what you think we should do."

I wince because that was my cue. "I think we should talk to the king and tell him how we feel."

That is my line. Well, it was suggested as my line. I've now done my duty and can go back to staring and hoping I look like I'm into this "impromptu" house meeting.

"You want to talk to him about this? Because you seem to avoid talking to him," Katy says, and there's no way to miss the accusation in her tone. "I mean if we're talking about people who are here for the wrong reasons, we shouldn't only talk about Shelby."

"What is that supposed to mean?" Hannah still has my back.

I spend most of my time with Hannah, Ashley F, and Riley. We cling together like a flock of baby birds trying to stave off an attack from the mean predatory birds. We're sitting in a cluster right now, with Hannah and Riley on my right and Ashley F staring a hole at Katy to my left.

"Yeah, if you're talking about Anika, I don't see a problem. She's not the one causing trouble," Ashley F says with a frown.

"No, she's the one hiding out. She's the one who production has to chase down when they need her to spend some time with Reg," Katy points out. "She's the one who doesn't belong here."

"No mention of production, please." Joe shakes his head and leans over to whisper something in Patrick's ear, his hand going behind Patrick's back.

Whatever it is he says makes Patrick's brow furrow.

Katy sighs and looks his way. "But it's true."

"We don't break the illusion on this show," Patrick says firmly, stepping away. "You should know that by now. You've been here for two weeks. You don't talk about production or cameras or anything that goes on behind the scenes. If you want to bitch about Anika, I can give you a million ways to do it, but you can't say production has to track her down. Talk about how annoying she is and how she throws herself in front of every train that's coming because she's got a martyr complex. She's dull as dirt and doesn't seem to want to be here, so she's taking the space of a woman who could truly love the king."

"Whoa," I say because I am not those things. "I don't throw myself in front of trains."

"No, but you do stick your nose into every fight," Riley whispers. "You play referee, and I don't think they're getting the fights they want."

Katy gives me a shrug. "Every time I try to cause some trouble you practically body check me. I'm trying here, Ani. Do you think I like being this bitchy? I'm a kindergarten teacher. I'm usually a happy unicorn, but they told me if I want any screentime, I better cause trouble."

"Again, nothing we should talk about on camera," Joe says, sliding out of his chair. He looks around to the crew. "We're going to take half an hour so the ladies can decide how they're going to handle this scene. Get a snack, people. Patrick, do you have those schedules I asked for?"

Poor Patrick. Normally a director barely knows the production assistants' names. Even the key PA. He got the micro manager. That can be tough, but he doesn't have to throw me under every bus he can.

"I thought we were talking about Shelby," Emily begins.

In the background I see Harper moving around, a tool belt circling her hips. She looks like she's working on one of the sconce lighting units, but I'm sure she's listening to every word we say.

"I'm sorry." I don't mean to hold everyone up. "I'll be faster with my conversations with the king."

Tiara Kate shakes her head, and I swear that fake crown doesn't move. I wonder if it's surgically attached to her head. "No. Katy has a point. You're the only one here who isn't crazy about the king."

"Crazy is a harsh word," Riley hedges. "I wouldn't say crazy."

"Then maybe you should leave, too," Katy shoots back.

"Can we stop policing other people's feelings?" I ask. "You know not everyone expresses their affection in the same way. I absolutely feel something for the king."

I think about Luca all the time. It's probably why I get nervous when production wants to shoot a scene between us. I'm insanely crazy about the Luca who sneaks into my bedroom at night and watches TV with me and argues about who the bachelor sends home and how he won't be so foolish. I'm falling for the Luca who blushed madly when he realized what happens in the fantasy suites, and that production really would prefer he pick a couple of us to sleep with.

It's not like the smooth and politic king he is in front of the cameras isn't charming. It's just that it feels fake when I know who he is underneath it all.

"Well, it doesn't show, and you're dragging the rest of us down," Katy says.

Harper has turned, and I see her eyes narrow. Oh, that could be a problem.

"How is she dragging anyone down?" Hannah stands up, facing off with Katy and the Tiara. "She's done nothing but help us all. When we don't understand what's going on, she explains all the production things to us. She tries to keep the peace so we don't all look ridiculous when the show comes out. I, for one, don't want to look like some stereotype."

"You're going to look like that no matter what you do," Tiara Kate says. "They're going to edit us all as they will, so you can give them nothing to work with and they'll give you the dull as dishwater edit, or you can give them some sparks and maybe you'll get something out of it."

It's the first time I've seen her admit she's not merely here for the king. "Really? Get something career wise? Because I think I got accused of not being here for the right reasons. Is my career not the right reason, but yours is?"

Katy huffs out an annoyed sigh. "Like Ashley F isn't already talking to the producers about doing their new dating show. Don't be a hypocrite. You don't need this show to get another show. You're a production assistant. You're like ants. There's always something for you to do. Do you think I want to be a teacher for the rest of my life? Do you know what it's like for us right now?"

I'm sure she's got horror stories. "Well, it's super fun to spend all my time catering to people like you. So you'll have to excuse me when I don't see the difference between you moving up on the reality show circuit and me trying to keep a job I love."

"So you admit you're not here for Reg," Emily says, shooting me a disappointed look.

"Neither are these two. And it's not like I don't like him. I do. He's a great guy. I just don't think a relationship like this can work," I point out. "It looks great on TV, but how much time have you actually spent with him? Getting to know him? Even if you've had a one-on-one, the cameras are there."

"I talked to him when they were repositioning the cameras." Hannah's looking at me with wide eyes like she feels the need to defend herself. "But I guess in the five hours we were gone it was only like an hour we got to talk without thinking about how things look on film. But it was a nice hour. Even if it was broken up with hair and makeup and lighting."

"Yes, we've all enjoyed our time with Reg." Katy locks onto Hannah. "You're here for the right reasons. You believe in the process. Anika admitted she doesn't."

"And you do?" I'm starting to get irritated. I stand because I see Harper inching toward us and I don't trust her with a wrench in her hand. "You think you're honestly coming out of this as the queen of Ralavia?"

Hannah snaps her fingers. "Ralavia. It's like saliva but with an R."

It's not. It's not in any way, but I ignore her and I ignore the fact that Ashley F is defending herself to Tiara Kate over possibly lining up a new gig even before she's eliminated from the old one.

"I believe in it a hell of a lot more than you do," Katy assures me. "You're here because production wants you here."

"Hey, she's been trying," Riley says. "She put on makeup and everything."

"Well, she doesn't share her room," Katy points out. "She's the only one of us with a private room. I wonder why that is."

I hope I'm not blushing because I know why I have a private room. Because Luca wants me in one. "The two women I was supposed to bunk with got eliminated the first night. It was just luck."

"Then why won't they let any of us move in?" Katy asks.

Hannah shifts on the couch, looking up at us. "I was told you have a sleep disorder."

"You asked to move into my room?" I hadn't been told. She'd said a couple of things a few days into shooting, but then I thought she'd let it go because I didn't hear anything else.

"Well, yes, because it was me and Riley and Ashley W packed into a room smaller than yours," Hannah explains. "But Patrick said you have sleep issues and I would be better off sleeping in the bathtub."

What the hell does Patrick have against me? He's rude.

"You don't want to move now, right?" Riley looks over at her closest friend in the house.

Hannah gives her a gentle smile. They've really connected, and I'm happy Hannah's found some friends. She's come alive in the last couple of weeks, and I pray she doesn't lose that light when Luca inevitably lets her go. "No. I'm happy right where I am, but it was tight for a little while."

"Anika is a diva," Katy interjects. "There's nothing wrong with her. She simply doesn't want to share. She heard her numbers were great the first night, and now she's better than the rest of us. I know I've heard she offered to be eliminated that first night, but boy, she's been playing it up ever since."

I'm confused. "Am I evil because I'm trying too hard or not enough? It can't be both."

Harper nods my way like I've scored a solid point.

"I think Katy is looking for drama." Ashley F seems satisfied with whatever she's told Tiara Kate and is back to the job of defending me. "If you trust the process so much, why are you constantly looking for ways to get other contestants kicked off? You think I don't know that you complained to production about my meds?"

"We're supposed to have only the things we brought in on the first night," Katy insists.

Oh, Shelby has made her look good in comparison, but she's kind of a cartoon villain. "She ran out of her inhaler. It wasn't like she smuggled in a pushup bra, Karen."

Harper snorts, but she's back to working that wrench in a way that doesn't have the potential to maim.

She's comfortable that I can handle this.

"How about we do this," I begin. "I'm not going to go to the king about any of you. He can figure it out on his own since that's the process. Katy, you can't get rid of your competition by creating drama around them. That will get you eliminated because this is not a dramatic man. If you can't tell that by now, you're in trouble."

"I'll admit he's too calm for me," Emily says. "But then my last two boyfriends were both pro wrestlers. I thought I would miss chair throwing less than I do."

"He's fine. He's who he's supposed to be." Katy's long blonde hair waves as she runs her hands over it. It's something she does all the time, and I wonder how all that hair fares against twenty kindergarteners on a daily basis. "He has to look like he's always in control. He's the king. I mean the poor man can't even kiss us, and it's obvious he wants to."

"Obvious?" I hate that the word came out of my mouth when I should have stayed so quiet.

"Maybe not to you since you're here because he's being forced to keep you," Katy shoots back. "But he's come close to kissing me."

"Me, too," Tiara adds. "So close, but then he had to pull away, and I could tell how much he wanted me."

"He kissed my hand," Hannah says. "But that's all. He's a gentleman."

"He's a man, and I'm sure he wants more than one of us, but he's constrained. That's my point. We have to make this show work, and Anika isn't helping." Katy shrugs. "That's all I'm saying. If she's not here for the king and she's not here to make the show better, and by that I mean more watchable, then why is she here? Do you guys want to be known as the most boring cast in all of reality TV or do you want to be talked about?"

"I want to get married," Hannah concedes.

A groan goes through most of the women, though I note that Riley puts a hand on her friend's shoulder.

"Well, I think it's safe to say none of us would reject the man." Katy's arms cross over her chest. "None of us except Anika. I could see her doing it. Look, I'm never going to see you as anything but someone production forced on us. I have to wonder if you're here to spy on us."

"Then I should do a better job." I'm sick of defending myself. "I'm not the one who is trying her hardest to take out the competition. According to your precious process, there is no competition. We're all supposed to get along and let the guy figure out who he's in love with. I'm trying to do that in my own way, and I'm not going to let you steamroll me into being someone I'm not. If you want to talk to the king about how much you hate someone else here and that you can't handle your own problems, *so please, please, Your Majesty, help the little girl out* then do it yourself. As for me, I'll take care of Shelby myself. Because I don't need a crown to be a queen."

"And cut." Joe is behind me, and he claps his hands. "Now that's what I'm talking about. That's the energy I need. We can edit that down so we're not talking about production. That was perfect."

Katy beams his way. "Thank you. I told you I could get her there. She's been kind of waiting to explode."

"Get me there?" I'm on the edge of exploding now because I'm beginning to figure out how much of this scene was set up, and I wasn't even allowed to read the script. They'd had a meeting I hadn't been invited to. "This was some kind of setup?"

Hannah shakes her head. "I didn't know. Neither did Riley."

But the rest of them were clearly in on it.

Ashley F gives me a sympathetic look. "Sorry. They told us they needed to see some emotion from you. You're the only one of us who hasn't cried in confessional yet. They're worried you come across as not wanting to be here."

I feel like a complete idiot. "So this wasn't about Shelby. This was about me."

Joe steps into the living room. "Of course it's about Shelby, and we still need to have a talk about how the house wants to handle her, but this was a good scene. I'm glad I kept the cameras rolling. That speech you gave? Fire. That last line is going to be around for a while, just watch it. Thanks, kid. You did good. Now take a break and we'll get back to all of you discussing Shelby."

I should have remembered that a "break" isn't a break if cameras are working twenty-four seven.

"I think I'll take my break in my room." I need to breathe because now my mind is rolling with everything these women have said to me. With the exception of Hannah and Riley, they've all allowed me to walk into some kind of trap that's likely going to get me way more screentime than I want.

"Be back in twenty," Joe says, and I can tell he's disappointed in me.

"Hey, you're welcome," Katy calls out.

"Leave her alone," Ashley F says. "She needs a minute. You got the reaction you wanted now leave her be."

I hurry up the stairs and into my room.

What would they say if they knew the truth? I like some of these women. I respect them all. Sure, I want to toss a couple of them into the Hudson, but I respect them.

The pressure of being stuck in this place is starting to get to me, and now I have to wonder if Luca is beginning to regret the whole no-kissing thing. Maybe he's connecting with these women the way production hoped he would, and he feels bad that he put himself in a corner. Maybe he's only coming around to see me because he put me in this stupid room and he doesn't have another choice.

"I could kill her and stuff her body in the foundation of the building we start on in two days," Harper says from the doorway. "I do that kind of stuff for the mob all the time. Part of being in the construction business in the city. Lots of bodies in foundations around here, you know."

I sniffle and sit down on the bed, a bit weary. "I don't like it here."

"Then why haven't you walked away? You can leave. They can't keep you here. If you're supposed to find dirt on the director, I don't think that's going to happen. I've watched him. The only woman who comes and goes from his private rooms is that Christy chick, and if they're banging, I would be surprised. They seem congenial. I take it we're looking for something a little more nonconsensual," Harper suggests.

I nod because it's not like Harper's going to talk. "There's a rumor he might be sexually harassing some of the women on his sets."

"I've met him three times now, and he's been perfectly lovely. We've talked about Gilded Age architecture. He didn't even look at my chest and I was wearing a serious bra, if you know what I mean. He did not fall into my honey pot."

And he hasn't come close to mine. Besides being a rat fink bastard who is giving me some low-key trauma, he's not bad to work for, though Patrick seems constantly on the edge. That's his problem, not Joe's.

I can leave if I want to.

I can walk out the door, and then I don't have to feel this way.

"Ani, come on. We can be home in fifteen minutes. Ivy's going to yell at me, but I don't care." Harper stands and offers me her hand. "We can have you packed up in no time at all."

Packed and gone, and I can call Jessica and tell her this whole thing has been a big old nothing burger.

"Oh, shit. You don't want to go." Harper is staring at me with something akin to horror. "I know it's not because of the friendships you've made along the way, so this is about Luca. Honey, what's going on. Is he still sneaking in here?"

I nod, and Harper sighs and sits back down, her hand finding mine.

"Have you changed your mind? Are you thinking you want to try to win this thing?"

The very fact that she's asked if I want to win makes me wince. "Luca's not a prize to win. He's been coming in to watch some reality shows with me. He didn't do a lot of research, so he's trying to figure out how it all really works. He didn't understand why the producers were upset he won't kiss anyone."

"Anyone but you."

"Not on camera," I admit. "No one knows he's coming in here at night. I mean except his bodyguard who sits out in the stairwell waiting for someone to try to murder him."

"Okay, that's weird," Harper allows, "but I think we're missing the salient point here. He's only interested in you, and it's obvious you're totally into him. I know what happened was annoying, but he's got a good reason he's doing this show. So I don't see the problem."

Then she hasn't been listening. "I can't be a queen."

"I thought you said that wouldn't happen."

"Luca's got it in his head that he needs to get married anyway, so he might as well go with someone he likes." He's been teasing me about it. "And he thinks it would be economically effective since the producers have to hand over seven million if we get married."

"A seven-million-dollar wedding?" Harper whistles.

"That seems cheap for a royal wedding, but yes." I can see she's already wondering what her bridesmaid dress will look like and how many glasses of champagne she can fit in on that private flight to Europe that would certainly be scheduled. "I can't marry him. He doesn't love me."

Harper groans. "Don't get hung up on a word. Some guys aren't great communicators."

"He's the head of his country. He's an excellent communicator." And he's an incredible kisser, and I'm worried if I do stay those make-out sessions are going to go further.

I'm more than a little worried that I want to know what it feels like to sleep with him, to have his hands on me, to not stop doing what seems to come so naturally between us.

"Watch his actions, not his words," Harper says quietly.

There's a knock on the door, and I can't help but start at the sound.

Harper crosses the space and opens the door, revealing a more irritated than normal Patrick.

"Don't you have a job to do? Like a light to fix or something?" Patrick moves out of the way to allow her to leave.

"I would love to fix the stick that somehow got shoved up your ass," Harper replies as she waves my way. "See you later, Ani. Think about what I said. You have options."

"No, you don't," Patrick counters. He moves into my room, glancing around. "You need to come back downstairs. Joe still wants a house meeting about Shelby, who I heard is on her way back from her one-on-one, so don't be surprised when she walks in. Or do be. Whatever Joe wants from you. Unless you're going to cry and run away because the girls were mean to you."

"What the hell did I do to you?" I'm sick of his attitude. "Do I look like the person who kicked your favorite puppy or something?"

"You're a pain in my ass." He stops and stares for a moment at the pink bear sitting on my bookcase. A long sigh runs through him. "And you're dumb as dirt. I can't even with you right now. Either get downstairs or let production know you're leaving."

He reaches out and picks up the bear, swiping it off the shelf in an angry gesture.

"Hey," I begin.

"You have five minutes." He walks out, carrying the bear with him.

What a jerk.

I've got the start of a headache from hell, and I still don't know what to do. I'm lying to everyone in this house and it's starting to get to me.

It might be time to leave.

But I take a deep breath and put on a smile because I can't do a damn thing until I talk to Luca.

Chapter Fifteen

When the secret door opens it's after midnight but I'm still dressed in the jeans and T-shirt I wore earlier for our house meeting. We all had to pretend to be surprised when Shelby walked through the door even though she'd been sitting in the kitchen most of the night, making way too loud comments on everyone in the house.

Ah, the joys of "reality" TV.

He smiles as he enters, his tablet in one hand. The door snicks closed behind him, but I can't forget the fact that Hans is out there. We're not ever really alone. "Good evening, Anika. I can't tell you how happy I am to be done with this day. I've spent hours waiting for them to let me know filming was done."

"I'm going to leave in the morning." There's nothing else to do but tell him. Be blunt and confident in my decision. Leave no room for debate.

Even though the debate is raging inside me. I'm not confident. I don't know what I want, and that's what's truly killing me.

His handsome face falls and he sets the tablet down, moving into my space. "What's gone wrong, *Schatz*? They said you had a house meeting. Did it go poorly?"

He can't understand how poorly it went. "I can't do this anymore. I can't keep lying to them."

He seems surprised to hear those words. "You're not lying to anyone."

I've been thinking about this all night, guilt weighing me down. "They all think they have a chance with you."

"My darling, I had a frank discussion with Shelby this evening, and she understands that I'm focused on one woman and it's not her. She doesn't know who it is, but she knows I'm only keeping her around because the producers asked me to. She's under no illusions about her chances."

Wow. No wonder Shelby had been particularly nasty this evening, despite the fact that all she would say was her date had been phenomenal. "Luca, you're not supposed to do that."

He shrugs. "I don't care. I would rather be honest. We're making an entertaining show. That's what I've concluded. Very few of the women who came on the show honestly believe they can find true love here."

"Hannah does," I point out.

I kind of do, too, but I'm not saying that to him. I would have said no, that's some silly talk right there a few weeks ago, but the truth of the matter is I'm falling hard for a man I can't have for so many reasons. I'm anxious and feeling like crap because no matter what kind of show we're making, the truth of the matter is we're lying because he's already decided the outcome.

"Hannah is smarter than you think she is." Luca is watching me with patient eyes.

That bugs me, too. He's watching me like this is all some part of my performance and if he waits long enough we'll get to a better part of the script. "She's going to get hurt when she realizes you never seriously considered her."

"Who says I didn't?"

I stare at him.

He shrugs. "How will anyone know that you are the only woman I want? I'll tell you something, Anika. I'm not talking just about this group of women. How will anyone ever know that you're the only woman I've wanted to spend time with in a romantic fashion in over a year? It's not that I don't like women. I do. More than half my advisers are women."

I snort at that thought. "And they let you do this?"

A single shoulder shrugs. "They all thought this was a terrible idea. But that's not the point. I want you to understand. The person I spend the most time with from my family is my cousin, Ella, who you'll meet when we go to Ralavia for the final ceremony."

I shake my head but he continues on anyway.

"What I'm trying to say is I've felt numb inside since my parents died. I've been in a dark place, and it was meeting you that seems to be bringing me out of it. I'm not willing to let you go. Tell me what's gone wrong and I'll fix it."

He's getting to me. "I told you. I don't like lying."

"You're not lying," he assures me. "If anyone's lying it's me, and I'll take that sin on myself. You don't have anything to worry about. Let me pick you for the one-on-one date this weekend. I don't want to spend another long evening with one of the others."

He's dodging the issue, and I have to bring him back to it. "Tell me you haven't already thought about how this plays out."

"Of course I have. You can't tell me the other men and women who've been in my position didn't know who their final four were very early on," he insists. "It's obvious who we get along with and who we don't. I suspect they were influenced by the producers the same way I'm being influenced. Joe made a point before the date to ensure that I would be keeping Shelby, despite the fact that I see through her. She's quite lovely to me, but the minute my back is turned, her claws come out."

"She makes good TV," I say.

He points as though I've fallen right into his trap. "Yes, and that's what we're doing. Making good TV, and if they didn't understand that before, they do now. Even Hannah. Like I said, she's smarter and more savvy than anyone gives her credit for. She's a nice young woman, and she's going to be fine at the end of this. And so are we. We're going to be better than fine. We're going to figure out if this thing can work between us."

"I thought you already had us married off."

"In my head I do. In my head I know this can work, but I see you need more time," he replies. "I'll give it to you. All you have to do is stay with me. Go through the rest of this process with me and then I'll show you how wonderful life in my country can be."

There are so many things wrong about this situation, but I hold on to one. It feels like the one thing that might save me. "Luca, I have a job."

"You could have a different one," he counters. "Or you could work with production companies to bring them to our country. You know this industry. When you think about it, you're perfect."

That was the problem. "Yes, I get the feeling I'm convenient for you."

A brow arches over his eyes. "Convenient. I assure you there is not a thing convenient about my life in the last several years, so don't be surprised if I try to hold on to the one good thing that's happened to me."

Just like that my walls begin to shake. So I find the next problem. The one he can't solve. "You don't love me."

His jaw goes tight. "I don't know about that. I've been wondering lately if I even understand that word. I know I want you. I know I think about you all the time. Do you want me to say it? I can say the words."

I shake my head. "No. I want you to mean it." I'm getting emotional. Getting? I'm past emotional. I've been trapped in this mansion performing like a marionette doll, and I thought I could handle it. "You're never going to mean it."

He moves into my space, and his hands come up to cup my cheeks and tilt my head so I'm looking into his eyes. "*Verlass mich nicht.* I'll show you. I'll prove it to you."

Then his mouth is on mine, and I can't think straight. I can't think about anything but him.

I know I should push him away, but my arms aren't interested in listening to that bit of logic. They wrap around Luca's muscular form and he leans over, getting his hands on my hips as his tongue surges against mine. Just like that I'm ready to give him anything he wants. Any way he wants it. I've never felt this crazy rush of desire in my life. Sex has always been something nice, a pleasant side effect of being in a relationship, but this isn't nice. This is necessary. This is like breathing to me.

I cling to him as he lifts me up and moves us over to the bed I've been using. He lays me out, and I know I'm not going to stop. I'm not going to tell him this is a bad idea. I watch as he drags his shirt over his head and tosses it to the side. He kicks out of his shoes.

"Take off the clothes, Anika. If you like them, take them off now before I rip them off you," he says, a savage look in his eyes.

That look should scare me. His words should have me arguing, but I simply lift my hips and shove my jeans off as I watch him drop the sweats he's wearing and get down to his boxers.

He's a freaking Greek god. It's not like I haven't seen him in his swim trunks. We're on a reality dating show. He's put in his share of time in a hot tub, but this is different. Those hours spent in a hot tub were playful. This feels real to me. So real.

Cool air hits my skin as I pull the shirt over my head and toss it aside. I'm not wearing a bra but I'm not cold. My whole body feels like it's coming alive for the first time.

I'm down to my undies when he eases his big body on mine, his lips on mine again. He kisses me until I'm breathless, whispering something in German I don't quite understand but I feel the words across my skin.

"*Ich habe schon ewig auf dich gewartet.*" He kisses my neck and all along my shoulder, sending heat sparking through me.

I let go of everything but what he's making me feel. I know this can't work but I'm going to have this night with him. I'm going to have these memories of being with him.

I'm always careful, but he makes me reckless.

His big hand cups my breast, and I bite back a moan.

"You're so gorgeous," he says. "I think about you always, *Schatz.* Tell me you won't leave me."

Treasure. His treasure. "I won't."

I can't. I think this was my last-ditch effort to get out of what I know is a dangerous to my heart situation. If he'd argued or been cold, I could have packed up and left, but he's figured out how to keep me close.

By keeping me really close.

I let my fingers find the silk of his hair as he drags his tongue over my nipple before sucking it behind his lips. Desire shoots through me, and I can feel every tug of his mouth between my legs. I'm already warm and wet and ready for him, but he seems determined to torture me. He moves between my breasts, one hand sliding down my body and teasing at my core.

He kisses his way down, leaving my skin feeling like a live wire everywhere he touches. He gets on his knees, my legs on either side of his gorgeous body. His cock is barely contained by those boxers he's wearing and his hair—usually so controlled—tumbles over his forehead, making him look young and reckless.

"I told you, Anika." There's the sexiest smirk on his face as he reaches down and rips the delicate lace on either side of my underwear, pulling it clear and tossing it to the side.

I can buy more underwear. I won't ever forget how it feels to have this god of a man loom over me, desire plain on his face.

He spreads my legs wide and lowers himself down. "Yes, *Schatz.* This is where I've wanted to be since the moment I met you."

He lowers his mouth to my core, and I swear it takes everything I have not to scream out his name. He takes his time, teasing me with his mouth and teeth and tongue. Over and over he drowns me with pleasure, and I can't think of why I ever fought this feeling. This is where I want to be. Every minute of every day.

When he gets back on his knees and shoves his boxers down, I'm ready to welcome him. I want nothing more than to have this man inside me, binding us together in the most intimate of ways. He proves he's always prepared by opening a condom he's brought with him. How long has he been planning this? I know I've thought about it since the moment I met him.

Maybe it was inevitable that we would end up here. Maybe there's been nothing I can do to get out of this trap I find myself in. All I know is if this is a cage, I'll lock myself in as long as he's with me.

"This changes things between us, Anika," he says as he settles himself between my legs.

I wrap myself around him, loving how he presses me down, the weight of him making me feel delicate and sexy. I pull him close for a long kiss as he gently works his way inside me. It's not hard since I'm more than ready for him, but when he moves, my breath hitches, my whole body clenching around him.

He mutters something in German and settles into a rhythm that has me panting. He feels so good, so right. Like I was born to be in this exact space with this man. Like something has fallen blissfully into place.

Then I'm flying as he hits the right spot, and I can't think of anything but the insane amount of pleasure he's giving me. When he goes over the edge, I hold on as tight as I can.

I hold on because I never want this moment, this feeling, to end.

I hold on because if I lose him, I fear I'll miss this man for the rest of my life.

Chapter Sixteen

When he returns from the bathroom, Luca tucks himself into bed next to me, his arm going around me to pull me back against him. "Come close, *Schatz. Ich brauche deine nahe.*"

My whole body is humming, and I feel warm. I think this is what total satisfaction feels like. "You have to speak English when we're in bed together."

"I will try, but only until you learn some German. I'm afraid my brain isn't at its best when you're naked. Another part of me takes over, and he only speaks German." He chuckles behind me, and we're so close I feel it go through his body. "Though you should know that almost everyone in Ralavia speaks English, too. My mother spoke Dutch, so she picked up German very quickly. Or you don't have to learn at all, and I'll ensure everyone speaks English around you."

I tilt back so I can sort of get a look at him. His arm tightens around me, and I realize he's worried he's pushing me. He doesn't seem to understand that he's kind of blown away all my walls. "I'll start learning as soon as I can get my phone back. Unlike Your Majesty, I haven't had access to any kind of electronics, and it's not like there's a tutor here. I want to know what you're saying to me."

He settles back down, seemingly calmer. "I'm saying how beautiful you are and how long I've waited for you." He kisses the nape of my neck. "Are you feeling better now? I meant what I said to you earlier.

You're not causing anyone harm. We're not hurting anyone at all."

I'm not so sure about that, but now that I'm here with him, I know I can't leave. "I don't want to think about the show right now. I want to be here with you for as long as we can."

Because in a few hours we'll be right back on set, and he'll be dating a bunch of women I've come to count as friends.

"Good. I don't either," he admits. "I want to think about you and the here and now. You should know that I've come to like your mother and her business partner very much. I might talk to her a bit when you're not around."

"I'm sure she's told you some stories." I try not to think about the fact that this is one of the reasons we can't work. Our circumstances are wildly different. We don't live in the same world. My mother makes sandwiches for a living and his was a queen.

"She has, and you're adorable in all of them. I think we get along quite well, though she did tell me to be careful with young ladies' hearts. Tonya seems to be watching me. Told me I should be careful. I was worried until I realized you're like a daughter to her, too. I was surprised to find out Harper has managed to get herself a job on set. I thought she owned her own business."

"Oh, this job isn't about money," I explain. "Harper is here to stick her nose directly into my business. She's trying to protect me and honestly, I don't know what I would do without her."

"Well, I hadn't seen her until earlier today and she has already threatened to use her sharpest tools on me if I hurt you, and I believe her. Please, my darling, tell her I have the best of intentions."

"I'll talk to her and my mom. Tonya can be a little intense. They won't poison you or anything," I promise him.

"Hans tests all my food, so it would be him," he says with a sober expression.

I turn, facing him. "Are you serious?"

His lips split in a delightful grin as he laughs. "Of course not. That would be ridiculous. No one is looking to take me out. Except your relatives and friends. I like that everyone is so protective of you."

He doesn't know the half of it. Somewhere in the city there is a tech goddess who is probably planning ways to destroy Luca on the Internet. "Oh, you have no idea. It's Ivy you really have to worry about. She's got a protective streak, and she's excellent with a computer."

A brow rises over his eyes. "So I've heard. I'll have to watch my step with her. You know I heard something earlier about an Ivy.

Production mentioned the name. I couldn't help but wonder if they weren't talking about your Ivy."

"I can't imagine why they would. Well, I can. She had this article released about how the whole Jensen Medical thing went down and then it came out that her CFO—who happened to be her boyfriend at the time—sold the whole company out. It turned out okay because now she works with her fiancé on a startup dealing with a matchmaking AI," I reply and my mouth keeps going. "Did you know that matchmaking in Victorian England was seasonal? They had a whole season for it. It started around Easter with a big debutante ball and ended on August 12th because that was the opening of grouse hunting season. What is a grouse?"

He chuckles, and his arm tightens around me. "It's like a goose. And you are filled with information. I promise not to give Ivy any reason to need revenge on me. It's obvious how many people care about you. Probably because you're kind and tenderhearted and an excellent friend." He punctuates each compliment with a stroke of my hair.

The sweet intimacy pierces me. Tomorrow we have to play our roles, but tonight we get to be Ani and Luca. Tonight we get to shut the world out and be together. "Do you have any friends you've had since you were a kid?"

I think it would be odd to go through life without deep friendships, without someone who understood what your childhood was like. We're so shaped by how we grow up.

"I wasn't allowed friends," Luca admits. "Not in the way you would understand. There were no playdates or football teams for me. I had mates at school, and I had my cousins, but my childhood was isolated. I'm the last of the line, and when my parents accepted that they wouldn't have another child, I'm afraid they became protective of me."

"Because they loved you."

He snorts, a not entirely unsexy sound coming from him. "No, because if I died one of my cousins would be the heir, and my father couldn't stand his brother or sister so keeping them away from the throne was of the utmost importance. No. It wasn't about love. They left me with nannies. There were always three, so they took shifts. When I was older, I went to school, and there was a bit of freedom in that, although it turns out raising a child only around adults makes one awkward. It took some time to build any kind of normal relationships with the other lads in my class."

That sounded terrible. "You should have been able to run and play.

My parents... Well, I don't remember a time when they didn't fight. They weren't a good match, but they tried for a long time. It was a relief when they divorced. After my dad decided he'd punished my mom enough, he was effectively out of my life. Even when they were married, it wasn't like he did his fair share of the childcare. I spent a lot of time on sets like this one. My mom or Tonya would pick me up and I would do my homework at the craft service table, handing out sandwiches. I knew how to make coffee way too young. But she always made sure I got time with my friends."

"I don't think I made a real friend until I was an adult," Luca muses. "It's hard because I have to put my people first. That means being friends with or dating me can be disappointing. I can't tell you how many times I have to cancel because of some emergency that forces me to return to the palace."

"Your girlfriend should understand that you have a thankless job that you never asked for." I feel for Luca in this. He never got to dream about what he would be when he grew up. His path was set the moment he was born, and it wouldn't change unless he was willing to leave his people behind.

"Perhaps it's why I've never had a truly serious girlfriend. I've never considered marrying any of them. The one I was closest to threw a huge fit when I had to leave our vacation in Greece to deal with a problem with parliament. Tell me what you would have done. Perhaps not thrown an empty bottle of Dom Pérignon at my head."

"No. I wouldn't have done that." I know exactly what I would have done. "I would have packed up and gone with you. If I couldn't, I would have followed you when I could. You don't have a nine to five job. You have a whole country depending on you. That's why allowances must be made."

There's a knock on the door that reminds me that despite our intimacy, we're never truly alone.

Luca sighs and kisses my forehead. "Remember that you said this, *Schatz*. The only reason Hans would interrupt is for a problem only I can handle." He stares at me for a moment. "I don't want to leave you."

Another knock.

I kiss him briefly. "It's okay. I understand."

He slides out of bed and retrieves his boxers and pants before opening the door. After a short conversation with Hans that has me wishing I knew more German, Luca sighs and nods his head.

"I have to go," he says as he pulls his shirt over his head.

"Apparently there are papers I have to sign. It's already morning at home, and parliament can't meet without them. I would have them come over here, but I don't trust anyone besides Hans with our secret. I'll see you tomorrow at the elimination ceremony. I can't wait to see what you wear." He winks. "Something short, I hope. You always look so beautiful, *Schatz*. Do you want to get rid of Shelby? This I will do for you if you think it will make the house calmer."

See, this right here is why I'm feeling guilty. "You can't discuss eliminations with me, Luca. I think you should talk to the producers. She does make for good TV, and you have to think about that. You're here for a reason."

He slips his shoes on, and he's so adorably disheveled it takes everything I have to not throw myself at him again. "Reasons can change. Or perhaps evolve is a better word. I still have to think about Ralavia, but that doesn't mean you're not a priority. You are, and I won't let you go easily." His lips curl up. "The good news is I still have two weeks to convince you. I think I'll practice looking pathetic so you can't deny me when I ask you to be my queen."

I laugh because if he asked me right now, I would absolutely say yes. I would chuck my whole future to be with him. He's straightening his clothes when I remember I wanted to ask him a question. "Where did you hear about Ivy?"

"Uhm, we're supposed to do something with a woman named Emma later this week," he explains. "She's coming in with your friend, Ivy."

My jaw drops. Well, she's found a way to get her ass in here. I shouldn't have doubted her for a second. "Emma's not a person. She's Ivy's matchmaking AI. They're going to run us through to see if we're compatible. Now I know why all the women were filling out forms earlier. I didn't have to. They already have mine."

He frowns. "You were going to allow a computer to find you a boyfriend?"

"You're allowing a reality show to choose a wife." I point out the obvious.

"No, I'm allowing a reality show to give me a pool of candidates and then I choose, and so far it's worked out well for me," he replies.

"Only because someone dropped out at the last minute. Otherwise, I would be the person getting you drinks," I counter.

"No, my darling, you would be the crew member I was secretly fucking and the reason none of this worked out because I'm so crazy about you. It's fate. You can't run from it. I don't care what that silly computer says," he returns.

Another knock. So Hans is getting impatient. "Go run your country."

"Fate, *Schatz.*" He winks at me and then he's gone and I'm alone again.

But his side of the bed is still warm and still smells like him, so when I settle back down I fall asleep.

It's no surprise that I dream about him.

Confessionals

Shelby

I don't care that they had a house meeting about me. They're sheep. I'm a lioness, so they should watch out for me.

Hannah

I think most of us are here for the right reasons. I don't know why they're going after Anika. She's a sweetheart. I mean, Riley's my closest friend here, but Ani's second. I'll be honest. I've never had a relationship quite like this one. It's easy and natural. Oh, I was talking about Riley. About friendship. But it's obviously not as perfect as my relationship with Reg.

Tiara Kate

I can't believe he picked me for the one-on-one date tomorrow. I'm so relieved. I didn't want to do that computer thing. Like, why should I believe what a computer says? Especially one Ivy Jensen programmed. Didn't she like get canceled or something? Wasn't she Tech Barbie for a while?

Riley

Who do I think is the nicest person in the house? Oh, it's Hannah. Hands down. I feel like I've known her my whole life. Like I don't even know that I care if I win anymore because of the friends I've made here. I didn't expect that.

Ashley F

That house meeting did absolutely nothing but send Shelby on a tear since naturally she found out about it. Drama. That woman lives to create drama. She'll make Reg's life hell if he picks her.

His Majesty

I'm more certain than ever that my queen is in that mansion. There's a treasure in one of those rooms, and I'm not a man to let a treasure slip through my fingers. You think I seem more relaxed? Well, perhaps it's because I'm back on a good exercise schedule. Nothing like exercise to relieve some stress.

Anika

How do I feel about being called out? By Katy? I feel like… I've been told not to say those things out loud. Lawyers. Yeah, I have feelings. Big feelings, but I'm going to be a lady about them. I mean, what are the right reasons? Can someone define them for me? Is wanting to get into that man's silky boxers the right reasons? Because I'm totally here for that. Wait. I probably shouldn't have said that. Can we edit that out?

Chapter Seventeen

I stand with Hannah three days later as Shelby walks out of the room where they're filming individual sessions with Luca and the team behind Emma. Katy and Emily have both been sent to the sequester hotel. I'm getting oddly comfortable with the elimination ceremonies, but I'm surprised at the emotion from Shelby.

It's clear from the sheen of tears in her eyes that she didn't get the outcome she wanted. "There's something wrong with that machine. Where is Joe? I'm not letting what that stupid computer said about me get out in public. I will sue everyone on this show."

I exchange a glance with Hannah, who's already had her session with Ivy and Heath.

Hannah shrugs. "She was super nice to me, though she thinks I'm not political enough to be a good match for Reg. She did say I should look for someone I'm comfortable with because I have a tendency to downplay my own wants and desires. I apparently need someone I can have a deep friendship with before we get physical. I liked her. Is it weird to call a computer her?"

They still call him Reg. I have to be so careful because one of the things I've figured out is there is King Reginald and then there's Luca. He's the man. He's my man.

Ashley F snorts. "Well, apparently the thing works because she didn't pick Shelby for Reg. That proves the computer is way smarter than the producers."

I'm getting nervous about this whole thing. They're using the forms I filled out months before. I wasn't looking for a guy then. I'm not now. I'm looking for a Luca, and now I worry I'm going to walk out of there with vengeance in my eyes like Shelby did. "What did Emma say about you?"

"That I need an ambitious man, one who matches my energy," Ashley F explains. "She didn't tell me anything I didn't already know. She said I would be a good pick, but I would likely be bored as queen."

"She confused me." Riley leans in. "I think the computer thinks I'm a lesbian. Which makes me wonder if I am a lesbian."

"I think that's something you just know." What kind of havoc is Ivy wreaking?

"Not necessarily," Tiara Kate says. Today she's wearing a bedazzled tiara with a big fake diamond at the center. She doesn't have to be here since she's going on the one-on-one with Luca. She's just hanging out to show us all…support? "Especially if you're naturally sexually fluid. But I think Riley being a lesbian should disqualify her."

"Hey." Hannah frowns TK's way. "She has every right to be here."

"Fox, they're ready for you." Patrick has one of his patented grim looks on his face as he holds the door open for me.

Teddy bear thief. I haven't forgiven him for that. I walk past him without a glance because he's one asshole I don't give more attention to than is absolutely necessary.

Luca is standing in the back of the mansion's grand ballroom. They've got it divided up into "sets," the largest being where we hold the king's choice ceremonies, and I can't help but remember there's one of those coming up fast. We're down to six of us. Me, Shelby, Ashley F, Tiara Kate, Hannah, and Riley. When we get to four, we're heading to Ralavia for the rest of the show, and I can't help but feel excited at the prospect. I want to see this place that is so important to the man who is rapidly becoming the center of my world. It also makes me nervous because the closer we get to the end, the more careful we have to be.

He's talking to Heath, Ivy's human golden retriever fiancé. He's one of the sweetest men I've ever met, and he balances out Ivy to perfection.

"I walked in here wanting to kill the man, but I like him, so now I'm thinking about murdering you because you got Harper in here and I've had to get all my information secondhand," an acerbic voice says.

I turn and Ivy's standing in the middle of the ceremony set, a cup of coffee in her hands. I've missed her. "Sorry. And I didn't get Harper the job. That was my mom."

I walk into her open arms, hugging her tight.

"I know. Your mom told me I didn't have any skills she could work with. I can make a sandwich," Ivy grouses.

Oh, I understood why my mom turned her down. Ivy is brilliant, but she's not what I would call a people person. "You're here now. That's all that matters."

"I've been worried about you," she whispers. "Are you okay?"

I pull back so she can look into my eyes. "I'm okay. It was hard at first, but…"

"But then you fell for him. At least that's what Harper told me. She said you have the chance to leave but you're not taking it. Are they holding you hostage? Blink twice if you need me to break you out."

"I'm fine," I promise her. "More than fine. I'm really getting to know Luca."

Ivy looks me over like she's trying to figure something out. "Like in a biblical way?"

That is none of her business. At least not here. When we have our after-show sleepover debrief complete with wine and cheesecake, I'll tell Ivy and Harper everything in way too much detail. "In an 'I want to see where this thing goes' way. I'm honestly okay. How did you manage this? I didn't know it was on the schedule."

"CeCe strong-armed your big boss into it," Ivy explains. "She's known Jessica for years. I'm not sure if she convinced her it was an excellent idea or if she has some dirt on her. I wouldn't put it past CeCe to blackmail someone. Anyway, I got what I wanted which is to see you, so that's all I care about."

"And you get to show off Emma," I point out.

Ivy's eyes light up. "I do. She's performing exactly how she should, by the way. I've been working on her language skills. She's got a great personality, if I do say so myself."

"You call that a great personality?" Joe walks up to us, a look of concern on his face. "Couldn't you tweak her so she's nicer about her matches? She hasn't said a single one of the contestants would be a great match for the king. I need something to work with. The only one she's been positive about is Ashley F, and I'm almost certain she's leaving soon."

Does he know something I don't? Maybe Luca's right and he understands the inner workings of this process better than I do. I know how things work from a production standpoint, but not how they're orchestrating things from the inside.

"Emma tells it like it is." Ivy gives him a shrug, and we start walking toward the office set where Heath seems to be showing Luca how Emma works.

"Did she have to point out that she wouldn't pair Shelby with Satan because no one deserves that kind of drama in his life?" Joe asks.

I bite back a laugh because no wonder Shelby was pissed.

"Hey, she's the one who filled out the forms," Ivy replies.

"That didn't come from forms." Heath's head comes up, and he waves my way. "Hey, Ani."

Luca is looking my way, too, a sexy smile on his face. Even though there's distance between us, I can practically feel his hands on me.

"What do you mean?" Luca asks, though his eyes remain on me. There's a small couch in front of the laptop that represents Emma. On screen it will look like we're in a cozy office, not on a large set with a team of fifteen people working around us. Sometimes when I'm with Luca, I forget, too.

"Part of Emma's process is to scour the Internet for a client's social media and anything else she can find." Ivy moves in around the desk, joining Heath. "Which is how she found out Shelby has asked for a lot of managers in her time."

"There's a whole TikTok profile set up exclusively for her," Heath agrees. "She's been screaming at retail workers for years. And did you know she's banned from four different Starbucks?"

"Shelby is here for very specific reasons," Joe allows.

"You needed a cast-iron bitch," Ivy replies. "Hey, no offense. I've totally been the cast-iron bitch in the reality show of my life. The point is that Emma looks at any number of factors to make her determinations. Shelby's Internet footprint was a big one. I thought the Satan thing was clever of her."

I happen to know that Emma is listening at all times. I often worry that at some point Emma will become self-aware and decide to take over the world, so I'm polite to her. "Emma, could you maybe use softer words during this assignment?"

The screen lights up, and a voice that sounds oddly like Heath's grandma comes out from the speakers. "Mom taught me that I need to speak my truth. Unvarnished and unapologetically. The advice I give is scientific and based on logic and reason."

That's a new feature. "Mom?"

Ivy's eyes roll.

Heath's whole face lights up. "It's because she's our baby."

"She's the only baby you're ever having if you don't get her to stop calling me Mom," Ivy says between clenched teeth.

Heath is unmoved by that threat. "Nah. I'll convince her we need a dog soon."

Joe sighs. "Well, I'll have to edit this so it looks like we've got some good candidates. What does she have to say about Anika? I'd like to know beforehand if I'm going to deal with another contestant walking out in the middle of the scene."

Luca moves to the couch and holds his hand out for me to join him.

I sit beside him, and he leans in.

"Hello, *Schatz*. You look gorgeous today," he whispers. "I don't care what the computer says. Remember that. She can be quite mean. And I think she thinks Riley isn't into men."

My anxiety notches up. What if Emma decides my perfectly normal obsession with Blake Lively means I'm into girls with ridiculously beautiful hair? I mean I wouldn't say no, but that only means I have eyes and am not a zero on the Kinsey scale. "What has she said about you? Or is she only tearing us apart?"

"Oh, I am a workaholic with a martyr complex when it comes to my people. Her words, not mine," he says smoothly as though we're talking about the weather and not our future engagement prospects. "Any woman who I'm with has to deal with the fact that the crown will likely always come first."

I did understand. "We've talked about that. I understand your job is unique. Now I'm worried about what Emma found on me. I use some weird memes."

"Stop freaking out," Ivy says as she types on the keyboard. "Like I said, Emma works beautifully. Emma, tell us about the king and Anika."

"Anika Fox is an excellent match for Reginald Lucannon St. Marten. Their values dovetail. They have the same beliefs, though the king sees things from a community perspective while Anika thinks about the individual. This could cause disharmony, but both are able listeners, willing to see viewpoints past their own. Anika is service oriented, which will be indispensable when it comes to working as a modern royal. The king has indicated that he will support and encourage his wife to pursue her own interests, something Anika will need to do. In the negative, Anika might find it hard to have all the public attention being royal brings about, but if the king handles it correctly, I believe she'll find her way."

Luca smiles at me. "I take back what I said. The computer is always right."

Joe frowns his way. "I thought we talked about this."

I was unaware they'd talked about anything.

Luca shrugs off his concern. "The cameras aren't running. I assure you I'll be a perfect gentleman when they are. I'm not going to molest the future queen of Ralavia on camera. I'll do that in private."

"Luca," I hiss under my breath.

It merely makes him grin.

Ivy is staring at us with wide eyes. It takes a lot to shock Ivy Jensen, but my showmance is doing the trick.

Heath, on the other hand, seems perfectly cheery. "Nonna did her research when I told her you were doing this thing. She gives you the thumbs-up, too, and says she wants an invite to the wedding."

"I will be pleased to have all of Anika's friends and family," Luca says smoothly.

I hold up a hand. "Nothing is settled. Absolutely nothing."

A look of pure innocence crosses Luca's face. "Of course. We're still in the middle of the process. We have to trust the process."

"Yeah, that's what you're doing. And it's a journey, not a process." Joe sighs and turns, gesturing for his camera crew to come in. "All right. Let's roll in ten. Check the lighting, please. Shelby kicked some of the equipment on her way out."

Luca stands, stretching and looking a little like a satiated lion. It's amazing what good sex will do for the man. "I'm getting some of your mother's scones. Can I bring anything back for you, darling?"

"I'm good. Thanks." I want to kiss him again, but I remember we're in a space with twenty people watching our every move. I'll be so glad when all of this is over and Luca and I can try to find some kind of normalcy.

"Okay, now I'm really worried." Ivy watches as Heath joins Luca, talking more about Emma and how they plan to market her. It's usually a conversation Ivy would never miss, but it's clear she's thinking about me. "Honey, are you sure about this?"

"I'm not sure of anything," I admit. "I just know I'm crazy about him. In the overused words of my fellow contestants, I'm falling for him. Or rather I've totally fallen for this guy."

"That would be great if he was an accountant or worked the counter of a deli on 42nd. Ani, he's a king. He will have to pick his job over you every time."

"That's a bit over the top." I argue with her even though I'm worried about it, too. "You're a workaholic. I hardly think you should judge."

"Less since Heath and I became a couple and we're working together," Ivy counters. "That's not what I'm talking about, and I'm not judging the guy. I told you I like him, but he has responsibilities we can't understand. Heath can chuck his career right out the window for me, and the only people it affects are me and him. That's not how Luca's world works."

"Well, I don't intend to make him pick between me and his crown," I reply.

"Yeah, well intentions are great, but the world has a way of forcing things on us," Ivy warns. "Just know that no matter what happens, we've got your back."

"She's right about that." Harper is suddenly beside us, her arms going around our shoulders, connecting us. "Come on. I want to show you something amazing."

"Is it original crown molding?" I ask because I've heard a lot about original crown molding.

"It is," she says with a grin. "I'm telling you this place is amazing. I could spend a year renovating it and not get bored even once. Come on."

I follow my friends, trying not to think about Ivy's words.

Chapter Eighteen

I watch from the raised dais where I stand with my daisy as Luca stares at the final two contestants. Tiara Kate is already crying, practically begging him not to let her go. Riley clutches her hand and looks over at me, Hannah, Shelby, and Ashley F.

"Kate, we've had so much fun, and I've loved getting to know you. You're insightful and smart."

She's bitchy and admitted that she was surprised at the ending of *Titanic*. Luca's being generous with the praise.

"Riley, we've connected on such a nice level. I truly believe we're friends and will continue to be so."

Hannah squeezes my hand, and I realize she's way more emotional at the prospect of Riley going home than she is of being out herself.

It's so nice that we've made good friends somehow. Even among all the craziness and chaos, there's still solidarity and friendship to be had.

"Riley, will you take this daisy and remain in the running to be my queen?" Luca asks.

Relief seems to pour through Riley, and she drops Tiara Kate's hand in a heartbeat. She has that daisy and is stating a happy *yes* before rushing over to hug Hannah.

"You're making a mistake." Tiara Kate pulls the tiara off her head and faces the king. "Not a one of these women are right for you. You think we can't all see who your favorite is? She'll be a disaster."

"Cut." Joe steps onto the stage. "Hey, you know we don't talk about what happens off camera, Kate."

She shakes her head. "We all know. He tries to hide it, but he looks at her all the time. I think he's sneaking into her room somehow because I swear I hear sex sounds coming from there. Don't try to deny it."

Luca's gone still, and I swear all the blood has left my body. How could she hear us? My room is all the way down the hall from hers. And we try to be quiet. Mostly. He does this thing with his tongue that makes me forget where I am and who I am and pretty much everything but what he's doing with his tongue.

"You've already picked Hannah," Tiara Kate accuses. "That's why you're keeping her best friend over me. It's not right."

I'm sure my jaw has hit the floor, but I simply pick it up and school my expression to an appropriately dramatic what-just-happened look.

Because I'm still trying to figure out what's going on.

"You think I've already selected Hannah?" Luca asks, as though weighing each word. "I can assure you I have not. Nor am I visiting her room at night."

"I share a room with her." Riley stands up for her best friend. "No one sneaks in. She wouldn't do that."

"Sure she wouldn't." Kate takes the tiara between her hands and cracks it in two. "You're all fools if you think something isn't going on. I guess I'll see you at the reunion show. I'll have a lot to say."

She storms off.

"Did anyone get that?" Joe is looking around at the camera operators, who all give him a thumbs-up. "Perfect. Someone go make sure she gets into the limo all right. Keep driving her around until she gives us what we need. Let's get the last shot so we can wrap for the day."

I'm feeling a little numb as we all hold up our champagne glasses and toast the fact that we've made it through another round.

"I'm the last bitch standing," Shelby says with a smirk as she passes the glass back to the PA. "That means I'm going straight to the final two."

"She's not wrong about that." Ashley F steps out of her shoes and bends over to pick them up. "The producers will want as much tension as possible. They'll want the viewers freaking out that he'll make a horrible mistake."

"Horrible is a lot," Shelby argues and then she sighs. "Look, guys, I know I'm being over the top. It's for show. Mostly. I mean, I actually kind of like some of you."

I glance over to where Luca is talking to Joe, both men with their heads down as one of the producers approaches. They all look serious, like Tiara Kate...I guess she's just Kate now since that tiara is currently being swept up by another PA...has sent them into a frenzy of conspiracy theories. Or they're trying to figure out how much of it to use.

"Does everyone think I'm sleeping with Reg?" Hannah sounds horrified.

"Of course not," Riley assures her.

Shelby rolls her overly mascaraed eyes. "Absolutely not. Though apparently you have a lot of nice dreams because I've heard some sounds, too. Look, Hannah, no one thinks you would try to cheat at this game we're playing. You're very trustworthy. Personally, I would bet you're a virgin."

"Am not," Hannah says with a frown. "I mean it depends on the definition."

"Nope." Riley takes her hand. "We're not talking about this. Good night, everyone. See you in the morning."

They walk off, and I think Hannah's started to cry.

"Hey, you could be nicer..." I stop because I'm talking to Shelby and that's like talking to a brick wall.

Shelby frowns my way. "I thought I was being nice. I told her she was all trustworthy and shit. I said I like some of you. You're not all boring."

I groan because I am not arguing with her tonight. "You know what, keep doing you. I'm sure it works out great."

I'm done for the night. I kick off my shoes and look over and Luca is still talking to the producers, though Joe seems to have left the scene.

I'm tired and still anxious from thinking we've been found out. The accusation opens a pit in my stomach, but I also know that when he shows up this evening, I'll welcome him.

And be very, very quiet, though with the dramatic exit of the contestant formerly known as Tiara Kate, I'm by myself in the west wing, a long way from the room Riley and Hannah share, and even further from Ashley F and Shelby.

"Anika, could I speak to you for a moment?"

I turn and one of the many producers who are all over this production is standing a few feet from me. I don't know his name because they kind of all look alike. They're all thirty-something dudes in suits that cost more than I make in a year. They're the guys who got the job because their dads or uncles are the executive producers or studio heads. One of these guys I recognize as Jessica's great nephew.

"Yeah," I reply, though all I want to do is run up to my room and wait for Luca because we need to talk.

After he does that thing with his tongue. I'm a little stressed.

He glances over as though trying to make sure no one is listening in. He gestures for me to follow as he walks over to a far corner, away from where the crew is cleaning and resetting the ceremony space.

"My aunt wanted me to talk to you," he says.

Ah, now I know who I'm talking to. Thad Wallace, Jessica's third and current husband's brother's youngest son. It's a lot, but knowing the hierarchy is a PA's best friend. "I haven't been able to talk to her. I can't exactly ask the director to break sequester."

"She doesn't want you to. She's seen the dailies and is thrilled with how the project is going," he says quietly, his hand in his pocket. "You're doing great, Anika. You're the perfect counterpoint to Shelby."

"I would think that would be Hannah."

"Oh, no. Hannah's got innocent-girl vibes, but you're like the girl everyone wants as her friend," he explains. "It's going to be a great finale. We'll tease the hell out of it that Reg chooses Shelby, and the whole world will be relieved when he picks you."

"He's picking me? Uh, I thought we didn't talk about stuff like this." Now I'm the one making sure no one's listening in.

He waves that off. "You're in the business, not one of these wide-eyed know-nothings. You know how this works. Anyway, she said she had a project for you and wants an update in the morning. She's insistent. She's checking out Helms, isn't she? She's going to give him the new franchise?"

If she hasn't told him, I can't. "I don't know what you're talking about."

He sighs as though he knows he's hit a brick wall. "I think you do, but you're one of those rules followers, aren't you?"

"Your aunt is the one who set the rules, so yes, I'm going to follow them," I reply. "Is she coming to the set?"

He pulls out a tiny cell phone. "She's in Sydney negotiating with one of the studios there. She wants to hit the ground running as soon as Helms is done with this project. If I'm right, he's going to hand everything over to us and the editors and take his place at the head of the biggest production Pinnacle has ever backed. Is that going to be a problem? I don't know what my aunt is doing, but I get the feeling you have some say in it. Which is weird because you're nobody. At least you were until this show. I guess now you're going to be the queen of Ralavia."

"That hasn't been determined yet." I take the cell and slip it into the bodice of my dress since no one thought I needed pockets. "So she's going to call me?"

"Before the shoot starts in the morning," Thad affirms.

At least I'll be able to give Jessica what she wants. Harper has tried to get Joe to hit on her, and he didn't go for it. He's been perfectly professional with me and all the other contestants. He kind of treats us like his kid sisters or daughters. Joe is seemingly kind and thoughtful.

"I'll take care of it," I promise.

"Good, and keep taking care of the king," he says with a weird smirk on his face. "He's going to be a star. It'll be worth the seven million to have exclusive rights to the royal wedding."

He turns and walks away.

He's kind of a jerk, but that's how producers are. And I want to be one, why? I walk down the hall, my shoes in hand and cell phone nestled against my boobs wondering why I want to do this.

Because since I was a kid, they were the people with the power. I grew up in this industry. Surrounded by it. It's all I know, and production has the power.

I want to be a different producer than the ones like Thad, who care nothing about the story they're telling or the people they're working with. It's not like there aren't great producers out there, but there are an awful lot of Thads.

At least Joe turns out to be a good person to work with. I round the corner to make my way to the residential portion of the mansion. Soon this will all be over, and Luca and I will have some time to figure out if this can work.

I'm starting to believe it can.

"I told you I don't want to do that," a familiar voice says.

I can barely hear him. It's Patrick, I think, but he's trying to keep it down. I wonder who's pissed him off this time. I feel for whoever it is.

"Stop," he says, and this time he's louder, and I can hear genuine distress in his voice.

I move toward the production office.

"You can't say you don't want it," another voice says. "After all, it's not like it's the first time, Pat. You know what happens if you don't do your job."

A chill goes up my spine because I know that voice, too.

Sometimes rumors get twisted. We see what we think we should see and forget that anyone can be a target. Not only women. No. We're equal opportunity sexual harassers in my industry.

So I do exactly what I would do if one of the women were behind that door. I throw it open and let Patrick know he's not alone.

I never realized how big Joe is, but seeing him with his hand around Patrick's throat makes it clear that the power imbalance goes far beyond their jobs. He's got Patrick backed against the wall, and I can't miss the sheen of tears in the PA's eyes. I also can't miss the fact that his hand is on Patrick's belt.

"Hey, are you okay?" He's not and I know he's not, but I can't think of anything else to say.

We've all been in this position. Every woman I know has had some man put his hands on her when she didn't want him to. From mild annoyance to outright rape, this is something women deal with on an everyday basis, and my heart aches and I'm also angry at myself because never once did I think that the person who Joe was harassing was a man.

Patrick doesn't deserve this, and I was sent here to make sure he doesn't have to put up with it a moment longer.

Joe's face is a florid red when he turns, his hands coming up as though he can show me he isn't dangerous. Except I've already seen behind the mask. "Everything is fine. We were just discussing tomorrow's shoot. Right, Patrick?"

Patrick is shaking as he nods. "Yeah. Tomorrow's shoot. I'm going home now to get some rest."

He rushes past me, his eyes not meeting mine.

"Anika, should we talk?" Joe asks me.

What is there to talk about? I saw what I saw, and I'm going to report it. Me standing here with him only places me in danger. I know when to retreat. I also want to let the monster stew in his own anxiety about what I'll do. I give him a smile. "Not at all. Sorry I interrupted."

He unleashes an audible sigh. "Sorry. My wife and I have an odd relationship. It's open, so if you're thinking about telling her, she won't be surprised."

Oh, she's not who I'm telling. "It's your business, Joe. On set affairs happen all the time."

I need to appease this man or I'm worried what he'll do to me. Tomorrow I'll have my talk with Jessica, and we'll have a new director shortly after that. I won't have to deal with him again, so I'm willing to say anything to get from point A, where I'm alone in a room with him, to point B, where I will never have to see this man again.

"I'm glad you understand. You've been in the business long enough to know how these things go. I have certain needs my wife can't fulfill."

"Because you're gay. Which is not a big deal in our business, so I'm not sure why you feel the need to hide it."

"I'm bisexual, and my wife understands my needs," he explains. "I come from a conservative, very wealthy family. If my parents find out, I'll be disinherited, and it will cost me a hundred million dollars. I've kept the secret this long. I might as well wait the fuckers out. Until then, I have nice casual relationships with men like Patrick."

It hadn't looked nice. He'd said no. "So you tend to hook up on set. That's a popular activity."

He stares at me. "Yes. Yes, it is. You should remember that."

Something about the way he says the words feels threatening, and I'm done with small talk. "Well, good night, Joe."

"Good night, Anika." He watches me leave.

When I hit the stairs, I run up them and down the hall to my room. I lock the door behind me. I really need a shower.

Chapter Nineteen

I'm practically vibrating with anger when Luca enters, the door opening without a single squeak. His eyes go straight to me sitting on the bed, a towel wrapped around me. I managed to scrub the makeup off my face and I'm feeling relatively normal again, but I haven't gotten dressed. He seems to immediately know something's gone wrong.

"What's happened, *Schatz*?" He sits on the bed beside me, his hand going to my thigh and a look of concern stamped on that handsome face of his. "Don't tell me nothing because you were smiling when I left you last. Was it Shelby? I knew I shouldn't have listened to the producers. I told them I wanted to get rid of one of the mean girls, and they talked me into Kate."

"It wasn't Shelby. She's perfectly happy with the situation. She's thrilled she's the last bully standing because she's sure that means she's making the final two." I don't care about the NDA in this moment. I need to talk to him. I need him to understand why I'm going to blow his relationship with an important person. "It's something else. Something serious. I caught Joe trying to force himself on Patrick."

"What?" Concern seems to turn to confusion. "Force himself?"

His English is so good, I forget it's not his first language. "I caught him and Patrick in a sexual situation. A nonconsensual one."

"But he's married." He shakes his head. "I'm sorry. That was a naïve thing to say. I'm a bit startled because I didn't know he was anything but the straight man he presents himself to be. I don't have a problem with it. I believe we're all born the way we're born and we accept it, but why would he hide it?"

I truly believe Joe told me the truth about this. Not so sure that his wife knows, but that doesn't matter to the situation at hand. "Apparently his parents are loaded, and he's concerned about them not approving of his lifestyle. He doesn't want to get cut out of the will."

Understanding dawns as he nods. "Ah, yes. Of course, and they are very religious in an... How would you put...old-school fashion. I've met them. They've done business with my country. Are you all right? Did he try to hurt you?"

He hadn't, though I had felt like it could happen. "No. I accepted his explanation that he's having an affair. Although I don't know he would call it that since he told me his wife knows about his lifestyle and they have an open marriage. I don't think Patrick would say they're having an affair."

"Did you talk to him?" Luca asks.

"I heard him saying no. He said it plainly, and he was crying when he did." My gut clenches because sometimes men don't understand. If you've never been in the position, it can be easy to wave it off. "I saw what was happening, Luca. I have zero doubt that Patrick didn't want what Joe was trying to do to him. I don't care if Patrick was having some kind of relationship with him. He has the right to say no at any point."

"Of course." He takes my hand, holding it to his heart. "You're right, my darling. So what are you going to do about it? How can I help you?"

I sniffle and lean into his strength. "I was sent to work on this show by the head of the company. She's been a mentor to me since I was an intern. She wanted me to take a low-level PA position so I could investigate some rumors she's been hearing."

His hand strokes over my hair. "Rumors about Joe. Rumors that he was hurting people?"

"Women," I correct. "I thought he was harassing the women around him. I assumed that was why Jessica sent a woman in. I'm young and potentially someone he might hit on. When he didn't and he seemed to treat all the contestants with respect and professionalism, I didn't even look at the men." I'm upset with myself for walking into this with a mindset that didn't allow for a different outcome. I had a specific scenario in mind and didn't think about all the times Joe would bark at Patrick to meet him in his office. Didn't see how tense Patrick would get. How angry he was all the time. "I should have known. Directors don't work that closely with production assistants."

"But Patrick is the head of the department."

"Which is why he should be working with Christy and the second unit directors," I explain. "I've never known a PA with such access to the director, especially one at Joe's level. I should have seen it."

He pulls me into his arms. "This is not your fault. No one saw it. But now we can deal with this problem. What does it mean for the production? I'm concerned for the young man, but I have to wonder what it means for the project. I can certainly handle a delay, but I've put a lot of my time and effort into this. I've spent a lot of money getting the palace ready for the shoot. What should I be expecting?"

"I don't even think there will be a short delay." I've thought this over because I know how much this project means to Luca. I've come to the conclusion that there's zero chance they'll shut down production. "The CEO sent me here to find this information, so she'll have a plan in place. The second director can take over. This is a flashy project for Joe, but it's simple compared to what he's used to. It's not the best use of his talent."

"No, it was a way for the production company to find out if he's a good bet," Luca surmises. "He told me he was doing this in exchange for the potential of heading a large franchise that will bring him millions of dollars."

"Yes. If he proved himself on this, Jessica was going to announce him as the head of what will end up being a billion-dollar franchise. But what it would really bring him is power," I reply. "I think he wants the power even more than the cash. After all, he told me he has millions waiting for him when his parents die."

He tilts my head up and stares into my eyes. "You're sure this won't shut down production? They can't throw it all away?"

I hate that he has to be so worried. "There's too much money but, Luca, you should know even if they were going to, I would still tell Jessica what I found out."

"Of course you would. You wouldn't be Anika if you didn't. I'm not telling you not to. I'm simply setting my expectations." He kisses me, and I feel my shoulders come down from around my ears. "I'm sorry you're in this position. Is there anything I can do to help you?"

"You didn't see it so you can't be a witness." I tilt my head back. "I don't want to cause trouble for you, but you'll be asked questions when it comes out. All you have to say is you never saw him acting inappropriately, but you believe his victims and stand behind them. I suspect we'll discover there are more Patricks out there."

He kisses me again. "Even if there's a delay, we'll work it out. Though it's hard to be patient. I want to get through the rest of this process. Excuse me, journey. I can't wait to get you home. I can't wait to show you off to my people. I know you don't think this can work…"

"I might be changing my mind about that." I cup that face I'm coming to love. There's a crisp brush of his beard because he hasn't shaved. He does that in the morning, so by this time of night, it rubs against my skin, and I've become addicted to the feel of it. "But I have to be able to work in some capacity. I know it seems like a hard business, but I do love it."

His mouth takes mine, and suddenly the towel drops away and I'm naked in his arms. "We'll work it out. Now stop thinking. I want to feel for a while. I spend so much time thinking and pushing away my own needs. This is the space where I get to be a man and not a bloody king. Only with you. Only ever with you."

I wrap my arms around him and let the kiss take over reality. This is where I need to be. I need to be with the man and not the king. I like the king, but I'm in love with the man. I accept that in this moment. I love Luca in a way I've never loved a man before. He's become vital to my life.

I'd been worried he would ask me to stay quiet until the project ends. Ivy had told me he would have to pick his country over me, but he's reacted exactly as I needed him to.

He murmurs something in German as he lays me out on the bed and gets to his feet to undress. I'm going to have to learn some German because every word is sexy, and I'd like to know when he's praising my body parts.

My mind flashes to the look on Patrick's face. I wonder how many times I've had that look on mine.

"Don't. Stay here with me," he urges as he tosses his shirt aside. "Stay here, *Schatz*."

I want to. I shove aside those dark thoughts because they have no place here between us. The day was long, and this is what we've both craved. This is our safe space from the storm that rages around us. From the heaviness of responsibility. From the anchor of our pasts. This is where we plan our future.

I shove off the bed and drop to my knees in front of him. I want to take some power. He's so dominant, so big and strong, but I can make him weak in the knees.

"Ani," he murmurs as my fingers work the ties of his pants. "Are you sure?"

I'm more than sure. He's got the tongue thing that makes me crazy. I want that, too. I have to experiment until I find what can have my big, gorgeous guy panting. "*Ja.*"

I know that much. Yes.

His hands sink into my hair as I pull down his pants and boxers and free his cock. He's thick in my palm, and I love how hard he is.

"Yes, I'm always ready for you," he promises. "Always."

We're going to make beautiful babies. One day. In the distant future. But the thought does go through my head as I lean forward and kiss him.

He hisses and his body tightens as I lick at the head, tasting the salty arousal I find there. His breath hitches, and I feel what I needed to feel. Powerful. In control. Giving to him, knowing how much he needs me, sends a wave of calm surety through me.

When I take him in my mouth and start to work him over with my lips and teeth and tongue, I forget all about the stress of the day. It's only me and him and this moment.

I alternate between butterfly kisses and sucking him deep, loving how his body has a fine tremble running through it. Those hot abs of his tighten even as he twists my hair in just the right way. My body feels alive. I want to swallow this man down, but I don't think he's going to let me.

"No," he says, pulling me off him. "I want to be inside you. I need to be inside you."

He kicks off his pants and hauls me up, tossing me on the bed. Before I can settle myself, he's on me. He drags me down the bed by my ankles, spreading my legs wide. I watch as he rolls a condom on, heat pulsing through me.

He's savage as he thrusts inside me. Luca can be so gentle and sweet, but I love this side of him, too. I love the man who can't seem to get enough of me because I'm certain I'll never get enough of him.

"Anika," he groans as he thrusts in and pulls out. "*Anika, du bist mein Schatz.*"

I know this one, too. You are my treasure.

He makes me feel like a treasure.

"I need you closer." He grips my hips. "Hold on to me."

I gasp as he lifts me up like I don't weigh a damn thing. He brings me close, my breasts crushed against his chest. I kiss him as he lifts me on and off his cock, his strength taking my breath away. He plunges deep inside me, and the pleasure rolls over my body like a tidal wave, washing away everything that came before it and leaving only him.

He groans my name as he takes us back down to the bed, wrapped up in each other. His head rests in the crook of my neck as he rolls us over. "I needed that."

I hold him tight. "So did I."

He rubs his cheek against my skin. "And now I need slow."

I lie back as he starts the process all over again. Journey. Now see, this is one journey I don't want to miss a second of.

Chapter Twenty

"I see," Jessica says over the line.

I've told her the whole story, and I can hear the disappointment in her voice. "I'm sorry. This isn't the way I hoped it would end. I thought I was going to tell you everything was great since I never once saw him be anything but a gentleman to the women on the cast and crew. He seems to be a genuinely nice guy when it comes to women."

There are predators everywhere. Straight. Gay. Bi. Doesn't matter. Predators are part of the human condition, but they do tend to prefer one type of prey over the other. Women aren't Joe's prey of choice, but that doesn't mean Patrick doesn't deserve to have one of us stand up for him. After all, we know what it's like.

"Yes. He's always been lovely around me, and my daughter thinks the world of him." Jessica sounds tired, but then it's late at night in Australia where she's working on the biggest project of her life. "I'm surprised. I assumed when I heard the rumors that they were about women. Well, I'll have to think about how to handle this. You've thrown me a curveball, Anika."

I ignore the annoyance I hear. It can't be for me since I'm merely the messenger. I've done my job, and now I have to lob the ridiculously hot potato back at her. It's going to be a hard couple of days for Jessica. "Like I said, I was hoping for a different outcome, but I'm glad you sent me in. I don't know what's been going on fully around here, but it's definitely bad, and we can spare Patrick from having to put up with it."

"Anika, what would you do in my position?"

She's been my mentor for years, so it's not surprising she's asking. Jessica loves a teachable moment. "I would fire Joe immediately. You have an eyewitness, so there's no need for further investigation about this incident. I would ask Patrick if he wants to file criminal charges against Joe, and I would release a statement to the press that we stand behind our cast and crew and always work to create a safe environment for them. Pinnacle Entertainment Group will not stand by and allow this kind of behavior. It's the only thing to do."

"Yes, I thought that was what you would say. There are nuances to the situation," she replies.

I should have known she would go here. It's inevitable. And honestly, it's smart. She has a company to think of. She has to get her ducks in a row. "So what I'm hearing is you want to talk to lawyers before you do anything."

"Such a smart girl," she murmurs. "Yes, I need to discuss this with legal. I have to remind you that you're still under contract."

So I'm to stay in position and not give away the game. Though I'm sure it doesn't feel like a game to Patrick. I feel comfortable that Luca isn't going to talk. "I'm not calling the press or anything. I trust you, Jessica. You'll do what's best for Patrick. If it helps, the assistant director is more than capable of finishing the project. I don't think there has to be a single day of shooting lost."

"That's good to know," she replies and sounds more energetic now. "All right, Anika. Give me some time to sort through this. What are you shooting today?"

"We've got a couple of one-on-one dates. We filmed the other three earlier in the week, and then the last king's choice ceremony here in the city," I tell her. I've already started packing. Luca had watched me this morning as he lounged on the bed. Lazy king. He'd fallen asleep with me the night before, and I bet Hans hates us both. I'm not sure if he slept on the stairs or went back to the room, but he was looking perfectly pressed when he'd knocked this morning and informed the king he was supposed to be on set for his "date" in an hour and production wanted to talk to him.

It's getting too normal to wave good-bye to my man as he goes off on a date with one of my friends.

Luca had kissed me senseless and left after telling me he wished we were filming our date today. We did that earlier in the week. He's already had one-on-ones with everyone before the last ceremony due to time constraints and where they were shooting. Our date had been to a Broadway show, and that was the night they would let us film with the cast. It had been magical. And if he'd cut me the night before, it would never have been shown.

Like Tiara Kate's time with him on a harbor tour.

It's going to be a long day since I won't see him until the elimination tonight.

"So you pack up after shooting ends this evening and head to Ralavia," she muses. "Well, the timing could be better, but there's nothing for it. I thank you for your work and for your discretion. They tell me you're doing surprisingly well at this."

I feel a blush cover my skin. "Yeah, it's not because I'm trying. I think I'm terrible at being on camera."

"I believe they call you adorably awkward," she replies. "You test quite well."

"I've been tested?" I sigh. "Of course I have. You're using focus groups on this project?"

It's something Jessica often does while a project is ongoing. She claims it helps the editors. What it helps them decide is who is going to be the bad guy. Or in this case girl. We'll get slotted into stereotypes. If it has to happen, the adorable weirdo is not terrible.

"Yes, dear. Normally we wouldn't, but this has big money behind it. And if the king marries one of you, it will be a huge ratings draw."

"It's funny you say that because Luca says the producers are hoping he breaks it off," I say with a little laugh.

I can practically hear her eyebrows rising. "Luca? I thought his name was Reginald? Such a stuffy name for a lovely man."

"He goes by his middle name." I feel my face heat. I shouldn't have given that away. "He's a nice man."

"So I've heard." There's a pause that lets me know she's thinking. "You know this project is important to me. Is there any chance that you didn't understand what you were seeing? If he's having an affair, it's a different story. If extramarital sex takes directors out of the running, I won't have anyone to hire."

"I know what I saw."

"But Joe said it was consensual." I can tell she's looking for any way out of this. I'm sure I've shocked her.

"What I saw wasn't consensual." I'm going to stand firm.

"But you haven't talked to Patrick yet," she says.

"He ran out. I haven't left my room yet, and he'll be out on the one-on-one dates all day. I won't have a chance to talk to him until the ceremony tonight." And I'm sure he'll be in a great mood after a twelve-hour workday with four more to go. I don't envy him the long days he has to work.

"Well, I'll handle things from here." She is silent for a moment, tension heavy between us. "You're a good person, Anika. Thank you for everything."

It seems like a weird thing to say, but I'm sure she's tired and she's got a ton of work to do now, too. "Of course. I'll see you when I get back from Europe. Unless you need me sooner."

The line goes dead.

I take a deep breath and try to banish the sense of dread that suddenly comes over me. I tell myself it's just nerves because this is a sticky situation I've stepped into. There will potentially be a legal fight if Jessica can't convince Joe to quietly resign.

There's a knock at my door.

I cross the room and open it, and Hannah and Riley are standing there, shoulder to shoulder, both with concerned looks on their faces.

"Did you hear they fired Patrick?" Riley asks.

"I mean he wasn't the most polite guy in the world, but he was very efficient," Hannah adds. "He was excellent at keeping us on time, and he made me understand why we have to eat before dates, not during. Even if the date food looks way more delicious." She blushes. "No offense to your mom."

Funny little trivia about shows like ours. Those fancy dates you see with all the fine food are strictly for show. The champagne is real and so is the food, but eating a burger on air isn't sexy. Eating anything is hard to film.

My heart clenches at the words. Though not the ones about my mom. She's fine. "None taken. What happened?"

Hannah walks in, setting herself on one of the unused beds. "No idea. I just saw him downstairs and it looked like he'd cleaned out his locker. I asked Lily, and she said the PAs had been told they have a new head. One of the older guys. It seems so weird. I thought he and Joe worked well together."

"I wouldn't say that was the vibe I got from them." Riley sits beside Hannah.

"What did you get?" I'm beyond curious. I have to believe that the situation with Patrick will be resolved when Jessica takes action. Though

Joe firing him means he can sue Pinnacle, which means more lawyers. "Did you see anything?"

"I think the director has a thing for Patrick, but Pat doesn't reciprocate," Riley says. "I've been in the situation before. You have a boss and he gets a little too close when you're talking. Hugs you a minute too long. Wants to be alone with you. You don't want to lose your job so you have to walk this balance beam of being polite and friendly with him, but not allowing it to go too far. I think Patrick fell off the beam."

"That sounds terrible." Hannah's head shakes in sympathy for those poor souls. "You think he gave in? For the sake of his job?"

Riley flashes her an indulgent grin. "No, silly. He'd likely be here if he had. I suspect he finally gave the old goat a hearty no. You seem unsurprised to find out the director's at the very least bi. That doesn't fit my wide-eyed country girl."

Hannah leans into her. "Well, my momma told me that everyone I met outside of the country would be deviant sex people, so I expect it. Though I didn't expect that Anika would be one of them. Why do you need condoms? Holy crap, are you having an affair with a member of the crew?"

I glance over to where she's gesturing and realize that Luca left the nightstand drawer open, and sure enough, there is a half-used box of condoms sitting there for all the world to see. I laugh—a thoroughly nervous sound—and shut the drawer. "I thought production left them all over. You don't have any in your room?"

Hannah looks at me like I've grown a couple of heads. "Yes, but they're in the bathroom emergency kit. They're not in my nightstand."

"Maybe those were left over from some preproduction nookie," Riley says, though she seems to be thinking, that brain of hers working over the problem.

I'm worried she's going to come to the proper conclusion. "That's probably what happened. So is Shelby on a rampage still this morning?"

"She's downstairs making flourless pancakes or something." Hannah waves her off. "I'm still bothered by the fact that Patrick's gone. Is there anything we can do about it?"

"I think production would definitely tell us to keep our fingers out of that particular pie," Riley says with a shrug. "But Joe should know that he's going to get a reputation eventually. It's not like Patrick won't talk."

He won't if Jessica gives him a big enough settlement to keep quiet.

Then all of this will be mere whispers and hints of rumors. Like what Jessica had heard, what had led me down the wrong path.

Which makes me wonder how many other Patricks are out there who've taken a deal in exchange for their voice. I don't blame them. Every person who has ever been put in this position has to judge for themselves what will make them safe again, what's right for them. I understand that going against a Hollywood machine can seem dauntless.

"I think we should take a minute and give it some thought." I only have to delay their going to the producers long enough for Jessica to set the wheels of justice in motion. It might be a couple of days, but she always moves swiftly and decisively. I honestly won't be surprised if she doesn't have him escorted off set tomorrow before they break everything down for the move to Ralavia. "We've got a big night tonight. Final four."

Hannah reaches for Riley's hand. "I hope and pray he cuts Shelby."

Riley shakes her head, pulling Hannah's hand against her heart. "It's going to be me or Ashley F. Ashley's right. She's the only big drama left. You're the ingénue. Anika is the dark horse. So that leaves one ambitious, girl-next-door slot, and one of us is going home before the big show."

I hate that she's compared us to a horse race, but she's not exactly wrong. "It could be any one of us. The king has a mind of his own. I know the producers put some bugs in his ear, but he won't do anything he doesn't want to do."

"Yeah, but I think he'll keep Shelby because he's only truly into one of us." Riley sighs and releases Hannah's hand. "I think he made his decision early on, and the rest of us didn't have a shot. But I also understand how he could have fallen for her so easily. She's the best woman in the house."

Hannah shakes her head, obviously confused. "Who are you talking about? Ashley?"

"I think she's talking about you." The way Riley's looking at Hannah makes me think maybe Emma was right.

"Me? I don't think Reg is in love with me," Hannah says.

"I guess you're not watching him carefully enough." Riley stands and moves toward the door. "I should go and pack. Need to be ready for tonight."

She walks out with the crisp step of an emotional woman. She's upset at the prospect of her fifty-fifty shot at making it to Ralavia. I agree with her on that. Luca will likely keep Shelby and Hannah around for exactly those reasons. But I also don't think Riley's upset at the prospect of losing the king.

I kind of think she is worried about losing Hannah.

Hannah stands up, watching her friend as she disappears down the hall. "What was that about?"

"I think she's worried she might not see you again after tonight," I explain.

Hannah blanches at the thought. "That's not true. We're best friends. I've never had a friend like Riley. I plan on seeing her every chance I get."

"But you could be in a foreign country," I point out. "Or back home. She'll be in Los Angeles. Relationships made on a set like this can be intense, but the real world comes back in and life settles down eventually. That's what Riley's worried about."

"Well, I don't think she has to worry about me marrying Reg." Hannah puts a hand on her hip and glances back to the nightstand. "I know I can be naïve, but I seem to be the only one here willing to tell the truth. Shelby is the one who put out the story that he's already picked me. She did it to mess with Tiara Kate. But she knows the truth the same as me. You know he's crazy about you, right? He watches you all the time. When we're not filming he asks me about the house, but it's always just a way to get around to talking about you."

What has Luca been doing? "What?"

"And you look at him when you think no one else is watching." Hannah frowns my way. "Which is why I'm confused. I thought you liked him. I was pulling for you."

I simply shake my head, so at a loss for what to say. I don't want to lie to her, but I can't tell her I'm sleeping with Luca.

"I'm disappointed, Anika. You and Reg—who you call Luca at least once a day and try to cover it up—are perfect for each other. Watching the two of you give each other longing looks makes Shelby fake vomit. If we turned it into a drinking game, we would all have to get our stomachs pumped."

Tears pool in my eyes because I hadn't thought I was being open at all. Did everyone know how in love with this man I am? How vulnerable to him I am? I'm an open book, but the trouble is sometimes open books get their pages ripped out.

"You do care about him." Hannah puts her hands on my shoulders. "Then why are you having an affair with some random crew guy?"

My mouth drops open. "I'm not sleeping with some dude from the crew."

"Then who are..." She stops, and a knowing laugh leaves her throat. "Of course. How does he get in here?" She shakes her head. "Nope. Don't want to know. But I'm shocked at how relieved I am that you're not cheating on the guy we're all dating."

I'm not going to confirm or deny, but she knows so I ask what I want to ask. "I would think a lot of people would see that scenario as cheating. Not with Luca, but on the show."

She seems to think for a moment and then nods. "You're talking about the contest to win the heart of an actual king. Yeah, I know I came into this whole thing believing exactly that, but I've had my eyes opened, and not in a bad way. This is a business, but crazily enough the process they talk about worked for one of us. I know we have to hold out for drama for the show's sake, but he's made his choice. There's nothing in my heart but love for you, Anika. I'm happy for you. And I'm happy for me because I think I found myself here. I know I found more than I ever expected."

I reach for her hand. "I did, too."

I thought I would find out if rumors were true and help out my boss. I never thought I would find the man of my dreams and make such amazing new friends.

She pulls me in for a hug. "I really am happy for you both." She sniffles and steps back. "I know I shouldn't ask, but if there's any way you can convince him to keep Riley, I would appreciate it. If you can't, that's okay, too. She's going to find out I meant what I said when I told her we're in for life now."

I watch her walk down the hallway a far more confident woman than the one I met weeks ago. Though she's managed to keep her innate kindness.

"I want an invite to the wedding," she says without looking back.

Shelby stops at the top of the stairs, and her nose wrinkles when she looks my way. "I better be there, too. It's going to be a massive shit show. I wouldn't miss it."

I frown. It's not going to be a shit show. It's going to be a perfectly lovely royal wedding.

My breath catches because I realize I'm going to do it. I'm going to throw all caution to the wind and marry this man.

I sit down, and despite all the terrible things that have happened, I can't help but smile.

Chapter Twenty-One

I check myself in the mirror before walking into the king's choice ceremony. There's a tension that's played through the house today because no one wants to go home fifth. Even Hannah, who deeply believes Luca is going to pick me and has been practicing her final rejection tears, is a little on edge. I think that's because she's worried about Riley.

"Hey, baby. You want some sliders? They're hot off the grill," my mom says as I start to pass her.

I stop and put my hands on my hips, showing off the designer gown I spent way too much on for this ceremony. Well, Ivy did, but I'm paying her back. She tried to tell me I could wear the sucker and return it, but I took the tag off because I'm going to need something besides yoga pants and T-shirts in my upcoming job. I'm not going to bankrupt my new country, hence I shall keep this shiny emerald cocktail dress around for entertaining. Queens entertain a lot, I think. "If I eat one of your sliders, I won't fit into this dress anymore."

"You look gorgeous, sweetheart." Tonya steps in beside my mom.

"Of course she does. That's why she can eat the sliders. She loves the sliders," Mom argues. She's frowning and when she stomps away, I'm left staring after her.

Tonya sighs. "Sorry. She thought she would get to see you more when she took this job. I'm afraid when she realized you would be a PA on set, she spent weeks making sure to work all your favorites into the mix."

My heart softens. I'm at a stage in life where I work almost all the time, and when I'm not working, I see my friends. I love my mom. She's great, but I haven't spent much time with her. "And that would have worked if I hadn't been shoved into a too-short dress and forced to compete in a blinged-out arena for a king."

Tonya snorts. "You always did have a way with words." She leans forward, her eyes glancing around as though making sure we're as alone as we can be on a set like this. "They fired Patrick, you know. Said he was behaving inappropriately. I have a hard time believing that since I've worked on four sets where he was the head of the PAs. I know he's on the hard-ass side, but he's a good kid."

"You know him?"

Tonya nods. "Yeah. Like I said, your mom and I have worked with him a few times, but I know him from more than just work. And that's all I can say about it."

I nod because I know what she means. If she can't talk about it, then she knows him from meetings. Tonya's been sober for more than twenty-five years now. I didn't know her before, but she's one of the most solid human beings in my life. Despite the fact that I wasn't her child, Tonya came to every school play and picnic. She helped me with homework while she waited for her cookies to bake. I adore this woman, and I hate that I can't tell her I'm taking care of the situation. "I wouldn't worry about it, and that's all I can say."

She stares at me for a minute and then snaps her fingers. "I knew there was a reason you took this job and it wasn't to end up marrying some king. Although you should know your mother and I think he's lovely. He comes by every day and talks to us."

I wince. "He should be more subtle."

"He is, but I'm your mom. I know when a guy likes you." My mom is back, and she's got a cup in her hand. "Here, baby. A green smoothie with ginger and some caffeine for energy. It won't make you bloat. I make this for all the actresses."

I take the peace offering because there's no need to fight with her. And I can probably use the energy. I take a sip and like usual, it's delicious. "Thanks. But he shouldn't show me any preferential treatment."

Tonya's lips turn up in a grin. "He only talks about you a little. He asks a lot of questions about your mom, though. I think he's trying to get close to her so he can be close to you."

"Or he wants to know if I can fit into royal society," my mom says quietly.

Is she worried about this? "He's not like that, Mom. I don't think his people are particularly posh. They seem very down to earth."

"Are you honestly thinking about marrying him?" My mom reaches out and takes my hand. "I don't want to screw this up for you."

I squeeze her hand. "You couldn't. Mom, if I thought for a second he wouldn't accept you, I wouldn't be falling for him. He's a good man. Though you might have to wear heels. Just kitten ones."

"I can't believe this is happening." My mom leans against the table, a little out of breath.

I take another sip. This probably isn't the time, but I can't leave her like this. "How do you feel about it?"

She takes a long breath and straightens up. "I'll be sad you'll be living on another continent, but as long as you're happy, that's all that matters to me. Though I'm not sure about the heels."

Tonya shakes her head. "I can get her in heels. She still has some. But I want you to be careful, sweetie. We've worked shows like this many times and I know the emotions can be real and intense, but they often don't last. I'm not telling you what to do. I'm merely advising you to guard your heart. I know you've been on set for weeks, but how much actual time have you been able to spend with him? I would bet the time you've spent with him by yourselves is less than an hour."

That would be true if he didn't sneak into my room every single night. I've spent hours and hours every night getting to know this man and his big heart. Hours learning the feel of his mouth on mine and how well he can love me. "I'll tell you some stories when all of this is done. I promise." I finish off the smoothie, and it hit the spot. I hug my mom and Tonya in turn. "I love you both, and I'll try to see you before we pack up tonight."

Because they won't be going to Ralavia with us. The basic crew is, but services like food would be picked up by a local catering company.

"You're feeling confident. I like it." Tonya winks my way.

My mom nods. "Be sure you do come by. I'll make you a to-go box because I've seen the fancy catering for the ceremony. Let's just say it'll keep you comfy in that dress."

"Anika, we need you on set." Lily holds her clipboard, a grim look on her face.

She's likely inherited a lot of responsibility she isn't ready for. I'm not going to make her job harder. "Coming."

She walks ahead of me into the grand ballroom. I can't help but look at it and wonder what it was like back in the Gilded Age. Harper's told me she would love to take a crack at restoring this place.

That would make an interesting show.

Luca is already in the center of the women, his glass of champagne in hand. He's the picture of masculine elegance in his suit, the blue of the tie bringing out his eyes. That man takes my breath away. I stop and stare at him for a moment. There's a tightness to his jaw that lets me know he's not excited about the coming night. He hates disappointing people, and I'm sure he feels crappy about keeping Shelby and letting Ashley F or Riley go.

He'll tell me all about it tonight.

"Ms. Fox, could I have a word?"

I turn and Hans is standing there. He's also in a suit, but he's built on bulky, super-muscular lines so I always think he's waiting to Hulk out and the suit will rip around him right before he saves Luca from whatever is coming his way. It's weird because I've rarely heard him talk. He's the silent but deadly type to a *T*. "Sure. Everything okay?"

One brow rises in a "would I be talking to you if everything was okay" way. "I want to tell you that Luca is a man who makes sacrifices for that which he loves. Don't forget that."

"Uh, are you trying to warn me about something?" If he is, he's being super cryptic.

He frowns and curses under his breath in German. "I'm telling you that sometimes plans don't work out the way we think that they will. So be ready."

"Anika!" A sharp bark pulls me away from the dude who's playing the role of conspiracy theorist number one in the scene I find myself in. It's Joe and he's standing with Luca, looking irritated as hell.

So I bet he's figured out I talked. Well, that was inevitable. I'm surprised he's still here, but it can take a while to sort things out. It's why I told Tonya not to worry about Patrick. He'll be taken care of in the end. I still have a job to do, so I suck it up and walk into the party.

Two hours later, I'm confused but I stand with my fellow contestants as Luca looks us all over.

He's been weird all night, and Lily's been glued to his side so even when we were filming our talk together, we weren't alone. I have to wonder what he's been through today and if he's been pulled into talks with the producers over how to handle the Patrick situation. If Jessica wants to move fast, she could up end a lot of Luca's plans. He might not understand that we can fix almost everything. The crew is solid. They'll be fine in the hands of the assistant director. But I can understand that it might feel scary for Luca. After all, he's betting his country's future on this show.

Hannah is standing to the side with her daisy, and Shelby's already gotten hers, too. The camera is set for his next selection, and I have no doubt they're going to play this thing for as much drama as possible so when he calls out Ashley F's name, I simply nod and smile, happy for her.

Riley sniffles beside me, and I move into the space close to her while Ashley F accepts her daisy and talks about how thrilled she is to be going to Ralavia.

"I'll miss her so much," Riley says so quietly I can barely hear her.

She's talking about Hannah not Ashley. I can see Hannah's already teared up. This is going to be an emotional night.

"Reset," Joe orders as everyone takes their places again. He's been terse and on edge, so I'm sure the man knows what's coming.

I glance over at Luca, but he's not looking my way. He's talking to Hans, who pats his shoulder and says something I can't hear that has Luca's jaw tensing again.

This is going to be hard on everyone, but I suspect that it'll feel bad even though I think all the other women know what's happening at this point. But we've made a little family, and it hurts to let anyone go.

The host steps in and gravely explains that this is the last choice the king will make this evening and if we do not hear our names, we must say good-bye and give up our hopes for the throne forever.

Riley is already crying, and I hold her hand.

I can't help but tear up, too. There were so many of us, and now I'm left with these women I've gotten to know and love. Well, most of them. The show is coming to a rapid conclusion, and these moments somehow feel precious to me.

"This is the hardest thing I've ever had to do," Luca says, his voice thick with tension.

Well, he's the head of a whole country so I doubt that, but we're playing for drama. I squeeze Riley's hand and hope I look nervous.

"I have to think about not only what is best for myself, but more importantly, what is best for my country. I need to select a queen who will embody all the things I love about Ralavia. The independence of her people, their willingness to come together during hard times and make tough choices that enrich the group rather than the individual."

His words kind of flow through me because I'm more concerned about how I'm going to handle this gently with Riley. Should I hug her and talk to her before I approach Luca? Or wait for the group good-bye?

"For these reasons, I'm giving my last daisy to Riley."

I turn to her, ready to give her a hug, but she's stopped and there's no way to miss the gasp that has gone through the room.

The world seems to still for a moment, and I look to Luca, who stares at me as though willing me to take this with some grace. He's not looking at Riley at all. He dumped me on camera, and he's trying to get me to walk away with some dignity. I don't know. I only know he's staring at me like I should understand why he did what he did.

I look to Joe, who's smug now, and I do understand.

I understand that I've been betrayed utterly by a person I believed in. Jessica isn't doing anything but covering up Joe's crimes. That's the only explanation. I mean, I guess I could believe Luca never cared about me and used me for sex and now he's dumping me, but the timing is too perfect.

They convinced him to give me up. They likely told him they would end production if he didn't. Hans just told me so. His words make sense now. I'm the sacrifice, and Ralavia is what Luca truly loves. It's his only love.

"Ani, are you okay?" Riley whispers the question.

I'm not okay. I'm gutted. I'm humiliated. I'm wrecked in a way I didn't think possible.

Tears pool in my eyes, but I'm not giving them what they want. Or maybe I'm giving them exactly what they want. What I won't do is humiliate myself. It's time to retreat. He's made his choice, and he never lied to me. He always said he would pick his country over anything and anyone. "Go on."

My heart fucking breaks as he kisses her cheek and hands her the daisy, asking if she still wants to be his queen.

"Of course," she says and runs to join Hannah.

Then it's my turn to say good-bye. I can't believe I'm saying good-bye. My hands shake as I step off the dais. Every camera is on me as I face Luca. His expression is blank as he steps forward, his arms out.

I can't. I can't hug him and tell him everything will be fine. I can't do that cheek-kissing thing when I remember how this man really kisses. I can't thank him for spending the last few weeks making me fall in love with him.

He told me who he was and I didn't believe him. I made the entirely feminine mistake of thinking I could convince him to believe in love when he told me he didn't. I believed Jessica when she said she wouldn't make other women go through what she had. I believed the system would work when I have so much proof it doesn't.

I love him. That's the hard part. I love him with all my heart and even as I stand here, I know there's the chance that he'll go through all of this, get what he needs for Ralavia, and be back on my doorstep one day. Hell, the way he's looking at me, he might be up for a backdoor affair right now. Which when I think about it, that's what we already have. He might think he can have his cake and eat me, too.

"It was nice to meet you, Your Majesty," I say, and I hate how my voice wavers. But I stand tall as I turn away from him. He no longer matters. Luca made his choice and it wasn't me. I walk toward the women I've grown to love. "But you guys… I'm going to miss the hell out of you. Come here."

They surround me, each whispering their shock as they hug me. Even Shelby hugs me tight.

"What's happening?" she asks.

"I'm going home," I reply surely because I am. I'm not about to go to whatever hotel they want to sequester me at. They can sue me.

I pull back and wave at the camera. The whole set has gone an eerie silent.

"Anika, I need you to talk to the king," Joe says, waving his hand for the cameras to move into place. "We'll edit it to make it look like you knew what you were doing. You say good-bye to the king first, and then to your fellow contestants."

"I've said good-bye to him." I'm not going to be his poseable doll. I step out of my shoes. They'll shove me in the limo and someone will pack up my things. I suspect I can have my mom pick them up and have them back tonight.

"Ani," Luca begins.

I shake my head because I'm done pretending. "It was lovely to meet you. I hope you get everything you need, Your Majesty." I turn back to Joe. "As for knowing what I'm doing, boy, it's obvious I haven't."

The director's eyes go slightly hard. "No. You obviously don't know which side to come down on. I would have helped you, Anika. I would have given you everything you wanted, but you had to play things poorly."

"What is that supposed to mean?"

He moves into my space, his voice going low. "It means I know what's been going on between you and Luca. I know he's been coming to your room at night, and he's been fucking you for weeks now. If you don't want that to get out and cause a scandal, you'll walk out of this room right now. I don't need your last shots. I can edit it all to make it look like your left with some kind of respect for yourself."

"What is going on?" Luca demands as he steps up.

"Absolutely nothing," Joe promises. "Get back to your place. Ms. Fox is leaving. Remember your contract when they put you in the limo, dear."

"Ani," Luca begins. "I'm sorry."

I'm sure he is, but he's made his bed and he'll lie in it alone. Or he'll take someone else and won't remember my name in a few days. The fact that Joe knows we've been sleeping together tells me Luca talked. It could only be him or me or Hans. I know it wasn't me, and Hans barely talks at all.

If it gets out that we were sleeping together during production, it could kill the project. Even as sad and angry as I am, I can't do that to him. He's a lonely man for a reason. He has to put his job above everyone else.

And that's why I would make a shitty queen. He's dodged a bullet, and maybe I have too.

It doesn't feel like it. It feels like I took one to the heart and I'm bleeding out for all to see. I need to get out of here. I need to get home so I can lick my wounds and figure out my next move because I'm almost surely fired, though they won't have to say that. They'll simply not find another job for me.

"Joe, this isn't over. I won't let it be," I say quietly.

"But it is and so are you. So go get in that limo and cry your little eyes out because it's the last time you'll be allowed anywhere close to this industry again," he whispers, but the threat is loud enough. "Do it or I'll have security take you out of here. If you don't, I can make sure your mother doesn't work either. You made your power play and you lost."

I hadn't even thought about my mom, though I know what she

would tell me to do. Still, I need to regroup.

"I don't understand what's happening," Hannah says, looking to Joe. "I get the feeling Anika's being punished for something, and I don't like it."

I'm not bringing Hannah into my mess. I give her a smile. "It's all part of the journey. The king has made the decision that I wouldn't be a good queen. And he's right. Your Majesty, I wish you luck. You can't go wrong with any of these ladies. They're all great."

"I don't like it, either," Shelby says, her arms crossed over her chest. "Something's going on that we don't understand. I agree with Hannah. Anika's being punished for something, and that's bullshit."

Joe stares at her. "The king made his choice."

"He made the wrong one," Shelby says, shocking me.

"That isn't your decision to make, and you can be the next one out if you like," Joe says.

I'm not getting anyone else in trouble. I move over to Shelby, ignoring the pleading look Luca's giving to me. To understand. To forgive him.

I can do both. Eventually. But not tonight.

"Don't fight him. I think the rest of the group needs you. Take care of them," I say as I hug Shelby. "Don't be too big of a bitch, and watch out for Joe. Do you understand?"

I pull back and she nods. "I will."

And then I'm being escorted outside where the cameras film me getting into the limo. I spend the next two hours with the producer trying to get me to cry on film. I don't. He finally gives up and drops me off at the sequester hotel.

I walk into the lobby and Ivy, Heath, Harper, and Darnell are all there. It's so late they're the only ones beyond the production assistant who's supposed to show me to my room.

Screw that.

I take the hands of my friends and walk back out into the night.

Confessionals

Ashley F

I don't know what to say. I'm in shock. What the hell just happened?

Riley

I know. I know. I need to stop crying. I mean I'm happy I'm still here. I wasn't ready to go, but losing Anika... This isn't what I expected. I thought I would come on the show and maybe meet this amazing man, but it's been more. I met my best friends. I met people I'm going to love for the rest of my life. It's just...it's been so much more than I expected.

Shelby

Well, I mean it's more time with the king for me. And that's a good thing. I guess he saw through her nice-girl routine. It's not exactly a routine. She's pretty cool, but I guess he decided he needed someone stronger for his queen. I'm ready. He's mine now. I can feel that crown on my head.

Hannah

I'm so glad Riley is still here, but I'm going to miss Anika. She's the sister I never had. Yes, I have three sisters, but they're all mean to me. Anika is the sister I've always wanted. Riley? No. Riley isn't a sister.

She's a friend. A best friend. I wish we could have talked to Ani. I can't imagine what she's feeling right now. We all thought she would be the one who married Reg.

His Majesty

Everything is hard now. I have to make the best decision for my country, and that doesn't always mean I get what I want.

Anika

What do you want me to say so I can get out of this limo? Do you want me to cry? Because I can do that. How about I talk about what truly happened in there? Do you want me to do that? I'll cry and tell you how I got screwed over by your boss. Fine. I want this over. I don't want to drive around Manhattan all night waiting for me to get tired enough to give you what you want. I'm devastated. I really lo…cared about him. I cared about all of them, and I'll miss them. And that's all I'm going to say.

Chapter Twenty-Two

"Is she still asleep?"

Ivy. She's the one who whispered the question. I can clearly hear her because I'm back at my teeny, tiny, costs more than my unemployed ass will be able to afford soon apartment. She's standing near the "kitchen," which is a hot plate and a microwave and a weirdly shaped fridge I'm sure was very modern in 1989.

They took me home and put me in bed last night after I'd cried for a solid three hours. When the tears started the guys had disappeared, but that was all right with me. I kind of hate all men right now. I know I don't really, but if I don't have to be around one for a few days, I'll be okay.

I'm not particularly fond of women in power right now either.

"You know Ani. She might sleep for a few days," Harper whispers back. "You remember when she broke up with Tommy Hammersmith in college? She didn't leave our dorm room for a week."

Yep. I'd hidden under the covers and lived off of protein shakes and pixie sticks. It had not been my best look.

"I don't get it," Ivy says. "I thought this guy was totally into her. Emma says they're an excellent match."

"Well, Emma doesn't know everything," Harper shoots back.

I want to stay in bed. I want to block the world out, but I can't. I have things I have to do, and they start with telling my friends everything I didn't tell them the night before. I'm so grateful they were there for me. If Harper hadn't been working, she wouldn't have known anything happened at all. They would think I was getting ready for the big move. "She knew enough."

"Hey, you're awake." Ivy hurries across the small space and sits on the edge of the bed. "I have some coffee and donuts. I can get something else if you like."

Harper joins her, but on the other side. I sit up in my Murphy bed that wouldn't have fit Luca at all, and I'm squished in by my two best friends.

"Does this have something to do with why Patrick was fired?" Harper asks.

"Yeah, she said something about a PA, but she wouldn't tell me because she said it had to do with the NDA you signed," Ivy replies, her expression beyond curious.

I sigh and wipe the sleep from my eyes. I'm weary as I sit back. "It doesn't matter now. Yes. I caught Joe sexually harassing Patrick. I pretended to take his explanation and called Jessica, who promised me she would take care of things. Apparently one of the things she needed to take care of was me."

Ivy's gaze goes steely. "Are you kidding me? Jessica, your mentor for years Jessica? Jessica, who talks feminism at every conference and talks about building your network of women and never letting them down because we all have to fight the patriarchy together? That Jessica?"

She's neatly summed up my boss. "The very one. I guess when she found out it was a man harassing another man, she decided she didn't need to give up her moneymaker for her principles."

"But that doesn't explain why Luca would dump you," Ivy says.

"Oh, it does." Harper leans into me, a familiar gesture of comfort. "They could close down the production. Jessica likely talked to her lawyers, decided they could cut Anika loose and save their prize director. Did she come up with some leverage against you?"

"My mom," I whisper.

"Fuckers." Ivy stands. She's the ragiest of my friends and the one most likely to plot some serious revenge. "All right. Let's figure out how to handle this. Should I go scorched earth, or do we want a slow burn where she thinks something's going wrong but can't quite put her finger on what's happening."

"We do nothing," I reply. "Except maybe talk to a lawyer because I broke my contract when I walked out last night. I don't think they'll challenge me on it because if they do I'll explain what happened, and that's what they're trying to avoid. I've thought about this and I need to talk to my mom, but I don't know if they can block her entirely. They can keep her off Pinnacle sets, but she's a mainstay in New York. She's had some clients for over thirty years."

"You want to talk," Harper surmises with a nod. "I think you should."

"I'll talk to CeCe and ask her to get a referral from Lawyer…," Ivy says and winces. "I should find out his name. I sometimes worry I'm becoming CeCe. But you know what CeCe Foust would never do?"

"Don't say sexually objectify someone because we all know her," Harper quips.

"She never acts on it," Ivy argues. "And she would never leave me in the lurch. Ever."

"Because she thinks of you like a daughter." I guess the betrayal from Jessica should hurt worse, and likely it will in the future. In the future I'll be able to shrug off this numbness and look at things rationally. But right now there's a hole in my heart and his name is Luca St. Marten. "Jessica has her own kids. I'm sure she would tell me she's doing this for the good of the company. She would say she's making the hard choices. The way a man would."

"Yes, but that's been our mistake all along." Harper sighs and holds my hand. "You definitely need to talk to a lawyer but until then, what are we doing about Luca? Do you think they put pressure on him to cut you?"

"I'm sure they did."

"Then he could still feel the same way about you," Harper hedges.

"He cut her cold with cameras filming her every move. He didn't give her a heads-up," Ivy argues.

But he kind of had. I hadn't taken the cues, but they'd been there. "He had his bodyguard tell me, but I didn't understand what he was saying."

"What did he say?" Harper asks.

"That I should remember Luca has to sacrifice." I sniffle. "I just didn't think he would sacrifice me."

"Asshole." Ivy is still pacing. "Like I said, there's zero coming back from this. I don't care if he's planning on trying to see her after the filming. We need a plan. I can probably take out his government with a few keystrokes."

"Ivy Jensen, you will do nothing of the kind." It isn't Luca's fault he was born the king of a country. It isn't truly his fault. He'd tried to warn me. He'd used Hans to do it, and Hans didn't understand how to plainly state *hey, girl, you in danger.*

Yeah, if Whoopi Goldberg had been Luca's bodyguard, I would have known to be on guard.

"I don't see why not," Ivy grouses.

"Because I'm moving on and honestly, Luca isn't the problem." I mean that. He has a goal and I got in the way of that goal, so I'm out. I know that now. It's a hard practicality that I have to find a way to accept because I'm not going to be the king's side piece when he gets out from under all the cameras.

Not that I feel very practical. I feel like drowning in my own tears. I want to stand in front of him without cameras running so I can tell him exactly how I feel. Anger. Rage that he could do this to me. I want to beg him to change his mind, to find a way to get what he needs while not giving me up. But I sit and I force myself to go numb. There still is someone I need to help. "Patrick is the problem now. Well, what happened to him is. I can't let it lie."

"Ani, what about your career?" Harper is always the reasonable one.

Reason has flown out the window. "They won't fire me, but I work on contracts. I'm assigned to different crews. I suspect there won't be a lot of work for me in the future. If I keep my mouth shut, they'll still work with my mom's company."

"Oh, I can take down Pinnacle, too." Ivy's gone a florid red.

I'm sure this whole thing reminds her of how she got treated in Silicon Valley. She knows what it's like to be a woman in a man's industry. Which is funny when you think about it. Women consume far more media than men, and yet the entertainment industry is still mostly run by and for men.

"I can connect them to some seriously dark shit and then call in some reporters I know. Jessica Wallace can go on a watch list and see how she likes getting the slow hand from the TSA every time she wants to fly," Ivy vows.

But this won't be settled in the court of public opinion. At least I hope it won't. "I need to go over all the scenarios. I feel comfortable when it comes to leaving sequester. Like I said, they won't want me to talk about why. But that leaves me in a bad spot, too, because it means they can edit my time on the show however they like. That could hurt Patrick's case if they get to control the narrative. Turning me into an angry, jilted almost-queen is good for the show and it could mean jurors later on think I'm being bitter."

"I want Ivy to figure out a way to shut the whole thing down entirely," Harper admits. "Look, if this was a home reno I would be your girl, but this is really more Ivy's world."

Ivy seems to think the problem through. "I think I can do it, but I might need some cash. CeCe can call Lawyer, who I am sure knows a couple of reliable black hats, though she'll probably just call them Criminals. I'd love to see one of those dudes deal with CeCe. It's all digital, right? All I have to do is fuck up the digital and all the backups and voila, no more dating show that hurts my bestie."

It's all super sweet. I mean seriously you want these women as your ride or dies, but I have to shut this line of thinking down. "I can't let you do that."

"Because of Luca?" Harper asks.

"Because of Luca. And Patrick and the crew, and those women I've grown to genuinely care about. That's the funny thing. We go in fighting over some man and we get maybe twenty minutes with him a day. But we spend all our time together. You really get to…" Huh. You really do get to know people. "I think Hannah and Riley are hooking up."

"Oh, according to Emma, they are a damn near perfect match." Ivy is nodding, leaning against the little bar. "I ran them through when I caught them holding hands where the crew couldn't see them. They are going to have a lovely life together."

"Unless one of them becomes the queen of Ralavia," Harper points out.

I doubt that will happen. Oh, he'll pick one of them and he'll do all the showy things he needs to do. Likely Shelby or Ashley F. He'll consider Hannah and Riley too easy to hurt. He'll make appearances with his fiancée and eventually announce it didn't work out.

Like he'd planned all along. I had been the bump in the road. I had been the detour he didn't want to take.

I wonder if he viewed the debacle with Patrick as a convenient off ramp. Was he out there relieved he never has to see me again? I doubt seriously I'll be invited on the *Contestants Tell All* show they always have right before the big reveal of who won.

Does he feel the loss or is he so used to sacrificing that it no longer bothers him?

Or there's a third scenario. He never cared about me at all. I was there and willing to have sex with him, and why should he turn me down?

My chest feels heavy. "I hope they make the right choice."

Ivy moves over and sits next to me again. "I'll call CeCe and get the name of a lawyer. Are you okay with me sparking a shit ton of rage in her so she'll get angry at the world and pay for everything?"

That sounds perfect to me. Especially since I can afford next to nothing. I don't feel bad about it either, because CeCe lives for this kind of drama. "Do you want me to cry in the background?"

Ivy pulls out her phone. "That's a good plan. Can you cry on cue now?"

I burst into tears because I give myself permission to relive last night's utter heartbreak.

Even Ivy looks scared. She presses in a number and holds the phone to her ear. "Thomas, I'm going to need to talk to CeCe. We've got a big problem."

Harper sniffles and wraps me up in her arms.

I let them take care of me while I try to purge myself of this awful heartache.

Chapter Twenty-Three

I'm showered and dressed in clean clothes by afternoon. My mom and Tonya have already been by, and I cried some more. Mom had only heard that I got cut. I told her the whole story, and she is vowing to spend her entire savings on a lawsuit. Tonya is vowing bloody revenge via cupcakes or something. I have to make sure no one gets poisoned.

Luckily CeCe is already on the case. I have an appointment in the morning with someone she swears will chew through whoever Pinnacle sends in. They've already accepted me as a client in what they call a wrongful termination lawsuit, though I haven't exactly been fired. It's something they can work through, they promised me. In addition, CeCe has vowed to sell all her shares in Pinnacle and advise others to as well.

I am unsure as to the legalities of that. Stocks aren't my thing. She might spend some time in the Martha Stewart wing of a prison, but I assure you she will do it with style.

I'm alone again as the afternoon wears on, sitting on my fire escape and watching the people walking by, a mug of tea my mom made for me in my hands. My aloneness is something I feel so sharply. I've lived by myself for years, but I wouldn't have called myself lonely. I feel the singularity of my existence now. I have friends and family, but without him I feel lonely. In the course of a few weeks that man became something necessary to me.

I sit here wondering if he's already on a plane for his home. I'm angry and restless, and there's a part of me that simply hopes he's okay. He was put in a position where he thought there was only one way out. Responsibility forced him to choose between his heart and his duty. He's a good king.

Can I blame him? Yeah. Irrational me can blame his ass all day long. The trouble is the reasonable me keeps showing up.

I think this is the first time I've really been in love because no matter what he did to me, I still want the best for him. It would be different if he cheated or lied. But he didn't. Circumstances happened, and he reacted like a king instead of a man because that's what he is.

I didn't pick a normal man to love. I picked one whose entire existence is dedicated to his people, to a crown. I thought I could help ease that burden for him, could work beside him so he would know he wasn't alone.

I feel tears well again when I hear a knock on the door. Will I ever stop crying?

My girls are back and earlier than expected. They promised they would return this evening with the finest New York street foods and the cheapest bottle of wine the bodega beneath me offers. We're going to sit and watch crap TV, and they will get me through another night.

I kind of want to be alone but I know how awful I would feel if one of them were in trouble and I wasn't allowed to help. So I sigh and stand up and wriggle through the window, not bothering to close it behind me. The air is warm and feels oddly fresh to me. I'm back in my tiny apartment, all the glamour of the Upper East Side left behind. I'm just me again, and now I have to figure out who this me is. The me without Luca. All I know about her right now is she cries a lot and she's not going down without a fight.

I set my mug on the counter and open the door, expecting to see my besties. "You're...not who I expected. How did you find me?"

Patrick stands in my doorway. Outside of work he's far more stylish. He wears perfectly pressed slacks and a bright blue polo under a fleece hoodie I've seen recently on several young stars. He's traded in his sneakers for a pair of designer loafers, and his hair is a bit curly when he doesn't slick it back. He's a hottie when he's not at work scowling at everyone. "I was your boss. I had all your paperwork. Besides, even if I hadn't known, I could have done this thing called looking you up. Unless you've recently joined a witness relocation program. Which you haven't. Can I come in?"

I stare at him for a moment. "You look different."

"I'm not working," he states flatly. "When I'm not working, I tend to like to be me. Are you going to leave me standing out here? You know you kind of owe me since you cost me my job and likely my career."

I feel my jaw drop even as I open the door and allow him entry. "What was I supposed to do? Let him rape you? Sorry. I didn't realize that was part of my contract."

He stalks in and glances around. "You live here?"

"For now. Maybe not much longer. Don't know if you heard but my ass got fired, too."

His expression goes grim. "Yeah, I did hear that you got cut from the show. Lily's a friend of mine. She's still working. I told her not to quit so she can give me all the gossip."

It's good to know he has someone on the inside. I wish I did. "Then you probably know more than I do since I got blindsided."

"You had to realize what was going to happen when they let me go," Patrick argues. "You had to know they would go into protective mode. It's a classic tactic for any large corporation."

"I've never been in the position before," I admit.

"What did you say to him after I left?"

"I was scared so I went along with what he told me."

He flushes, his cheeks going bright red. "And what did he tell you? That I wanted it? That we were having an affair?"

I didn't want to go into the specifics and make him feel worse than he already does. "Something like that."

He stares at me for a moment like he's trying to figure me out. "You should have believed him. It would have been easy to, and it would have saved you a lot of trouble. Why did you think it was nonconsensual? We could have been pretending."

"You weren't pretending."

"You can't know that. If you went along with him, why did they fire you? I know why they fired me. He didn't want to get caught again so he got rid of the *temptation*, as he put it," Patrick explains. "You must not have sold him. You're not exactly an actress. He knew you knew, and that's why you got the boot. Lily told me she knew something was up when the producers took the king into private meetings most of the day. The two dates they were filming got cut way short. They must have been worried he would react poorly to you being let go."

"They had to convince him to let me go." I realize why Patrick looks different. Why he's acted the way he has. "You dress down so he won't think you're dressing for him. How long has it been going on?"

"I met him last year on a set and he asked me out. I told him I don't date married, straight men and that was that," he says. "Then I got this job. I thought since it was a large shoot, I would be okay. I can get a dude's coffee, but he started asking me to talk to him privately."

Patrick's eyes close, and his chest moves as he takes in a deep breath. A long moment stretches between us, and I know he's making a decision. He'll either bring me in or push me away, and I'm almost certain he'll select the latter. He seems to have learned that it's better to protect himself than to trust others. His eyes open, and he turns to the window. "I need air."

I follow him out on the tiny fire escape, and we sit for a moment, our shoulders pressed together as the hum of the crowd forms a soundtrack to this scene of ours.

"This would be a good place for a confessional," he says quietly. "I mean if you could get a camera out here and it wouldn't drive the sound person up the wall. The light at this time of day is excellent. It's an extremely New York place to confess your secrets."

"You don't have to confess anything." I know what I saw, but I also know that it's sometimes hard to admit that you're a victim. "I'm sorry if I caused you trouble. I didn't mean to. I thought I was helping you."

He growls a little. "I keep trying to poke holes in your goody-two-shoes persona."

I'm offended by that. I recently had a torrid affair with royalty. I should get some cred for that. "I don't have a persona, and I'm certainly not a goody-two-shoes. What does that even mean? Everyone wears two shoes. I would hope they're good."

He snorts at my rebuke. "It's an old saying. My parents are in their eighties. They're actually my grandparents. Mom died and Dad hit the road, and I was a two-year-old left with super-conservative grandparents who were looking forward to retirement."

And he was gay, which had to be hard on him. "I'm sorry."

For the first time he smiles and there's no wariness behind it. "Don't be. They were great. They loved me and supported me and they were...a little shocked when I first came out, but then those two people who went to church every Sunday were taking me to pride parades. My dad...I call him dad because that's who he is...told me I shouldn't ever be ashamed of what God made me. And then he promptly told me I couldn't be alone with any male friends in his house. He was probably right about that. That door being open saved me many a misstep."

It's the first time he sounds like a genuine person to me and not a walking ball of irritation. "I'm glad to hear that."

"Anyway, sometimes I sound like an old dude because I'm around old people most of the time. I like to listen to their lives. They have a lot to say, but not many people listen. They would absolutely call you a goody-two-shoes and tell you you're naïve." He rests his head back. "I assumed you would think I wanted it."

"Why would you assume that my eyes don't work?" I ask. "I saw you. You were not consenting."

His gaze turns my way. "Ani, do you think this hasn't happened before? Joe Helms is one in a long line of predatory men who think anyone beneath them is theirs for the taking. The funny thing is when I work for an out gay director, I never have trouble. It's the ones in the closet who think they can take whatever they want and have zero consequences."

"And you're stuck in the job because if you quit or cause trouble, you might not get another one." I know the business. "I don't know if he bought my act or not. There's a whole lot more to the story. I called the CEO of Pinnacle and told her what happened. I was literally there to find out if Joe was having trouble. She thought he was harassing women."

He whistles. "That explains a lot. I have to admit I was surprised when you took the job. I assumed you were there for some weird reason that was likely about watching me. Paranoid, I know, but it wouldn't be the first time. I was probably awful to you because I suspected you were there for nefarious reasons."

I'm curious. "Why would you think that?"

"I asked around. You're way overqualified. You should have been the boss, though even that would have been a step down for someone like you. So I didn't trust you."

"Well, I was there for something other than a paycheck, so you were right about that," I admit. "Are you still mad?"

"I'm not mad. I'm at a loss. No one's ever done anything like that for me. The couple of times I complained I was either let go or told to keep my mouth shut because I'm a man and no one is going to believe I didn't want a little sex."

My heart hurts for him. "I'm sorry. I believe you."

"I know, and that's both comforting and scary," Patrick admits. "What did they do to you? What did they threaten you with? Did they find out you were hooking up with the king on the sly?"

It's my turn to be surprised. "How did you know that?"

He gives me his dumbass-said-what look. "Anika, why do you think I took that pink bear out of there? You were the only one with a bear in your room. I need you to put on your thinking cap for this one."

Revelation dawns on me, and I realize Patrick saved me from a much worse possible fate. I also feel some relief because Luca isn't the one who told them. They already knew. They might have even used that footage to get Luca to agree. "It was a nanny cam."

He points my way. "She shoots, she scores. I can't believe you didn't catch that trick. Man, if something shows up in your room on a shoot like that, you have to suspect there's a hidden camera. You were the golden girl of that shoot. They wanted something on you in case they needed leverage. I know these particular producers and they're usually cool, but there's money on the line this time. I took the camera but it had a wireless connection, so me destroying it didn't destroy what they already had on you."

But he'd hauled that dumbass bear out of there before the night Luca and I made love for the first time. I'm shaking slightly as I put a hand on his arm. "Thank you, Patrick. All they would have caught was us watching TV on his tablet and a couple of make-out sessions."

"But they would have gotten more if I hadn't ridden in like the white knight I am?" he asks as though he already knows the answer.

I nod. "A lot more. I loved him."

Patrick sighs, and his expression is softer than I've seen before. "See. That's naïve right there, and Anika, I wish it had worked out for you. I'm sorry. You can tell them I won't talk. Get your job back and maybe you can get your man back, too."

As if. "He's not my man if he can't stand up for what's right. And I don't want a job where I have to be silent. You should know I've already contacted a lawyer."

He turns, looking me straight in the eyes. "It's not going to work. Any lawyer you can afford will be easily defeated by the unholy amount of money Pinnacle can throw their way."

"It took a long time to bring Weinstein down, but they did it. Two women reporters risked their careers to do it. Nothing changes if we aren't willing to take a risk."

"They were getting paid to do that job," he counters. "I don't know about you, but I don't have the money for a lawyer. They've already reached out to me with a piece of crap offer."

My heart clenches. I might end up the loser in this war. The only one who loses it all. "What did they offer?"

"Twenty thousand if I sign an NDA." He sighs. "I could use that money."

If he won't talk, then I have no leverage. I'm nothing more than a bitter voice speaking out against a man who likely turned me down. That's how they'll play it, and they'll use the show to paint me as the worst woman in the world. I'll be getting the villain edit.

"But I think I can use my freaking dignity more," he says firmly. "I talked to my parents, and they want me to go after him. They said a lot of stuff about David and Goliath and how no matter what I'll rest better if I fight so no one else has to go through this again. It'll be easier if I'm not alone."

I squeeze his arm. "You're not alone."

He nods, and there's a sheen of tears in his eyes. "I knew you would be trouble, Fox."

So much trouble. At least I have some good news. "And don't worry about money. My best friend has this mentor and she has mountains of cash that she likes to spend...well, mostly on shoes and her dog, but occasionally she'll take up a cause. She also thinks Jessica Wallace is a faux feminist. Jessica thinks she's stepping on a PA with no power, but she's about to find out she's really fighting CeCe Foust."

His eyes widen. "Are you kidding me? *The* CeCe Foust? Billionaire tech investor?"

"Yep. I've known her since I was in high school and she scared the crap out of me," I admit. "She mostly calls me Ivy's Little Blonde Friend, but she slipped up today. She knows my name."

It had been oddly satisfying to hear after all these years.

His jaw tightens, and I can see him getting emotional. "We have a chance?"

"We have a chance. Someone is going to contact you tomorrow about taking in your story," I admit. "I should have called but I was busy crying."

"Because you loved him."

"Because I loved him."

He puts an arm around me, the gesture awkward as though giving affection isn't normal for him. "Thank you, Ani. Thank you for seeing me. I'm sorry about the king."

"I hope he picks Shelby and she makes his life hell." I don't, but I need some bravado right now.

"No, you don't." He sees right through me.

We sit there as day becomes night and get ready for the fight.

Chapter Twenty-Four

I stand in the lobby where all this crap started and wonder why I bothered to show up. Jessica's assistant called the night before and asked if I would take a meeting with her at noon. It's been three long days since the king gave me the cut direct. I'm calling him the king for now. I'm sure I'll get back to thinking of him as Luca, but for the foreseeable future I have to pretend that Luca didn't really exist. I'm sure a therapist would call it a coping mechanism.

"She's ready for you." Abby, Jessica's longtime receptionist, gives me a sympathetic look. I don't know if she's aware of what's truly happened, but it's obvious she knows I'm in trouble. "Are you okay? Can I get you anything before you go in? Some coffee?"

I shake my head because I'm not thirsty. I'm curious more than anything. Why did she offer this meeting when it would be easier to simply let me go? I wasn't going to contact her again. In fact, I suspect Lawyer would tell me I shouldn't walk into that office.

I'm kidding. His name is Dave and he's lovely, but he would be upset that I'm about to talk to her.

"Thanks, but I don't think this will take long." I stride to the door and open it, letting myself into that magnificent office with views of Central Park. I'd hoped to be here one day, but now I think I would have to sell too much of myself.

Jessica stands at the window overlooking that swath of brilliant green in the middle of the city. She turns slightly when I join her, and I'm surprised to see she looks tired. She's never less than perfect, but today she looks closer to her actual age. "Anika, thank you for coming in."

So we're going to be polite. "Thanks for getting me kicked off the show in a deeply painful fashion."

Well, she's polite. I guess I'm a little bitter.

She frowns my way. "I know you won't believe this, but you'll thank me for that one day. Anika, you can't honestly think you were going to marry that man and become the queen of...whatever country he owns. It was all for show. He wants a bump in tourism. That's all. The most you were going to get out of this is a few weeks of press on the other side, and then a month or two with him before he gently broke it off. European royals don't marry girls from Hell's Kitchen."

"We'll never know now." It's not like I haven't thought every word she's saying. It's just that when I was with him, it felt right. It felt so right that the gaps in our experience and backgrounds didn't seem to matter. It felt so right that at the end, I was ready to take on the challenge of learning how to be a queen for him. I was ready to embrace his world because he'd become the center of mine.

Such a silly girl to dream that love was enough.

"I know." She turns to me, her expression going grim. "What do you think you're doing, Anika? I heard that the production assistant has hired a rather expensive lawyer. There's zero way he does that unless you're willing to talk. Do I need to explain your nondisclosure agreement to you?"

I shake my head. "An NDA can't bind me if criminal behavior is witnessed. The NDA means I can't talk about why I was there. That's all it covers. I had a lawyer look it over."

"Of course you did."

"Someone taught me to always know what I'm going into. I screwed up this time because I genuinely believed that you wanted me to find the truth. You've taught me a lot. I won't forget this lesson. It might be the greatest lesson you ever teach me."

"Damn it, Anika, I was going to take care of the kid," she says with a huff as she strides over to her desk. "I was going to write him a large check and avoid all of this. The truth of the matter is I already signed the contracts with Joe. We're announcing the project as soon as he returns from Ralavia. Though now apparently that's a clusterfuck of a situation."

"What do you mean? And why would you sign the contracts before

I gave you my report? I thought that was the whole point."

She puts a hand to her head as though trying to stave off a headache. "Because you hadn't found anything and he was considering another job, one that would conflict with ours."

"So he strong-armed you into making a bad decision."

"You have to understand that we've spent millions on this project already, and the actor attached is insistent on having Joe as the director."

I know exactly who she's talking about. Kent Osbourne is the hottest action star working today. His last three films collected almost a trillion dollars in worldwide box office. He started his career with Joe, and it looks like he was standing up for his boy. But there was a problem. "I suspect Joe isn't sexually harassing Kent."

Her eyes close as though she's willing herself to be patient. When she opens them again, she settles into her "let's be reasonable" face and gestures to the chair in front of her massive, elegant desk. "I suppose not. I know you think I'm fine with this, but I'm not. I'm shocked. I had no idea he cheated on his wife."

I lower myself down because I would like to hear this explanation. "Did you know he was bi? I don't get that. It's perfectly okay to be out in our industry. I got the whole 'but my parents' thing. He's a grown man. He's wealthy on his own. How much money does he need? Also, that's zero excuse for what he did. I forgot to ask. Do you believe me?"

She sighs, a weary sound. "Yes. I believe you saw what you saw, and I heard it in his voice when he called me. He told me the same thing. He told me he's bisexual. I explained that I didn't care. I do care that he hurt people in my employ. But there's so much money riding on this."

"He'll do it again. If you hand him the reins that will put him back on top, there will be no stopping him. You're making a monster worse. He'll understand that there are no real repercussions to his actions, and he'll behave accordingly." I have a few questions to ask. "Would it be different if I'd found him molesting a young woman? If the PA had been Lily or me instead of Patrick, would you still be asking me to stand down?"

She sits back. "I don't know. I think it's far harder to prove that a man is harassing another man."

"Why?"

"Because they tend to be sexual creatures, and Patrick is gay," Jessica offers. "There will be people who say he likely wanted it and when he didn't get everything he thought he should, he cried foul."

"Like they don't say that about women all the time? Jessica, you have been my mentor for years and I've respected you, but if you can't see that this is the same, I'm disappointed." Not words I ever thought I would say to this woman.

Her eyes are steady on me. "I have to be realistic."

I give her back some steel of my own. "He has every right to a safe work environment."

Her head shakes as though she's already negating that argument in her head. "There won't be a work environment if this all goes to hell. I doubt Kent Osbourne will come down on the side of a PA when the man who gave him his big break is already whispering in his ear that this is all a big misunderstanding and a production assistant is trying to blackmail him for cash. He's good at this."

I wasn't playing games. "Then he can deal with the press when the lawsuit gets filed because Patrick doesn't intend to blackmail him. He intends to have his day in court so Joe doesn't do this to anyone else. He's the hero here, Jess. He's in the right, and you're making decisions that put you in the same group you claim is everything that is wrong with our industry. That's what I don't understand."

Her eyes narrow, anger obvious in her stare. "Don't vilify me. You have no idea how hard it is to sit behind this desk. It's easy for you. You don't have to choose between a company you've spent your whole life building and your moral center."

"I assure you none of this was easy for me," I argue. "Did you know they would bug my room?" Again, I'm curious.

She bites her bottom lip. "Ah, so that's how they knew you were seeing the king off set. I was rather surprised to find out you of all people would cheat like that."

"Cheat? You need to decide which it is. Either the show is pure fantasy and then my relationship with the king is meaningless as long as we play by the rules on camera, or it's a real thing and then maybe you shouldn't have producers try to influence his every decision," I shoot back. Now that I'm sitting here, I'm surprised at how easy it is to spar with her. I would have been afraid before, afraid to disappoint her, afraid to rock the boat.

Sometimes the boat needs to capsize.

"Joe means to use that footage of you if you don't back down," she warns. "I'm having to deal with that as well. If that footage gets out, I don't know if we'll be able to air the show. The reality show isn't as important as the film franchise, but it's got surprising buzz behind it. If he puts out the story that you and the king had a deal before filming ever started, it's going to be bad for you both."

"So this is the part where you blackmail me." I've already thought about this possibility. It's kind of hard not to when you discover you've made something of a sex tape. "Luca's a big boy and the network needs this show. I don't think you're going to throw me under this particular bus, and if you do, the resulting scandal will likely bring Luca the press he wanted anyway. Instead of the king looking for a bride, he can become the bad boy of European royalty. He's a smart man. He'll figure out how to get what he needs."

"And what about what you need?" Jessica counters. "I know you seem to think I've fired you, but no decisions have been made yet. I'll take care of Patrick financially and you can come back to work. I'll even give you whatever project you want."

If only it were that easy. I want to take the offer. I can make a difference from the inside. But that would leave Patrick behind. It would leave a lot of men at risk for the same treatment, and the longer it goes on behind the scenes, the more other powerful men learn that as long as they have cash, they can get away with anything. Someone has to hold the line. I never imagined it would be me. "No."

"Why are you being so obstinate? I thought I taught you that we have to work around the system sometimes," Jessica argues. "I thought you were smarter than this."

"And I thought you had more integrity. Everyone who faces a situation like this has to make their own decision, and I won't judge a victim if they feel like they need to take a check and get some closure for their own mental health. But I wasn't traumatized. I'm a witness, and if I don't stand up, who the hell am I?" I rise from my seat because this is getting us nowhere.

She looks as close to tears as I've ever seen her. Jessica Wallace is a rock, but this seems to have shaken her. "Can't you see? Sometimes the boss has to make the hard decisions."

Like Luca had. He made the decision to sacrifice me over his people.

I will always miss him, but deep down I suddenly know I'm going to get through this. I will find my way to the other side and be stronger for it. I am more than my relationship with one man. I'm more than a love affair or a TV show I was briefly on. I am more than my job.

I am a product of the people who love me. My mom and Tonya. Harper and Ivy and Heath and Darnell. I am my own unique being, and I have to make decisions, too. I have to decide what I can live with and what I can't, what actions build me up or tear me down and strip pieces of my soul away.

I have to decide what I'm willing to fight for. What I am willing to sacrifice for the good of the people around me.

Like a queen.

"I'm sorry it had to end this way, Jessica. I really do thank you for everything you've done."

Her hands fist on the desk. "Anika, this is a stupid emotional reaction, and you're going to regret it. You can't beat him."

"Maybe not. But I'm going to give it a hell of a try." I stride to the door and only turn when I've opened it. "I don't suppose I'm going to get to have my say on the contestants-tell-all show?"

She shakes her head. "My darling girl, he's going to eviscerate you in edits. No. You're going to be the villain, and it might take years to get your reputation back."

She's right, though there's a simple solution. "Is this one of those decisions you're making as a boss? Because you own that footage."

Her lips purse. "It's out of my hands."

"It's not. It's a decision," I say gravely. "Own it. This is your choice to try to cover it up and ruin a couple of lives to save that piece of crap. So now we know where we stand. I noticed your stock was down today. I wonder why."

Her eyes narrow. "Are you starting rumors?"

"I don't have to. I can tell the truth," I reply simply, and my heart aches because this is the end of an era. I did love her. I looked up to her. I'm so sad she is less than I thought she was.

"Anika, are you still talking to him?" Jessica follows me out into the empty lobby.

"Joe? No. The next time I see him will be in court." I'm going to take it all the way.

"No, the king. He's causing trouble on the set or something," Jessica admits. "They were supposed to start shooting today, and he's not there."

"He's not in Ralavia?" That doesn't sound like Luca. He's done a lot to keep the show going. I would have thought he would be happy to be home and to almost be through.

"He got on the plane, but he didn't show up for his call this morning. I have to wonder if you're causing this trouble." Jessica crosses her arms over her designer blouse. "It won't work. We can't possibly bring you back."

"I'm sure he got called away on some business. He is a king, you know." This is no longer my problem. "Good luck with all of that. And don't expect me to keep my mouth shut. If you don't give me a space on the show for my side of things, I suspect there are reporters willing to talk with me. Good luck, Jess. I really do thank you."

Her face flushes. "I wish it didn't have to end like this."

I feel tears spark. "Me either."

I turn and leave that part of my life behind. It's time to build again.

Chapter Twenty-Five

I have an iced latte in my hand as I walk up the street toward my apartment building. It might be my last for a while because that sucker cost seven bucks, and I'm about to beg my mom for a job baking cookies while I regroup. It's going to be a while before I find another job in production. If I ever get another. I should be more upset about that, but I'm honestly feeling okay. It's a little like Galadriel in the *Lord of the Rings* movies. I got tempted by something evil and turned away, and now I can go with the other elves to the western lands and do whatever they do in the western lands. Probably not work as a production assistant. The point is, I was tested and I feel like I passed.

Righteousness, though, won't keep me in lattes. I've got some money saved up, but I suspect Joe's going to clobber me in edits. He'll start making promos where I'm the good girl gone bad, and soon I'll have an invite to *House of Villains* or something. Reality TV is about to come seriously calling, and I'm planning on ignoring it all.

I'm likely going to lose my tiny apartment and I'll be back at my mom's, but there are worse things that can happen. She could live in Jersey, for example. She could still be married to my dad. I decide I can handle being cooed over by two women who know how to cook for a while until I find my feet again. Harper and Ivy will be there, too. I'm not alone.

Maybe I'll ask CeCe for suggestions. She's been the bad girl of the finance world for a long time, and she seems to love it. Of course I suspect the whole bad-girl rep is easier when you're a billionaire and a competent woman of whatever age CeCe claims to be. I would never argue with her. If she says she's thirty-five, I'm going with it.

I turn down my block and notice there's a limo outside the door and a man in uniform rummaging around the trunk. Huh. I didn't know there was anyone in my building who could afford a limo ride, but good for whoever.

My cell trills and I glance down at it. Harper. I've got my hands full of purse and latte and treats to go along with the latte, so I decide to call her back when I get upstairs. As soon as I start to slip the phone back in my pocket it rings again.

I stop and check the screen. This time it's Ivy.

Okay, so something's happening. Or they want to know how my meeting with Jessica went. I gingerly balance the latte and my bag of snacks from the bakery—Danishes are the best breakup food—and manage to answer the phone with one hand. "Hey, what's going on?"

"Thank god," she says in a rush. "Anika, you need to get down to Times Square. Something's happening."

Like I'm buying that. "We don't go to Times Square. We avoid it like the plague."

I'm serious about that. I skip right past midtown whenever I can. It's a mob of tourists and ticky-tack shops, and yes, all the mega screens are super cool at night, but it's not worth the forced intimacy with three thousand people I do not know. Although the world's largest Olive Garden is tempting.

Don't judge me. My ancestral food is salted fish.

Out of the corner of my eye, I see the limo driver stepping onto the sidewalk, though he's left the trunk open, so I guess he's waiting on his client. I hope the poor dude doesn't get stiffed. It would be exactly like one of my neighbors to pull a prank. I want to tell him this neighborhood isn't the place for limos, but Ivy's talking again.

"I'm serious, Ani. Get down here. One of the networks is about to run something on the big boards. Some kind of story about Luca. I got a text from a guy Heath knows in the newsroom," Ivy says.

I sigh. "Well, I'm sure I'll hear about it. I'll check their website."

The last thing I need is to watch some promo story about Luca's final four on the big screens, my humiliation shining bright for all the tourists to see. I can be humiliated in the comfort of my own home, thank you very much.

"Ani, you have to come down here." Harper seems to have taken the phone. "I'm serious."

"And I'm serious about drinking my last latte," I shoot back. This is some kind of prank to get me in a better mood. "Guys, I'm fine. I don't need a pick-me-up. Though if you want to grab some breadsticks and come over and watch TV, I would be up for that." There is one person in our community who hasn't yet had the chance to console me. "Or I can cry a lot and ask Lydia to make us some ziti."

"Now that is not a bad idea," Ivy says.

"Hush," Harper chides. "Anika, I'm not joking, and this is not some consolation surprise. You need…"

That's when someone walks up behind me, wraps an arm around my waist, and starts hauling me backward. Right there on the street. It's everything people outside of the city fear. You know those stories moms tell their daughters to keep them far from the scary city. Don't go to New York or they'll kidnap you right off the street and you'll be carrying a latte that you really wanted and it's going to fly out of your hand while some asshole drags you…

…to his limo?

"Hey," I start to yell. I might have dropped my Danishes and my latte, but I keep that phone firmly in my hand. If I'm going to be murdered and chucked in the Hudson, I'm taking this phone with me.

"Calm down," a deep, strangely familiar voice says. "I've been waiting here forever. This is tradition. In you go."

Hans? I realize that Hans is the one in the limo driver's uniform, and he's hauling me up like I weigh nothing and dropping me into the trunk. Which is weirdly furnished. I catch sight of soft blankets and a bunch of pillows, and I smell lavender. Like someone tried to make sure the trunk smells fresh, and the murder victim has a smooth ride before dying.

"What the hell, Hans? What are you…" I'm so shocked that I let him get a hand on the door to the trunk.

"I told you. It's tradition," he replies with a grin that I think he meant to be cheeky, but it's more like he's going to enjoy murdering me. He needs to work on making his expressions more humanlike.

"What is happening?" I hear coming from my phone.

"Relax, please," he says right before he slams the door shut. "*Ich habe sie. Ich bin unterwegs.*"

"Hey!" I kick at the top of the trunk. "Use your English words, Hans. What the hell is going on?"

"Ani?" Harper's voice comes over the phone.

He's a terrible kidnapper because he's left me my phone, and I'm using it against him. I bring it to my ear as I feel the driver door open and shut.

"I need you to call the police. Hans just kidnapped me and threw me in the trunk of a limo," I say, trying to feel around my new prison. "I think Luca wants him to murder me or silence me or something."

"Uh, he kidnapped you but he left your phone?" Ivy asks.

"I guess they don't have *Dateline* where he's from. He's not good at this," I shoot back because she is missing the salient point. I am being driven to my… I don't honestly think Luca means to murder me, but this could be some kind of play to get me to shut up.

The limo starts to move, pulling away from the curb.

Did anyone look up from the native New York game of pointedly not noticing other people or anything else going on around them long enough to witness my kidnapping? Or did they simply shrug and move on?

I bet someone got my Danish. I wanted that Danish. I bet a rat got my Danish. They're fast, and they know a good thing when they see it. They're city rats, and according to a recent study there are three million of the suckers living in the city, so I'm probably right.

I'm panicking, and I need to focus.

"Calm down, sweetie." Harper's voice is soothing over the line. "Something is going on. Ivy and I got texts thirty minutes ago telling us to come to Times Square, and there are a whole bunch of cameras here. Like a small crew, and I recognize them from the show. I thought the crew was going to Europe."

There was crew in Times Square? "They are. They should have left days ago. But Jessica said Luca didn't show up on the set today."

"I think he might be here," Harper says. "Though I haven't caught sight of him. Something big is going down because they've blocked off a huge square. There's police and everything."

What the hell is going on? And why is Hans going so slow? I twist in my comfy prison, and something soft caresses my cheek. Are there rose petals strewn all over the trunk Luca's had me kidnapped in? "Hans! What the hell is going on?"

"Hold please," Hans barks.

"We're not on the phone, asshole," I shout back. "And if you're trying to take 9th, don't. I don't care that the Internet says it's two minutes on a good day. There are no good traffic days in the city."

The car swerves as though he's taking my advice. Two minutes my ass. More like half an hour, and you'll be lucky to get there in one piece because the streets are a *Mad Max* fight between the yellow cabs and the Ubers. Which is why I walk.

I put the phone back to my ear. "What is going on?"

"I don't know, sweetie," Harper replies, "but I don't think he's trying to shut you up. If I'm right, this might be a grand gesture fit for a king."

"It better be groveling fit for a king," Ivy grouses. "I mean it. I better believe that man or he's going to get the full-on hacker treatment, and I might sic Lady Buttercup on him. I know she's small, but that little bitch can bite."

I force myself to relax because it's obvious I'm not going anywhere, and Hans seems to be moving this train along now. "Why would he come back? He didn't finish the show. The show was the most important thing in the world to him."

"I tell you why he does what he does." Hans's voice is clear and unmistakable even though I'm stuck in the trunk and there's a whole stretch limo between us. I hear him say something in German I don't understand. "Why are you so surprised?"

"Because you told me he was going to sacrifice me."

"No, I tell you that sometimes to win the game the king must sacrifice the queen," he replies.

He is so rewriting history. "That is not what you said, and even if you did, I got the message. I didn't understand it at the time because you're so cryptic. If you're going to warn a girl she's about to get her heart stomped on, you should say it plainly."

"I see you." Ivy sounds excited. "At least I see a limo and it's got flags on it. Like the ones heads of state use. The police are waving it in. What is even happening right now?"

"I say this as plainly as I can. Any Ralavian would have known exactly what was going to happen," Hans says without a hint of sympathy in his voice.

"Well, I'm not Ralavian," I shoot back but my heart is starting to thud in my chest because the limo slows, and I can hear the crowd all around us.

The limo stops, and I feel the door open.

It's a mere moment before the trunk swings up and I blink in the sunlight. Hans stares down at me. "I hope when you are, you will learn to be more logical. This is my king's gift to you. *Alles Gute zur*

Verlobung."

He helps me climb out of the trunk, and I don't need the phone anymore because I see Harper and Ivy behind the police lines. I look to Hans. "I don't know what that means."

For the first time I can remember he smiles at me, a look of pure amusement. His eyes light with mirth, and he bows before me. "You will, *meine Königin*. Watch the boards. I think you will find them illuminating."

"Ani, tell them to let us through!" Harper yells.

I look and the policeman is waiting for me to say yay or nay. Like I have some power here. I nod and he allows my friends through as the big board changes and a network news anchor comes on.

"This is crazy." Harper holds my hand.

Ivy's lips turn up. "I think this is going to be one hell of a grovel."

"Big news from the set of the Pinnacle production of the reality dating show *The King Takes a Bride*," the well-manicured news anchor says. "Hollywood will surely be up in arms over the revelation that acclaimed director Joe Helms has been caught admitting to sexual misconduct."

My jaw drops. What has Luca done?

"We have exclusive outtakes of the hour-long conversation between Helms and Reginald Lucannon St. Marten, the king of the tiny country known as Ralavia. It's apparent to this reporter that Helms didn't know he was being recorded. The king was involved in a sting operation to hold the director to account after an incident on the set led to one contestant leaving and a production assistant being fired."

My eyes are wide as the scene changes and there's Joe sitting in a luxurious seat, a glass of Scotch in his hand. Which is funny since he recently left rehab. It's obvious they're on a private jet and the camera is set up behind Luca, but I recognize his voice.

"But, why, Joe? You could find a willing partner. Why would you force that young man?"

Joe's eyes roll. "He wanted it. Yeah, I know he said all the right things, but what you have to remember about men like Patrick is they are always playing games. So I play with them. I wouldn't touch a woman in his position. Way too dangerous, but you know how it is."

"I think I know what it means to be placed in a situation I don't want to be in," Luca says.

"I assure you he wanted it no matter what that little bitch says. Now he'll be paid handsomely to keep his mouth shut, and she will, too." Joe takes another drink.

"I don't think Anika will back down. I think Anika will fight you."

I feel tears roll down my cheeks. He did this for me. All of it. He's putting himself and his plans at risk, and he couldn't have done it if he hadn't cut me. If he hadn't done what Joe wanted, there's no way he could have gotten him talking.

"She'll lose." Joe waves a hand. "Women like her mean nothing in this business. Relax, Luca. You're going to get everything you want out of this. No one expects you to actually marry any of these idiots. It's all for show, and they'll move on and settle for whatever chumps they can get to marry them and no one will remember their names."

The feed cuts back to the anchorman. "But apparently the king has no intention of forgetting Anika Fox's name. He does, however, hope she will change it."

I turn and the crowd parts, and I see Luca standing in the middle of the pedestrian walkway that cuts through the center of Times Square. He's dressed in a military uniform, looking more stunning than I have ever seen a man look. There are thousands of people around us, but in that moment he's the only thing I see.

"He didn't sacrifice me," I say, my eyes holding with his.

"Only for a moment," Hans says. "Only so he could give you what you need, my queen. At least I hope you'll be my queen."

"That's a good grovel." Ivy Jensen of the cold-heart clan, as she calls it, is crying. "It is acceptable."

"Tell me you're going to say yes." Harper's got tears in her eyes, too. "I mean if you're not going to, we'll get you out of here but this is some next-level shit here, Ani."

I turn back to my friends. They should know better. "Be my maids of honor."

I'm already running to him when they shout back.

"Always."

I don't care about the cameras or the people. I don't care that we're standing in the epicenter of my country and everyone is watching. All that matters is him.

He smiles and proves he knows me because he braces himself, his arms coming up to catch me as I throw myself into them.

I wrap myself around him, arms around his neck, legs around his waist.

I breathe again because I am home.

"I'm so sorry," he whispers. "I know I should have walked away the minute they came to me, but it wouldn't have helped Patrick."

I squeeze him tight. "You did great, babe. You did perfect."

He sets me down and there's a somberness to his expression as he steps back, and I realize my mom and Tonya are standing at the front of the crowd.

My moms. I should have called them that all along since Tonya's always been there for me.

"By all the traditions of Ralavia..." Luca starts.

Oh. He sounds super serious and this is an important moment, but I am who I am and everyone should get used to it. "Babe, is that why Hans threw me in the back of a limo? He wasted a good latte, and somewhere the Internet is waiting for the appearance of Danish Rat."

A smile splits his handsome face. "Yes. It's from our Viking ancestors. Almost no one does it, but it's now a tradition among royals in Ralavia. Hans should have explained it to you."

"Hans needs some lessons in communication."

"Can I continue?" he asks, but there's nothing but pure joy on his face.

I nod. My heart feels like it's going to beat out of my chest.

He drops to one knee. "Anika Christina Fox, will you marry me? Will you stand beside me and all the people of Ralavia as queen?"

I'm going to be snotty and red in the face in all the pictures, and I don't care. I manage a nod because words won't come.

He might never say the words *I love you*, but it's there in his actions, in his willingness to put me first, to trust me with his precious country. I'd been told that words can lie but actions never do.

Unless someone bungles the heads-up he was supposed to give a girl.

Luca rises to his feet and hauls me into his arms, kissing me right there in the middle of Times Square as the crowd erupts in cheers. So they're tourists and that's a good thing because if he was doing this in the middle of Brooklyn, they would congratulate us and tell us to move it along because they have places to be.

But this is a slice of fantasy, and everyone seems to love a royal wedding.

He cups my face and puts his forehead to mine. "I love you, Anika."

"You don't have to say it." I have everything I need from him.

"I do. I was afraid of it, but this feeling, this beautiful space you fill inside me, I think this is love," he admits.

"I love you, Luca," I reply.

My mom and Tonya surround us, and then Ivy and Harper join the group hug, and even Hans seems a little moved.

I stand in the center of my universe, and I don't need a crown. I'm already a queen.

Confessionals

Shelby

Well, I said it would be a shit show, and it was. I mean we didn't even get to film in the country we spent weeks talking about going to. That seems like poor planning. But yeah, I'm happy for them. I'm also available for other dating shows.

Hannah

I'm happy about how everything worked out. I learned so much about myself, and I can't wait to see what life has in store for me. I came here to fall in love and I did. I fell in love with the city and the friends I made, and I fell in love with me for the first time. That's what makes it possible to really love another person. I found out I deserve love, and there she was.

Riley

This was the best experience of my life. Hey, you know none of us got to do the crying in the limo thing. Why don't you send me and Hannah out in one of them? Yeah, I just want to make out with her in a limo. Though in the regular seats. The trunk thing was weird.

Luca

I got everything I came here for. More, really, since I'll be honest, I wasn't sure this would work. But I found my queen. I found a strong, beautiful, honest, and loyal woman to live my life with. I found someone I can't ever sacrifice. With Anika, I can be a king, but I'm also a man.

Anika

I know. It's huge. It's like three carats or something. It's kind of heavy, actually. How do I feel? Like I'm here for the right reasons. I'm here for him, for real love. Oh, is that Danish I smell? Because I lost a perfectly good Danish.

Joe Helms

On the advice of counsel, I plead the fifth.

Epilogue

The Royal Palace
Ralavia

"Fox, are you really wearing that? Did you murder the designers the studio sent?"

Patrick is still Patrick. Even six months and one criminal case in which he was the star witness—though not the only one—later, he's still a pain in my ass.

I'm wearing jeans and a sweatshirt that declares *Ralavia is for Lovers*. That was totally my idea. We have merch and everything.

And the tourists are pouring in for the royal wedding. We even have a couple of Windsors showing up for this sucker. Of course I'm not wearing jeans to my rehearsal dinner.

Which is being filmed along with the wedding for twenty million that's going straight into the coffers. When Pinnacle dropped the project, another production company picked it up and paid through the nose for it. They re-edited it and *The Road to a Crown* became one of the biggest hits of the year all around the world. "No. There's a nice dress waiting for me, but I got hungry. You know damn straight no one's going to let me eat the food at the dinner."

"Because it looks terrible on camera. No one can eat pretty on camera. It's an awful gross process, and I won't be filming it," Patrick says, an implied *duh* in his tone. He glances over at the lighting crew. "Hey, be careful with the stained glass. Harper gave me a whole lecture about how it's five thousand years old, and I'll be stabbing history in the back if we break anything." He sighs. "She's going to be fun to work with."

I smile. Patrick's got a new job. He was hired to run production on the royal wedding specials, and he's got a brand-new reality show. *A Gilded Renovation.*

Also my idea. What we realized was that Ralavian Production Studios didn't have to just shoot in Ralavia. We have seed money and our first big project. We'll be filming the renovation of a Gilded Age mansion with a world-famous designing brother duo and the most amazing construction manager I know. Harper. It doesn't hurt that Harper and one of the brothers hated each other on first sight and have a whacked-out chemistry. I can't wait to see where it goes.

We're going back, all three of us. Me and Harper and Ivy. Back where our dreams began, where my love story grew, where we learned to dream. The mansion in the Upper East Side is getting a glow up.

But first I'm getting hitched.

"You could have taken the other job," I say as I walk past the ballroom toward the craft service table.

"The *Hannah and Riley Show*?" Patrick shakes his head as though it's the most terrible idea in the world. "Save me from small-town lesbians taking on the big city and fighting injustice."

"I think it's going to be fabulous." Shelby is already dressed to kill. She'll be starring in *Island of Skanks*…I mean *Lovers*. We joke, she and I. We've gotten kind of close, though she Karens out every now and then. "I, for one, want to see the moment she tells her preacher father that she went on a reality show to try to marry a king and ended up with a graphic designer with spectacular tits."

Riley grins from her makeup chair. "And they're real, too."

Hannah's eyes roll, but she chuckles. "He handled it better than I thought he would. Though he told me he's planning to show the first episode to his bible study group. I'm not sure that's going to go so well. I think he means it as a cautionary tale. He told me if I went to New York, I would become a lesbian and I did."

"Uh, you always were one, babe." Riley winks her way. "Me, too. I was afraid to admit it until I found someone worth risking everything for."

"Eww, they're so mushy." But Shelby sits beside them and starts talking to Ashley F.

The gang's all here. My bridal party. My friends.

Up ahead my two maids of honor are talking to my moms. That's how I refer to them now. Mom and my bonus mom. Tonya's been a far better parent to me than my dad.

"I like the relaxed look." Tonya nods with approval.

"I've got an hour or so," I hedge. "I will look stunning when the cameras roll. I'm sure there's a makeup artist waiting to make my eyelashes look like they were made for a fashionable Godzilla."

Ivy blinks. "Yeah, they're ridiculously long. You know where I don't have to wear a ton of makeup? When I'm coding. It's the best job because no one expects me to be beautiful."

"And yet you are," Heath says from where he's sitting with Darnell, both of my amazing guy friends looking dapper in suits.

"Hey, did you see the news?" Darnell asks. "Jessica Wallace is out as CEO after the stock drop and how she handled the Joe Helms case."

Ivy frowns. "She still got a fifty-million-dollar severance package. At least Helms got jail time."

It had been deeply satisfying watching them take him away. He's only doing two years in a minimum-security prison, but he won't be in a position of power anymore.

I feel sad about Jessica, but I did what I had to. "The money won't mean as much as her reputation. Where are the moms?"

It's what we call CeCe, Ivy's mom, Diane, and Heath's grandma, Lydia. They've formed their own weird girl gang.

"Oh, they're at the casino," Tonya explains. "They invited us, but your mom insisted on overseeing all the catering."

"My baby is getting married. It's the biggest most important production of my life," my mom announces. "I'm not leaving this palace until the job is done."

Tonya smiles brightly. "But then we're heading to someplace called Ibiza. CeCe and the girls invited us along. I think it's going to be fun."

Heath waves at me. "I've got a plan in place to bail them out when the inevitable happens. Don't worry. Your honeymoon is safe."

"CeCe would never let them get arrested," Ivy promises. "She'll bribe the cops or use her mob connections."

"Not making me feel better," I shoot back. "She's like the queen mother now. Or she's about to be."

"I don't think that's how that works." Darnell always has to be the smartie.

"Baby, I made a sandwich for you," my mom says. "I also made some pasta but it disappeared."

Ivy winces. "I was really hungry. It wasn't just me. Heath and Darnell are pasta thieves, too."

Harper looks stunning in her blue cocktail dress. "I didn't eat a thing because if I do this dress will explode, and I've been told it's perfect for the lighting in here. I'm going to hate getting what I wished for, aren't I?"

She's nervous about the show. "You're going to be perfect."

"I know someone who is already perfect," a deep voice says.

Just like that my heart rate jumps. I turn and Luca is there. He's not ready either. So there, Patrick. He's looking deliciously rumpled in his riding clothes. Or maybe they're his polo clothes. I don't know. I'm still learning. I only know he looks absolutely sexy.

"I like the way you think, Your Majesty," I reply with a grin.

"I like the way you do everything, Your Majesty." He moves in and hauls me up into his arms. "I think I need a shower before we film. Come along. You'll find this is one of your sacred duties as queen."

"Get a room," Ivy calls out.

"I don't need a room. I have a whole palace," Luca replies without looking back.

"I would never shirk my duties," I vow. *"Ich liebe dich, mein König."* I've got a tutor now.

"I love you, too, my queen," he says, and he carries me away to our future.

* * * *

The Park Avenue Promise series will continue…

Discover the Park Avenue Promise Series

Three young women make a pact in high school—
to always be friends and to one day make it big in Manhattan.

Built to Last
Coming 2025

Harper Ross has always dreamed of working on one of the magnificent brownstones of Park Avenue. Now a well-known businessman has hired her firm to do the construction work on his latest acquisition. He wants to showcase the renovation on a television show for his brand new network. It's the same grand home she and her friends had promised themselves they would be able to afford one day. Working on it isn't the same as living in it, but it's all a part of Harper's grand plan to grow her father's construction business into one of the biggest in the city. The only obstacle—the designer on the project.

Reid Dorsey believes in the balance between beauty and functionality. As one of Manhattan's new voices in design, he's excited to get to work on a true Gilded Age property. If only the owner had selected a contractor he enjoyed working with. Oh, Harper was brilliant and her work was excellent, but she had an opinion on everything. Everything, and it was usually the opposite of his.

Over the course of the job, these enemies start to see different sides of each other and suddenly their fights don't seem so bad. But when the project is threatened, they might have to choose between their jobs and the beautifully designed future they could share.

* * * *

Start Us Up

Now available.

She's a high-tech boss who lost it all...

Ivy Jensen was the darling of the tech world, right up until her company fell apart completely after she trusted the wrong person. Her reputation in tatters, she finds herself back in the tiny apartment she grew up in, living with her mom. When a group of angel investors offer her a meeting, she knows she has to come up with the new big idea or her career is over.

He's an up and coming coder...

Heath Marino has always been fascinated with writing code. He's worked on a dozen games and apps and is considered one of the industry's more eccentric talents. But now he's back in New York to spend time with his grandmother. She was known as one of the city's greatest matchmakers, and he wants to know why. Surely there's some kind of code in his grandmother's methods, and he's going to find them.

When Ivy meets Heath it's instant attraction, but she's got a career to get back to and he just might be her on-ramp. It could be a perfect partnership or absolute heartbreak.

Book Club Questions

1. My Royal Showmance takes place in the world of reality dating shows. How do you feel about shows like The Bachelor? Do you think it's possible to find a real relationship in such a setting?

2. The hero of My Royal Showmance is the king of a small (and fictional) European country. What does it mean to be royal in the modern world? How do Luca's responsibilities affect his views on love and dating?

3. Both Luca and Anika have parents who had complex relationships. How do you think their views of their parents' marriages affect their reactions to one another?

4. Luca and Anika break the "rules" of the show by meeting secretly in her room. How do you feel about that? Is it fair to the other contestants?

5. Anika is sent to the production to figure out if the director is harassing the women on the set. When she doesn't see Joe doing anything she would consider harassment, she's almost ready to clear the man until she witnesses him with Patrick. As a society, we tend to associate sexual harassment victims with women. History—especially Hollywood history—has shown us men often are subjected to harassment as well. Should Anika have seen the situation sooner? Do you agree with how she handled it once she understood? Why do you think it's hard for men to come forward?

6. There's a lot on the line when it comes to handling the sexual harassment issue—both money from the production company's end and Luca's hopes for his country. Anika refuses to accept the idea that her silence can be bought in exchange for the "greater good." Do you think she's being naïve? Would Patrick be wrong for accepting a deal? How do we treat survivors and their needs versus the idea of justice?

Discover More Lexi Blake

The Bodyguard and the Bombshell: A Masters and Mercenaries: New
Recruits Novella
Coming August 6, 2024

The Bodyguard...

Nate Carter left Australia's elite SASR unit after a tragic accident.
Shattered by the experience, he thought taking a job in the States might
be a good way to start over. His father's former employer, McKay-
Taggart, has a position for him in the bodyguard unit. He never
imagined himself risking his life for celebrities and the wealthy, but it
will do for now. It will also give him a chance to reconnect with old
friends, including the girl who'd been like a little sis to him ten years
before.

These days, however, his feelings for Daisy O'Donnell are anything
but brotherly.

The Bombshell...

Daisy O'Donnell is a girl on a mission, and it does not include
falling for one of her brother's best friends. She has plans, and while
chaos always seems to follow her, she's determined to see this through.
Daisy finds herself in need of a bodyguard when a job goes terribly
wrong. She's sure her dad will find someone suitable, but she didn't
expect a big, gloriously masculine Aussie to show up ready to take a
bullet for her. Maybe spending some time with Nate Carter won't be so
bad after all.

An explosive match...

Thrown together by danger, Nate and Daisy can't resist the insane
chemistry between them. But when his past and her present collide, they
must decide if they can hold it together or go their separate ways
forever.

Tempted: A Masters and Mercenaries Novella

When West Rycroft left his family's ranch to work in the big city, he never dreamed he would find himself surrounded by celebrities and politicians. Working at McKay-Taggart as a bodyguard and security expert quickly taught him how to navigate the sometimes shark-infested waters of the elite. While some would come to love that world, West has seen enough to know it's not for him, preferring to keep his distance from his clients—until the day he meets Ally Pearson.

Growing up in the entertainment world, Ally was always in the shadow of others, but now she has broken out from behind the scenes for her own day in the spotlight. The paparazzi isn't fun, but she knows all too well that it's part of the gig. She has a good life and lots of fans, but someone has been getting too close for comfort and making threats. To be safe, she hires her own personal knight in shining armor, a cowboy hottie by the name of West. They clash in the beginning, but the minute they fall into bed together something magical happens.

Just as everything seems too good to be true, they are both reminded that there was a reason Ally needed a bodyguard. Her problems have found her again, and this time West will have to put his life on the line or lose everything they've found.

* * * *

Delighted: A Masters and Mercenaries Novella

Brian "Boomer" Ward believes in sheltering strays. After all, the men and women of McKay-Taggart made him family when he had none. So when the kid next door needs help one night, he thinks nothing of protecting her until her mom gets home. But when he meets Daphne Carlton, the thoughts hit him hard. She's stunning and hardworking and obviously in need of someone to put her first. It doesn't hurt that she's as sweet as the cupcakes she bakes.

Daphne Carlton's life revolves around two things—her kid and her business. Daphne's Delights is her dream—to take the recipes of her childhood and share them with the world. Her daughter, Lula, is the best kid she could have hoped for. Lula's got a genius-level intelligence and a heart of gold. But she also has two grandparents who control her access to private school and the fortune her father left behind. They're impossible to please, and Daphne worries that one wrong move on her part could cost her daughter the life she deserves.

As Daphne and Boomer find themselves getting closer, outside forces put pressure on the new couple. But if they make it through the storm, love will just be the icing on the cake because family is the real prize.

* * * *

Treasured: A Masters and Mercenaries Novella

David Hawthorne has a great life. His job as a professor at a prestigious Dallas college is everything he hoped for. Now that his brother is back from the Navy, life seems to be settling down. All he needs to do is finish the book he's working on and his tenure will be assured. When he gets invited to interview a reclusive expert, he knows he's gotten lucky. But being the stepson of Sean Taggart comes with its drawbacks, including an overprotective mom who sends a security detail to keep him safe. He doesn't need a bodyguard, but when Tessa Santiago shows up on his doorstep, the idea of her giving him close cover doesn't seem so bad.

Tessa has always excelled at most anything she tried, except romance. The whole relationship thing just didn't work out for her. She's not looking for love, and she's certainly not looking for it with an academic who happens to be connected to her boss's family. The last thing she wants is to escort an overly pampered pretentious man-child around South America to ensure he doesn't get into trouble. Still, there's something about David that calls to her. In addition to watching his back, she will have to avoid falling into the trap of soulful eyes and a deep voice that gets her heart racing.

But when the seemingly simple mission turns into a treacherous race for a hidden artifact, David and Tess know this assignment could cost them far more than their jobs. If they can overcome the odds, the lost treasure might not be their most valuable reward.

* * * *

Charmed: A Masters and Mercenaries Novella

JT Malone is lucky, and he knows it. He is the heir to a billion-dollar petroleum empire, and he has a loving family. Between his good looks and his charm, he can have almost any woman he wants. The world is his oyster, and he really likes oysters. So why does it all feel so empty?

Nina Blunt is pretty sure she's cursed. She worked her way up through the ranks at Interpol, fighting for every step with hard work and discipline. Then she lost it all because she loved the wrong person. Rebuilding her career with McKay-Taggart, she can't help but feel lonely. It seems everyone around her is finding love and starting families. But she knows that isn't for her. She has vowed never to make the mistake of falling in love again.

JT comes to McKay-Taggart for assistance rooting out a corporate spy, and Nina signs on to the job. Their working relationship becomes tricky, however, as their personal chemistry flares like a wildfire. Completing the assignment without giving in to the attraction that threatens to overwhelm them seems like it might be the most difficult part of the job. When danger strikes, will they be able to count on each other when the bullets are flying? If not, JT's charmed life might just come to an end.

* * * *

Enchanted: A Masters and Mercenaries Novella

A snarky submissive princess
Sarah Steven's life is pretty sweet. By day, she's a dedicated trauma nurse and by night, a fun-loving club sub. She adores her job, has a group of friends who have her back, and is a member of the hottest club in Dallas. So why does it all feel hollow? Could it be because she fell for her dream man and can't forgive him for walking away from her? Nope. She's not going there again. No matter how much she wants to.

A prince of the silver screen
Jared Johns might be one of the most popular actors in Hollywood, but he lost more than a fan when he walked away from Sarah. He lost the only woman he's ever loved. He's been trying to get her back, but she won't return his calls. A trip to Dallas to visit his brother might be

exactly what he needs to jump-start his quest to claim the woman who holds his heart.

A masquerade to remember

For Charlotte Taggart's birthday, Sanctum becomes a fantasyland of kinky fun and games. Every unattached sub gets a new Dom for the festivities. The twist? The Doms must conceal their identities until the stroke of midnight at the end of the party. It's exactly what Sarah needs to forget the fact that Jared is pursuing her. She can't give in to him, and the mysterious Master D is making her rethink her position when it comes to signing a contract. Jared knows he was born to play this role, dashing suitor by day and dirty Dom at night.

When the masks come off, will she be able to forgive the man who loves her, or will she leave him forever?

* * * *

Protected: A Masters and Mercenaries Novella

A second chance at first love

Years before, Wade Rycroft fell in love with Geneva Harris, the smartest girl in his class. The rodeo star and the shy academic made for an odd pair but their chemistry was undeniable. They made plans to get married after high school but when Genny left him standing in the rain, he joined the Army and vowed to leave that life behind. Genny married the town's golden boy, and Wade knew that he couldn't go home again.

Could become the promise of a lifetime

Fifteen years later, Wade returns to his Texas hometown for his brother's wedding and walks into a storm of scandal. Genny's marriage has dissolved and the town has turned against her. But when someone tries to kill his old love, Wade can't refuse to help her. In his years after the Army, he's found his place in the world. His job at McKay-Taggart keeps him happy and busy but something is missing. When he takes the job watching over Genny, he realizes what it is.

As danger presses in, Wade must decide if he can forgive past sins or let the woman of his dreams walk into a nightmare...

* * * *

Close Cover: A Masters and Mercenaries Novel

Remy Guidry doesn't do relationships. He tried the marriage thing once, back in Louisiana, and learned the hard way that all he really needs in life is a cold beer, some good friends, and the occasional hookup. His job as a bodyguard with McKay-Taggart gives him purpose and lovely perks, like access to Sanctum. The last thing he needs in his life is a woman with stars in her eyes and babies in her future.

Lisa Daley's life is going in the right direction. She has graduated from college after years of putting herself through school. She's got a new job at an accounting firm and she's finished her Sanctum training. Finally on her own and having fun, her life seems pretty perfect. Except she's lonely and the one man she wants won't give her a second look.

There is one other little glitch. Apparently, her new firm is really a front for the mob and now they want her dead. Assassins can really ruin a fun girls' night out. Suddenly strapped to the very same six-foot-five-inch hunk of a bodyguard who makes her heart pound, Lisa can't decide if this situation is a blessing or a curse.

As the mob closes in, Remy takes his tempting new charge back to the safest place he knows—his home in the bayou. Surrounded by his past, he can't help wondering if Lisa is his future. To answer that question, he just has to keep her alive.

* * * *

Arranged: A Masters and Mercenaries Novella

Kash Kamdar is the king of a peaceful but powerful island nation. As Loa Mali's sovereign, he is always in control, the final authority. Until his mother uses an ancient law to force her son into marriage. His prospective queen is a buttoned-up intellectual, nothing like Kash's usual party girl. Still, from the moment of their forced engagement, he can't stop thinking about her.

Dayita Samar comes from one of Loa Mali's most respected families. The Oxford-educated scientist has dedicated her life to her country's future. But under her staid and calm exterior, Day hides a few sexy secrets of her own. She is willing to marry her king, but also agrees that they can circumvent the law. Just because they're married doesn't mean they have to change their lives. It certainly doesn't mean they have to fall in love.

After one wild weekend in Dallas, Kash discovers his bride-to-be is more than she seems. Engulfed in a changing world, Kash finds exciting new possibilities for himself. Could Day help him find respite from the crushing responsibility he's carried all his life? This fairy tale could have a happy ending, if only they can escape Kash's past...

* * * *

Devoted: A Masters and Mercenaries Novella

A woman's work

Amy Slaten has devoted her life to Slaten Industries. After ousting her corrupt father and taking over the CEO role, she thought she could relax and enjoy taking her company to the next level. But an old business rivalry rears its ugly head. The only thing that can possibly take her mind off business is the training class at Sanctum...and her training partner, the gorgeous and funny Flynn Adler. If she can just manage to best her mysterious business rival, life might be perfect.

A man's commitment

Flynn Adler never thought he would fall for the enemy. Business is war, or so his father always claimed. He was raised to be ruthless when it came to the family company, and now he's raising his brother to one day work with him. The first order of business? The hostile takeover of Slaten Industries. It's a stressful job so when his brother offers him a spot in Sanctum's training program, Flynn jumps at the chance.

A lifetime of devotion....

When Flynn realizes the woman he's falling for is none other than the CEO of the firm he needs to take down, he has to make a choice. Does he take care of the woman he's falling in love with or the business he's worked a lifetime to build? And when Amy finally understands the man she's come to trust is none other than the enemy, will she walk away from him or fight for the love she's come to depend on?

* * * *

Adored: A Masters and Mercenaries Novella

A man who gave up on love
Mitch Bradford is an intimidating man. In his professional life, he has a reputation for demolishing his opponents in the courtroom. At the exclusive BDSM club Sanctum, he prefers disciplining pretty submissives with no strings attached. In his line of work, there's no time for a healthy relationship. After a few failed attempts, he knows he's not good for any woman—especially not his best friend's sister.

A woman who always gets what she wants
Laurel Daley knows what she wants, and her sights are set on Mitch. He's smart and sexy, and it doesn't matter that he's a few years older and has a couple of bitter ex-wives. Watching him in action at work and at play, she knows he just needs a little polish to make some woman the perfect lover. She intends to be that woman, but first she has to show him how good it could be.

A killer lurking in the shadows
When an unexpected turn of events throws the two together, Mitch and Laurel are confronted with the perfect opportunity to explore their mutual desire. Night after night of being close breaks down Mitch's defenses. The more he sees of Laurel, the more he knows he wants her. Unfortunately, someone else has their eyes on Laurel and they have murder in mind.

* * * *

Dungeon Games: A Masters and Mercenaries Novella

Obsessed
Derek Brighton has become one of Dallas's finest detectives through a combination of discipline and obsession. Once he has a target in his sights, nothing can stop him. When he isn't solving homicides, he applies the same intensity to his playtime at Sanctum, a secretive BDSM club. Unfortunately, no amount of beautiful submissives can fill the hole that one woman left in his heart.

Unhinged
Karina Mills has a reputation for being reckless, and her clients

appreciate her results. As a private investigator, she pursues her cases with nothing holding her back. In her personal life, Karina yearns for something different. Playing at Sanctum has been a safe way to find peace, but the one Dom who could truly master her heart is out of reach.

Enflamed

On the hunt for a killer, Derek enters a shadowy underworld only to find the woman he aches for is working the same case. Karina is searching for a missing girl and won't stop until she finds her. To get close to their prime suspect, they need to pose as a couple. But as their operation goes under the covers, unlikely partners become passionate lovers while the killer prepares to strike.

About Lexi Blake

New York Times bestselling author Lexi Blake lives in North Texas with her husband and three kids. Since starting her publishing journey in 2010, she's sold over three million copies of her books. She began writing at a young age, concentrating on plays and journalism. It wasn't until she started writing romance that she found success. She likes to find humor in the strangest places and believes in happy endings.

Connect with Lexi online:

Facebook: Lexi Blake
Twitter: authorlexiblake
Website: www.LexiBlake.net
Instagram: www.instagram.com

Discover 1001 Dark Nights Collection Eleven

DRAGON KISS by Donna Grant
A Dragon Kings Novella

THE WILD CARD by Dylan Allen
A Rivers Wilde Novella

ROCK CHICK REMATCH by Kristen Ashley
A Rock Chick Novella

JUST ONE SUMMER by Carly Phillips
A Dirty Dare Series Novella

HAPPILY EVER MAYBE by Carrie Ann Ryan
A Montgomery Ink Legacy Novella

BLUE MOON by Skye Warren
A Cirque des Moroirs Novella

A VAMPIRE'S MATE by Rebecca Zanetti
A Dark Protectors/Rebels Novella

LOVE HAZARD by Rachel Van Dyken

BRODIE by Aurora Rose Reynolds
An Until Her Novella

THE BODYGUARD AND THE BOMBSHELL by Lexi Blake
A Masters and Mercenaries: New Recruits Novella

THE SUBSTITUTE by Kristen Proby
A Single in Seattle Novella

CRAVED BY YOU by J. Kenner
A Stark Security Novella

GRAVEYARD DOG by Darynda Jones
A Charley Davidson Novella

A CHRISTMAS AUCTION by Audrey Carlan
A Marriage Auction Novella

THE GHOST OF A CHANCE by Heather Graham
A Krewe of Hunters Novella

Also from Blue Box Press

LEGACY OF TEMPTATION by Larissa Ione
A Demonica Birthright Novel

VISIONS OF FLESH AND BLOOD by Jennifer L. Armentrout and
Ravyn Salvador
A Blood & Ash and Fire & Flesh Compendium

FORGETTING TO REMEMBER by M.J. Rose

TOUCH ME by J. Kenner
A Stark International Novella

BORN OF BLOOD AND ASH by Jennifer L. Armentrout
A Flesh and Fire Novel

MY ROYAL SHOWMANCE by Lexi Blake
A Park Avenue Promise Novel

SAPPHIRE DAWN by Christopher Rice writing as C. Travis Rice
A Sapphire Cove Novel

EMBRACING THE CHANGE by Kristen Ashley
A River Rain Novel

LEGACY OF CHAOS by Larissa Ione
A Demonica Birthright Novel

Love the Way You Spy
Masters and Mercenaries: New Recruits
By Lexi Blake

Tasha Taggart isn't a spy. That's her sisters' job. Tasha's support role is all about keeping them alive, playing referee when they fight amongst themselves, and soothing the toughest boss in the world. Working for the CIA isn't as glamorous as she imagined, and she's more than a little lonely. So when she meets a charming man in a bar the night before they start their latest op, she decides to give in to temptation. The night was perfect until she discovers she's just slept with the target of their new investigation. Her sisters will never let her hear the end of this. Even worse, she has to explain the situation to her overprotective father, who also happens to be their boss.

Dare Nash knew exactly how his week in Sydney was going to go—attending boring conferences to represent his family's business interests and eating hotel food alone. Until he falls under the spell of a stunning and mysterious American woman. Something in Tasha's eyes raises his body temperature every time she looks at him. She's captivating, and he's committed to spending every minute he can with her on this trip, even if her two friends seem awfully intense. He doesn't trust easily, but it's not long before he can imagine spending the rest of his life with her.

When Dare discovers Tash isn't who she seems, the dream turns into a nightmare. She isn't the only one who deceived him, and now he's in the crosshairs of adversaries way out of his league. He can't trust her, but it might take Tasha and her family to save his life and uncover the truth.

* * * *

"Okay, I am trying to fully grasp what happened here." Cooper sat back. "Someone piece this together for me because I do not understand."

Kala's lips curled up. "Tasha and the new target." She used her thumb and forefinger to make a circle which she pushed the forefinger of her other hand through back and forth while making squeaking sounds.

Such a bitch. "I didn't know he was the target."

"Hey, he wasn't the target then," Tristan pointed out.

Zach was staring at his cell, likely reading through the reports Drake had sent. Of all the people in the room, he looked the most grim.

"Tash couldn't have possibly known," Lou argued.

"Tasha slept with Darren Nash." Cooper seemed to need a moment to wrap his head around that reality. "When? I wasn't aware you were seeing anyone. When did you have the time to meet this guy? Did you know him back in the States? I thought he was Canadian."

Captain America was in the house, and she wasn't going to let him make her feel slutty. He didn't mean it. Coop had been raised like the rest of them to be open about all their needs, but he could also be overly protective. He reminded her so much of his father, Alex McKay. Uncle Alex, though there wasn't a drop of blood between them. Kenzie had stopped calling him anything but Mr. McKay by the time they were ten and she'd realized the ramifications of the relationship. Like Tash herself, Cooper had been adopted and didn't look anything like his father or mother, but the gestures were so familiar they didn't need things like hair color or eye color to make it clear they were related.

Tasha enjoyed being told how like her mother she was. Her mom was the best. Her mom would know how to handle this situation.

"I didn't know him before. It was a one-night stand," Tasha explained. "Like you've had one-night stands. And the twins have had one-night stands."

"Mine ended in me stabbing someone," Kala admitted. "I didn't know he was a Russian operative. I just thought he was hot. I didn't actually get to sex, so it was more like a one-night violence. Kenzie is a true-love girl. Zach has had his share, but he's discreet. Coop is the manwhore here."

A light pink stained Coop's cheeks. "I thought we weren't going to use hurtful words anymore."

"Well, I've never had a one-night stand." Tristan acted like he was adjusting his halo. "As the purest person here, I'm proud of Tash for getting some."

"I didn't say she shouldn't have a good sex life, but it might have been nice if it hadn't been with the freaking target," Coop shot back.

"Hey, it's not Tash's fault, and this conversation is doing none of us any favors," Zach proclaimed.

Kala's expression had lost its humor, and Kenzie had gone quiet.

"Well, I think I'm probably purer than Tris since I've never had a three way." Lou filled in the awkward silence. "And I'm proud of Tash, too. He seemed like a great guy. I spent a lot of time talking to him.

What are these rumors?"

Tasha wasn't sure she wanted to know the answer to that question, but here she was. "Cooper, can you give us a report on what you know about the target?"

She'd called Dare the target. It made her stomach roll.

But the op was important. It wasn't terribly dangerous. Not compared to some of the stuff they'd been through, but there was a reason this op had been selected as their first solo mission. It was supposed to be fairly easy, with Kenzie and Kala tag teaming a man profiled for his harmlessness. They were to listen and evaluate relationships. If they had a chance to gather more intel in a safe fashion, they had the go ahead. Easy peasy. In and out.

If this op went well, they would be allowed more freedom.

She might have screwed that all up.

On Behalf of Blue Box Press,

Liz Berry, M.J. Rose, and Jillian Stein would like to thank ~

Steve Berry
Doug Scofield
Benjamin Stein
Kim Guidroz
Chelle Olson
Tanaka Kangara
Stacey Tardif
Chris Graham
Jessica Saunders
Ann-Marie Nieves
Dylan Stockton
Kate Boggs
Richard Blake
and Simon Lipskar

Printed in the USA
CPSIA information can be obtained
at www.ICGtesting.com
JSHW081755220324
59629JS00001B/5

9 781957 568737